STABLE

A novel

BY KATE GEMMA

For Jack,

If you ever wonder what I did during your naps...

Contents

May 30, 2000
Settlers Hill Daily Tribune

A three-day manhunt for four missing children—Maura Bennett, Charles Mitchell, Sawyer Swenson, and Gregory Fitzpatrick—has come to a happy ending. All four children have been found alive in Settlers Hill, New York. The children are currently recovering at Mountain View Medical Center. At this time, police have declined to comment other than to say that they do have a suspect in custody. Sheriff Harvey Barton will give a press conference at Settlers Hill Town Hall tomorrow evening at 6 p.m.

KATE GEMMA

CHAPTER 1:

2000

"**S**top it! You're going to kill him!" Charlie Mitchell screamed, his fists vibrating by his side. He watched Boyd Barton pummel his friend Greg Fitzpatrick into the dirt for the second time that week. Greg's red hair fell in ribbons over his brow. His cheeks flushed in between his freckles so he rolled beneath Boyd's fist like a bruised orange.

Boyd glanced up from his victim momentarily. He let out a cackle, his trademark chipped tooth glistening in the sunlight. "So, what? I'd like to see you try to stop—"

Boyd's words were cut short when a set of knuckles slammed into his front teeth. He fell back, clenching his mouth as blood trickled between his fingers. His chipped tooth landed in the mud beside him.

Maura Bennett stood over Boyd and wiped her blood-covered knuckles over her yellow sundress, staining its blue flowers red. She pulled the hem of her dress just above her knees and knelt down in the mud beside him. Gripping the frosted tips of his spiked brown hair, she leaned in further and whispered, "Leave them alone or I'll gut you like a fish."

Maura could feel a presence behind her before she turned to see who it was. "What the hell is going on over here?" Coach Carlsen, the football coach, boomed as he reached out his hand to Boyd to help him up. Everything about Carlsen was large. His height, his voice, even the frown he was scowling down at Maura. She tried to say something, but her voice got caught in her throat at the sight of him.

Once upright, Boyd cupped his free hand over his bleeding mouth then spit the blood out into the mud. "You all right, kid?" Carlsen asked Boyd. He didn't bother asking Maura if she was all right or who'd started the scuffle. That was because Maura wasn't his up and coming start player.

"Boyd was picki—" she started before Carlsen cut her off.

"Doesn't look to me like Boyd was the one doing the picking," he growled.

Boyd played up the victim card, moaning quietly and leaning up against his Coach.

Carlsen pointed a finger at Maura. "You're going to be in Principal Jenning's office first thing in the morning. Get out of here." He waved her off. "Scat!"

Greg had made a run for it when he saw Coach Carlsen approaching. Greg knew Carlsen didn't like him ever since he quit the middle school's football team after one practice. He felt bad leaving Maura by herself but she could handle Boyd better than anyone.

Maura was the only one who didn't take any of Boyd's crap. It wasn't the first time she'd hit him, just as it wasn't the first time Boyd had pummeled Greg. Greg was Boyd's favorite and easiest target. Maura sighed. A part of her wished her friend Sawyer has been there to see her level Boyd, but he always had to go home right after school to get his homework done. His moms were strict like that.

By the time Maura reached the soccer fields where Greg and Charlie had retreated, a crowd surrounded Greg and Charlie. Eager faces, hungry for gossip, regarded Charlie as he reported the news. As she got closer, she heard Charlie yelp out, "...and then she lit him up! Right in the mouth!"

Some laughed and others cheered. Boyd had a lot of enemies—all of his own creation.

Greg washed the remainder of the blood from his face in a nearby puddle, leaving a thin film of dirt on his skin as it dried. "I could have taken him. You didn't need to do that," he shouted back to Maura as they headed to Sawyer's house. They took the path just beyond the soccer fields and around the small traffic circle at the center of town. It was a long walk, but the adrenaline from the fight was the wind at their backs.

Charlie walked beside Maura. Greg was sulking, licking his wounds, and lagging a few feet behind. Patting Maura on the shoulder, Charlie shouted backward, "Get a grip, Greg! You were as good as dead!"

"And fine! If you really want me to leave you, next time I'll let Boyd Barton have you all to himself!" Maura laughed. She knew that time would never come. There was no way she could stand back and watch one of her best friends take a beating without stepping in. She rubbed her fingers together as she walked. Boyd's dried blood felt like chalk on her skin.

Greg leapt forward to catch up and pivoted in front of Charlie and Maura. He bounced his finger between them. "The two of you aren't going to tell Sawyer, ok?"

Maura and Charlie nodded their heads in congruence. Greg turned and continued to walk. And Maura and Charlie shot each other a menacing smile.

Greg, first to the porch, rang the doorbell and Sawyer answered the door. Sawyer had just entered a major growth spurt and it seemed to Greg, Maura and Charlie that he looked an inch taller every time they saw him.

Greg shifted from one foot to the other, trying to peek around Sawyer's shoulders. "Where are Shelly and Ramona?"

Sawyer rolled his eyes, grabbed his backpack and closed the door behind him, "You know they don't like it when you call them by their first names."

When Maura and Charlie reached the porch, Maura pushed past Greg. "Let me just wash my hands before we go." She reached for the doorknob behind Sawyer.

Sawyer grabbed her hand and turned her around. "I wouldn't go in there."

Maura snickered, "Why not?" She had never been denied entry into Sawyer's house before.

Greg's home was a different story. Greg's mother, Bea, was the town judge and a harsh, critical woman who did not allow strangers in her home. And anyone outside of her immediate bloodline was considered a stranger and therefore, an enemy.

"Come on, Sawyer, I really need to wash my hands. Got to get Boyd Barton's blood out from under my fingernails." Maura waved her fingertips in Sawyer's face giddily.

"She had chemo today, okay?" Sawyer's lip twitched, a distraught tell. His mother, Shelly, had been diagnosed with Stage II breast cancer just one month before. Ramona had been working overtime, waitressing at Empress Diner to cover medical bills. "Let's just go before it gets too dark," he said and locked the door behind him.

Maura dropped her hand. Sawyer walked ahead, adjusting the backpack on his shoulder. Greg, Charlie and Maura looked at each other and shrugged. The brawl with Boyd Barton evaporated into the air, and soon became the most trivial part of their day.

CHAPTER 2:

2018

Pavement turns to dirt and the 2015 Honda Civic I rented from the airport rattles over the gravel road into Settlers Hill. My hometown sits in between two sister mountains that stare at one another's rocky faces and plush trees. A stream runs between the sisters, where the children of Settlers Hill catch frogs and chase salamanders. "There are more silos than people in Settlers Hill," I would tell my new friends in New York. Maybe that's why I ended up in the Big Apple after college; I needed to meet only the eyes of strangers when I walked down the street. Anonymity promises infinite opportunities to fail and start over again.

I already know one thing about Settlers Hill has changed—Charlie is dead. They say he fell after he lost his footing up on some jagged rocks just off the trail.

By the time anyone found him, wild animals had gotten to him. The thought makes me nauseous. Thirty years old. It wasn't supposed to end like this. After everything we've been through, I can't believe that this is how his story ends.

Charlie was the good one, the traditional one. He had a good job, a pretty wife, a home— white picket fence and all. Charlie was the one who always made Greg, Sawyer and me come back together when we were at odds with each other. He was a calm voice in the madness and a port in the storm. He reminded us that we only got mad because we cared.

A knot of anger sits in my stomach where sadness should reside. Anger is easier than sadness. Anger makes me feel strong. No one feels strong sitting in a corner balled up in the fetal position crying. So angry is what I'll be.

I glance at the time on the dashboard. The funeral starts at 9:00 a.m. and it's already 8:57 a.m. I'm going to be late, as per usual.

With no GPS and no cell service, I search for St. Brigid's Church from memory. Though the Pharmacy on Main Street turned into a Walgreens, not much else seems to have changed geographically. I find myself reading street signs only to realize that they might as well be written in hieroglyphics. I lived in Settlers Hill for half a lifetime and I don't suppose I looked at one street sign. Instead, I used landmarks as a visual GPS. If you are coming from the high school, make a left at the town pool and cross three streets to get to Greg's house. To get to Grandma Marylin's, make a right after you pass the white house with blue shutters where I had my first kiss.

Settlers Hill at an aerial shot is the perfect little mountain adjacent town. The downtown area is paved, and clapboard shops, coffee shops and vintage clothing stores line its streets. On the corner sits the only bank in town. The tellers never ask for your ID because not only do they know your name, but your mother's maiden name and how long your first dog lived. St. Brigid's Church takes center stage, the apex of its cross piercing the sky. At just the right time of morning on the west side of the church, the light from the east comes streaming through the stained glass so you can walk right through the stations of the cross on that sidewalk. As the town sprawls out, clearly designed by someone who took classes on crop circling from aliens, the suburban homes circle out, gaining more land per lot the further you get from the church until you're met with farmland.

I pull up to the new street light at the South end of Main street. After the light, the road splits, with the road on the right continuing on to St. Brigid's Church. To the left, the road turns to dirt after a hundred feet, leading to hiking trails and the Old Salem Farm. Sitting at the red light, with my right blinker tinkering like the second hand of a clock, my eyes shift to the left and down the dirt road and toward the farm. I don't have the courage to stare at it head on. Even at a distant glance I can see the outline of where the fire ate at the wood. I tense like it might reach out and grab me. Pull me back in. Lock the door. The scars on my back burn. The light turns green. I slam my foot on the gas.

It begins to drizzle as I pull into the church parking lot. Sawyer and Greg are standing up ahead, next to a beat-up robin's egg blue pick-up. Sawyer is leaning on the hood as he watches Greg smoke a cigarette. In the cold, damp air I can see their breath coming out of their mouths as they talk.

I step out of the car and don't bother locking it. There's no need to here. Greg sees me and flicks his cigarette to the pavement and stomps the ember with the heel of his steel-toed boot. I'm happy to see he's wearing a suit—even if it is one size too small and paired with workman boots. Greg always thought fighting the subtle conventions of society made him stand out from the crowd. But we tried to tell him that as a six-foot, 220-pound, freckled red-head, he stood out whether he wanted to or not.

Greg squares his large frame toward me and stomps playfully forward. "Get over here, stranger!" The smell of gasoline and pot wraps around my body as he hugs me and hoists me up in the air.

"Nice," I say as he places me back on the ground. "I thought you were done with that." I motion toward the flattened cigarette, smoke curling to the sky. Apparently, it isn't the type of cigarette I thought it was.

Greg adjusts his tie and shoots me a cheesy smile. His yellow teeth speak of a lifetime of smoking. "Oh, come on now, let's not start off like this. It's just pot, which is basically legal now." He nods his head back at Sawyer. "If ol' US Marshal over there isn't giving me shit for it, then the big city photographer should probably cut me some slack."

I raise an eyebrow, "Just pot?"

Greg makes an "X" over his chest. "Cross my heart and hope to die."

I smile, though a piece of me doesn't want to give him the satisfaction. I want him to try harder, be better for himself—to himself. But today is not the day to lecture Greg about his drug problems. He feels the pain of Charlie's death just as Sawyer and I do, and if anything, he may be worse off. His coping mechanisms always proved more harmful than helpful. "Ok, then. Well, you look good."

"Well that means a lot coming from a girl who dates movie stars!" He shuffles around, straightening out his suit.

I didn't want to talk about ex-boyfriends today. I try to laugh off the comment and slap Greg's arm, pushing him off to the side. Greg may be twice my size, but he was never very steady on those giant clown feet. I walk past him towards Sawyer, who's smiling at me, arms crossed as he shakes his head.

"Look out, here comes Mad Dog Maura," he chuckles. He's dressed in a suit that I can tell he wears for work. I can't tell the brand, but from the softness of the material I bet it's expensive. It crisply sits over his body like it was freshly prepared by the cleaners. He's wearing a dark forest green tie, which brings out the leafy green in his hazel eyes.

I snort out a laugh. "I think my Mad Dog days are over." Thankfully, my old nickname has remained trapped in the town of Settlers Hill. I plan to keep it that way.

"It's been a while," Sawyer lies. He shifts his weight off of the truck and walks toward me with his hands in his pockets. My heart speeds up. I pray what I'm feeling doesn't show on my face. "At least you're on time," he glances down at an imaginary watch on his wrist. "-ish."

I feel a playful pinch on the back of my arm. "I don't know about you, but I need a drink, honey." The familiar sandpaper voice crawls into my ear.

I breathe a sigh of relief. Aside from Greg and Sawyer, Grandma Marylin is the only one I actually want to see in Settlers Hill. With no children or grandchildren to speak of, she took on Charlie, Greg, Sawyer and me as her own—all at different times and for different reasons. At one point in her life, she was one of the wealthiest, most well-known socialites in New York City. Back then, she didn't follow fashion trends—she set them. To be invited to one of her famous, themed cocktail parties was a badge of honor among those on the Upper East Side.

But then, her marriage to a man named George Tinton from Settlers Hill brought her barreling into our lives. It was a riches to rags story, except she kept the money. Instead, she tossed aside her notoriety for love and the simple life her new husband lived. George passed shortly after their tenth anniversary, but since Settlers Hill was where she felt closest to him, she never left. Instead, she became a pillar in the community, not to mention the woman who rescued us more times than we can count.

Grandma Marylin took Charlie in after his parents' fatal car accident and I came to live with her after my father's deadly overdose, after which my mother abandoned me. Greg spent almost as many nights there as Charlie and me, in order to escape his harsh mother. And Sawyer's mothers both worked, and Grandma Marylin was the only person they trusted to look after their son while they weren't home. Her money kept us fed and clothed, and her heart kept us safe.

"A drink? You read my mind." I turn to face her. As usual, she looks absolutely perfect. Despite living in a small town where most men wear a suit jacket over their overalls for a "fancy" night out, Grandma Marylin never once abandoned her New York City style. Ready for the runway, she's wearing a long black Gucci dress with a grey cashmere throw draped across her shoulders. Her diamond earrings draw little attention away from her perfectly coiffed hair, which is black with a carefully placed silver streak running through the front.

Greg throws his cigarette—a Marlboro Red this time—to the pavement and crushes it under his shoe, hoping Grandma Marylin won't notice. She shakes her head at him and then turns her attention to Sawyer.

"Well, hello handsome," she crosses her arms, smiling.

Sawyer's shoulders reach for his ears and he shoots her the soft, genuine smile of a complimented child. He leans in and gives her a kiss on the cheek. "I second that drink."

She links her arm through Greg's, who stands straighter with her at his side. This is the first time I've seen her since her diagnosis. Multiple sclerosis. She leans slightly, into Greg's side, betraying her usual sturdy stance.

"This is the second funeral I've been to this month," she says.

I cock my head.

"Harriet's boy. Car accident. Absolutely awful. I prayed I'd never know her pain, but here I am, only one week later," she says. "I'm going to sit with Natalee up front."

Natalee is Charlie's wife. Until this moment, I haven't even thought of her.

Grandma Marylin takes in my vacant expression. "You're all welcome to join us, but knowing you, you'll be a few rows behind." She winks her trademark wink but it's different today. Her lids are the levy holding up bulging dam waters. Charlie was the closest thing she had to a son, just as I was basically her daughter. I have no doubt in my mind she's three martinis deep and seated on a Xanax cloud—not that she doesn't deserve every vehicle it takes to get her here today.

Giving us each a kiss on the cheek and tight squeeze, she tells us to meet her out front after the funeral. Then she walks through the church doors and I swear I see her pause at the threshold, like a strong wind has pushed her back before she thrusts onward.

Just behind Greg's pick up, the hearse pulls up. This is when it all sinks in. Until now, it felt like we were just three old friends catching up, waiting for Charlie to get here. Call it denial, but a part of me half expected this whole thing to be one big practical joke. Even on the way here, I repeated my wish like a mantra. Charlie's not dead. This is just a way to get us all together. Our separate and busy lives have made it hard to stay as close as we once were. Though, one may argue that distance may be the best thing for friends like us.

Once, a few months after we'd been rescued from our abduction, a therapist told each of us, in our respective sessions, that we were too codependent on each other. She said it wasn't healthy. Charlie claimed she didn't know what she was talking about and the rest of us agreed. We needed each other.

Time slows as the doors on the hearse open. I can't look at the casket, so I focus on a spot in St Brigid's stone facade as I walk in behind Sawyer and Greg. The entire town is here. Prolonged eye contact and head nods become a proxy for words. Good. I don't want to talk to anyone. I worry that if I open my mouth, I'll start sobbing uncontrollably. I hate crying in private let alone in front of every person I've known since birth.

Sawyer, Greg and I find our seats. There's more than enough room for our trio to sit comfortably, but we sit tightly—shoulder to shoulder, hip to hip. The pain in my chest deepens. I wonder what emotional pain would feel like if we didn't have these physical symptoms of it. Would we feel it at all? Or would it just be a nagging voice in the back of our minds, reminding us that things will never be the same.

Charlie was supposed to die with all of us in that stable. And even though we came out of that alive, I still never prepared for Charlie, Greg, Sawyer and I to die separately from each other. All this time, I've kept this fantastical idea that our fates were forever linked, hand in hand.

The casket remains closed, as suggested by the funeral home, who despite their best handiwork were unable to mask the irreparable damage done to Charlie's body. Natalee had to identify the body. I don't envy her for that. I'm desperately holding on to the image I have of Charlie, happy, smiling, whole—it's something Natalee no longer has.

I can see Natalee and Grandma Marylin through the gaps between mourners. They're seated in the front pew, Natalee's head locked forward. Sunlight pierces through the stain glass leaving colored streaks across Natalee's bleach blonde hair. In high school, I envied her good looks and popularity, despite her incessant use of the word "like." No one cares what comes out of your mouth when you look like that.

I knew for sure was that I didn't envy Natalee now. Though I'd seen Charlie through the years, I hadn't seen Natalee much since their wedding five years ago. Charlie planned his visits to New York around her girls' trips and during the rare times I'd ventured back into Settlers Hill for a holiday, Charlie would come to Grandma Marylin's while Natalee would go to her family's house.

I look up at the altar. Father Donahue, resident priest of St. Brigid's, speaks briefly of Charlie and at length about Charlie's relationship with God. Father Donahue did not know Charlie well, so he falls back on what he does know—God. And I can't help but think that if Charlie was attending his own funeral, he wouldn't be pleased.

CHAPTER 3:

2000

"Hurry up! The sun's going down soon. And we can't miss dinner, you know that," Maura said.

Charlie lagged four feet behind Maura, Sawyer, and Greg on the sidewalk just before reaching the crosswalk that lead to the mountain's hiking trails.

"I mean it!" Maura shouted back to him. "Grandma Marylin will freak out if we're not home for dinner."

"Wouldn't want to upset Miss Marylin," a voice sprouted up beside them. Pulling up in a black sedan with "Sherriff" in gold lettering was Sherriff Harvey Barton—Boyd's father. He had a head of thick, brown hair parted to the side and hazel eyes that caught the dying sunlight.

Harvey kept one hand on the wheel and one arm draped out the driver's side window, as he moved the car forward at a snail's pace.

Maura just about jumped out of her skin. Did the Sherriff know she'd just knocked out his son's tooth? Given the smile on his face, she thought not.

"Hi, Sherriff" and "Hi Mr. Barton" rang out from the four as they slowed their pace. Harvey had only been the Sherriff for a year or so, so some of the children in town called him Sherriff, while others stuck to the original Mr. Barton, or even at times "Officer". Harvey never corrected anyone, whatever they called him, as long as it was respectful.

"What are you kids up to? Don't you have homework?" Harvey said in that gleeful tone adults use for children when they are pretending to give them a hard time.

Charlie stepped toward the curb eagerly. "We're going up the hiking trails, we're build—"

Maura raced up and jutted Charlie in the ribs with her elbow to shut him up. "Just exploring," she said.

Harvey nodded. "All right, well you be safe out there and get home before dark. Coyotes can be a little scary, but I'm sure they've got nothing on Miss Marylin waiting at a dinner table with cold food."

Maura, Sawyer, Greg, and Charlie laughed.

Harvey started to pull away when he stopped again. "Oh, and you should invite Boyd with you to go exploring sometimes. Better than being cooped up playing video games all night." He chuckled and winked. "Now, don't you tell him I said that."

The children nodded and watched him drive away.

Once Harvey had rounded the corner and was out of sight, Greg doubled over laughing. "Oh, yeah, let's invite Boyd!"

Maura, Sawyer, and Charlie snickered.

Maura turned to Charlie. "What was that? You're not supposed to tell anyone about the treehouse."

"I didn't!" Charlie said.

"Yea, because I stopped you," said Maura.

"Next thing you know and Harvey's sending Boyd to meet us at the tree house and then Boyd would take it and kick us out," said Greg. "Don't be an idiot."

Maura, Charlie, Sawyer and Greg hiked their way up the North Woods Mountain. They spent most days after school hiking up there until they reached their secret hideout. And though the secret hideout was neither hidden nor much of a secret, they'd started to build a tree house there, in the largest, most level tree they could find on the mountainside.

A few feet past the marked entrance to the trail, there was a stick figure adorned sign. It told people to pick up after their dogs and reminded hikers that the trails close after dark. Just beyond the sign, the three trails split. There was the red trail, the green trail and the blue trail. The red trail took you to the west side of the mountain. It was steep and rocky, and the least habitable of the three trails. The green trail ran on level ground, over tiny brooks and streams that cut through the woods. And the blue trail wrapped around the eastern side of the mountain and boasted a sweeping view of Settlers Hill. The teens took that trail every day to their level tree, which they'd named Odin.

They were creating the hideout as a place to escape from their small town to be all by themselves. Charlie had drawn out the blueprints and Greg had stolen his dad's old tools for the job. Greg's dad had been gone since before he could remember and he knew his mom wouldn't notice them missing. Even still, they all knew what a risk it was to take them. Judge Bea, Greg's mother, was the town's resident hangman both in the courtroom and at home.

Thick foliage restricted the view into town and the town's view of the trail, making it the ideal spot. Small birds landing on fallen branches on the forest floor echoed sounds of a larger animal approaching. Charlie was always the first to flinch.

Greg laughed. "Why do you always freak out? When have we ever even seen a bear around here?"

"I'm not afraid of bears, idiot." Charlie clenched his jaw.

"Sure, you aren't. Besides, it would only be a black bear. They don't bother you unless you bother them. It's not like we'd see a grizzly bear," Greg pressed on.

Sawyer, a few steps ahead of the rest, stopped and turned around, "Yeah, Greg, they're just like giant squirrels." He rolled his eyes.

"Kind of!" Greg agreed excitedly as Sawyer's sarcasm skimmed right over his head.

"Ok, ok, let's keep walking. We don't have much time before the sun goes down." Maura said, trudging on ahead of the rest.

At the very end of the Blue trail stood Odin. Its thick oak trunk stood as a sturdy base for its branches that grew so long, they curved to the ground. At certain angles, Odin resembled one of those Japanese hand fans.

Sawyer was the one who had named it. His grandmother was Norwegian and would read him stories about the Norse gods. Odin was the god of wisdom as well as battle, magic, prophecy, victory, war, and death. Just what they were looking for.

So far, Odin was only flanked by a makeshift ladder—ten two-by-fours nailed into its trunk. Now that they had access to its branches, the hard part was about to begin. They raced toward Odin and climbed the steps, stumbling over each other before they each found a branch to dangle their feet from.

"Did you bring the supplies?" Charlie asked Greg, perched on a branch.

Greg unzipped his backpack revealing two hammers, a box of nails and sandpaper. Each time he borrowed them, he made a point to return them promptly. He knew his chances of being caught were slim since Judge Bea wasn't handy, but he wasn't about to take any unnecessary risks.

"You know he likes you, right?" Sawyer whispered over to Maura. She sat a few feet away from him on an adjacent branch.

Maura curled her lip in disgust. "What are you talking about?"

"Boyd Barton, that's who he's talking about!" said Greg, eavesdropping. He pulled four pieces of gum out of his pocket. He tossed one in his mouth then one to each of his friends.

"Right. Just shut up." Maura said folding the gum wrapper into a neat square.

The boys shot each other knowing glances from their branches. "Come on," said Sawyer, "you know that's why he comes after us. He wants your attention and he knows how to get it. I mean, the guy's a jerk, but he could kick your ass in a hot minute if he really wanted to. At least you get him good—you've saved my ass more than once. But really?"

Maura felt like someone had pressed two hot irons against her cheeks. Why was Sawyer giving her such a hard time? It wasn't like him. "Get a grip." Her hands fumbled and she dropped the gum wrapper.

"I bet Boyd would love to get a grip on you!" Greg shouted, cackling the hardest at his own joke, as he often did.

"Why do you still have that on?" Sawyer said to Maura, pointing to the Band-Aid on her knee. It had been on so long that the edges were worn down leaving a ring of glue and dirt around it.

Maura placed a hand over the Band-Aid. "It's so stuck on there because I waited too long. I don't want to rip it off. It'll kill."

"Let me see," Sawyer shifted himself to sit closer to her and gently peeled back her fingers. "Just relax," he said and looked up at her. He maintained eye contact, steadying her gaze on him, and then ripped the Band-Aid off her knee in one swift motion.

Maura yelped. Her face contorted in anger. She opened her mouth to scold him, she was interrupted by the sudden sound of a blaring siren.

CHAPTER 4:

2018

A town car pulls up after the hearse leaves. Charlie had told me that Grandma Marylin had been occasionally hiring a driver after her Multiple Sclerosis diagnosis. Her fatigue and unreliable right foot made it dangerous for her to drive. I know it must be killing her. She's a woman who's pride rests on her independence and perseverance.

I slide into the town car and sit next to Grandma Marylin. Her powder-based perfume settles my nerves. I look down. Her hand is draped over mine. Her palm is warm against my knuckles. It's only been a few months since I've seen her, yet so much has changed. She came to New York and we'd hopped around to all of her old haunts, places I couldn't afford to eat in or sleep in without her financial backing. My heart wrenches when I realize that that was the last time she would be able to move that freely, with so little planning or care.

I try not to think of it. I'll need to do a lot of compartmentalizing today. A piece of me still refuses to believe that Charlie won't be at Hannigan's for his own funeral after party. I want to ask Grandma Marylin if she believes Charlie's death was an accident. I can't bear to bring it up. I don't want to make today harder than it has to be. And I could be wrong, right?

Hannigan's is the only bar in town. It's a total dive. Drinks are cheap and its patrons can be found there as early as 10:00 a.m. At all times, the TV's behind the bar are turned to TNT, playing Law and Order reruns. Cream painted bricks line the front door, chipped with drunken messages. My personal favorite was always "Ray loves Tori" with a line through it, next to a clearly written "Tori is a whore." I like to imagine that Ray left Tori in the bar to have a cigarette outside, biding his time by immortalizing their love on the brick, only to return to the bar to find her making out with some other guy. Perhaps then he rushed back outside to correct his mistake.

When we were kids, Old Man Hannigan owned the place and was strict about not letting anyone underage drink under his roof. But each night, he'd have a few too many and would pass out on his cot in the back room. Then we'd take the liberty to serve ourselves. But as I survey the bar in front of me, I can see that Hannigan's has changed since my last visit.

"Well, isn't this fancy?" Sawyer announces, stepping out of the front seat. He reaches back and opens the door for Grandma Marylin and me before our driver can scurry around.

Hannigan's painted brick has been restored to its original red façade. The shingles on the roof look as though they have never seen so much as a heavy rainstorm. The sign over the door reads, "Hannigan's Bar and Restaurant" in navy blue block lettering, while a neat chalk board sign on the sidewalk reads: "Happy Hour 4pm - 8pm, Monday through Thursdays."

"Old Man Hannigan really dressed up the place, huh?" I nudge Greg's arm.

Greg nudges me back. "Old Man Hannigan was like 90 years old last time you were here."

"Duh. I guess Barry has it now?" I ask. Barry Hannigan was Old Man Hannigan's son.

Sawyer cocks his head. "Barry's a lawyer in DC. Ran into him a few years ago working on a case."

Grandma Marylin steps out of the car. "Coach Carlsen owns it now."

"Did he retire from harassing kids? I mean, coaching high school football?" Sawyer asks.

"In fact, he did. From both." Grandma Marylin whips back her shawl, places a hand on either hip and points her chin to the Hannigan's front door. "Coming with me?" It was a silly question. We'd follow her anywhere.

Soon, the bar is packed. People pour in, wearing suits and black dresses. Too distracted at the funeral, I failed to recognize how hauntingly familiar each face is. This might as well be a high school reunion. There's Ella Espenson, the former head of student counsel and class president. Her blond hair still tickles her butt and her rosy cheeks are illuminated under the fluorescent lighting. She was one of those rare girls who seemed to have it all and was genuinely friends with everyone. Not far from her side is Tucker Randall. He was the reason people came to basketball games. He wasn't the best player on the team, but he was easily the best-looking, and he always knew how to work the crowd. He'd have us all cheering like winners even when our team hadn't even made a basket yet.

But not everyone I see is from high school. Off in the corner, holding a beer an looking as if he is waiting for someone to come talk to him, is Dr. Greenberg, everyone's favorite pediatrician. Wearing a tight-lipped smile, he shifts from leg to leg. I heard his wife died a few years back. She was always the social one. It seems that without her, he's lost the ability to engage. In that respect, he's the one I identify with the most with right now.

The reality of reentering my past hits me. I can feel my muscles tightening, my shoulders reaching up to my ears. What am I nervous about? My mind tells me not to worry, but my stomach screams otherwise, tightening into a hard knot.

A large hand at the small of my back. Sawyer. My shoulders drop and the knot in my stomach loosens like he's pressed some sort of release button. It's his signal that I don't have to face it all alone. Can he sense my nervousness, or is he just using me as a human shield to push through the crowd? It's probably a little of both, but I choose to assume the former.

After finding an open high-top table by the bar, I offer to get our drinks. Glenlivet on the rocks for Sawyer, dirty martini—extra olives—for Grandma

Marylin, a gin and tonic for me and a Pepsi for Greg. I reflexively move to order Charlie's whiskey sour and painfully have to stifle the urge.

"Maura!" a familiar voice transcends the chatter before I can reach the bar. It's Joanna Winters, our eighth grade English teacher. She throws her arms around me, squeezing tightly as she whispers in my ear. "How are you, sweetheart?" She pulls back, keeping her hands on my shoulders. Alcohol crawls off each of her breath and I do my best not to sneer at the stench. I can tell from its potency that the drink in her hand is not her first of the day. The redness of her lipstick has faded, leaving only the lipliner. Her curly, frizzy hair reflects the fluorescent bar lightning and hangs like a dusty storm cloud.

"Hi, Miss Winters. How are you?" I say.

"I'm well. I was so sorry to hear about poor Charlie. He was always such a sweet boy. One of my favorites, to be honest." She wavers slightly on her feet.

"Charlie would have loved to hear you say that. Between you and me, he always had a little crush on you." Joanna Winters, originally from Minnesota, came to teach in Settlers Hill just after a divorce—a marriage that lasted only a few years and bore no children. She arrived young and eager to teach, looking for a new beginning, no doubt. I know how that goes.

Most people who are born in Settlers Hill die in Settlers Hill. That's made Joanna so exotic; a new person from a distant land who had a twinge of an accent none of us could place. Her o's were long and cute, and before class we'd all perform our best imitations of her. All of the boys liked her, but Charlie loved her most of all. He saved every single one of his papers that she graded. He would make us all nauseous with his insistent rantings of how one day he would marry a woman like Miss Joanne Winters. Now she stands before me, drunk and disheveled with no ring on her finger. She's even wearing in the same clothes she'd worn when she taught me the difference between "your" and "you're."

"Aw, that warms my heart." Color returns to her cheeks and for a brief moment, she looks slightly less wasted. "So, what have you been up to?"

"I'm a professional photographer for Smooth Magazine."

Joanna's eyes widen. "Smooth Magazine!" she says excitedly. "I've had a subscription for years! Oh, I love all of their relationship tips and that section on beauty blunders. Oh, and of course the Smooth Man of the Year edition every December." She winks. "It must have been so difficult to get a job there."

"I guess I must be a damn good photographer then," I say with a tinge of defensiveness. As a woman in the corporate world, you get used to people undermining you so often that a simple, harmless phrase can turn on you. "Sorry," I catch myself. "How are things with you? What are you doing?" I become increasingly conscious of the fact that I need a drink and that I have three people waiting on me.

"Still teaching. It can be a little redundant teaching the same thing year after year, but I try to stay busy with scrap booking and my book club and baking, of course."

"Very nice." I smile, hoping it ends the conversation. There is something odd about talking to someone as an adult who you had only known as a child. I have to keep reminding myself that I'm an adult now, too.

She glances over my shoulder to Greg, Sawyer and Marylin, and her eyes well with tears. "Charlie would have loved to see you all together again."

With no premeditation, I wrap my arms around her. It's an unfamiliar reflex but it just feels right.

I walk over to the crowded bar and see Coach Carlsen. His t-shirt is tucked behind his suit jacket and his belly has grown round and hard since I saw him last. He's lost more than a few brown strands of hair from the top of his head. His cheeks are rosy from the heat of the bar. Coach Carlsen can fill a doorway. His heavy chuckle can be heard on the other side of a fire door. With so many patrons tonight, he's fluttering back and forth, sloppily spilling drinks as he delivers them. This clearly is not part of his job. He's the owner. But given the volume, his bartenders need all the help they can get.

I'm able to grab the attention of some young bartender, a girl with her boobs up to her chin, who's otherwise demurely dressed in black. She dressed for this funeral like teenage girls dress for Halloween: sad/scary, yet sexy. She hands me all four drinks and I do my best to stabilize them against my body so I can get back to the table without spilling. The last thing I want to do is take two trips. No more conversations with ghosts of the past before I can get this gin in my stomach.

As I approach the table, I see that Greg's mother, Judge Bea, is standing there. Grandma Marylin, Sawyer and Greg are seated at the high-top and Grandma

Marylin has used her Birkin bag to save a seat for me. I instantly want to find a new place to sit. But where else would I even go? The only people I want to see here—or anywhere, really—are right in front of me. I take a moment to brace myself for impact, lift my chin and make my way over.

Greg is staring into his lap. Sawyer's stoic eyes sail beyond Bea, completely ignoring her. But Grandma Marylin's eyes are fixed on the Judge, focused and steady.

I set the drinks down on the table. "Judge." I nod.

She silently nods back. Judge Bea is a tall woman who wears heels to appear even taller. Her hair is tightly pulled back into a neat bun, which only accentuates her sunken eyes. Her cheekbones could cut glass. Her monotone voice is at all times soft but accusatory, with the innate ability to make you second guess yourself. Grandma Marylin used to say that if Bea could, she would have walked around with gavel in hand at all times. She has the highest conviction rate in four counties, and no one in Settler's Hill dares look at her sideways. Well, almost no one.

Bea picks up the dirty martini I'd set down and drinks it all in one sip. She sets it back down on the table and dabs her mouth with a napkin.

"Oh!" Judge Bea clasped her hand to her chest. "Marylin, was that your drink? I do apologize."

Grandma Marylin smirks. She is no fool to the game Bea is playing. "It's ok, dear. You need it more than I do."

Bea squints. "I guess those of us who have to work for our money do need a drink at the end of a long week."

Grandma Marylin's smile does not break, knowing better than to feed in chummed waters. Sawyer and I know better than to speak up when Bea and Marylin are at it. Greg fidgets in his seat. I worry the Judge's presence might drive him over the edge. It must be hard enough for him to sit here in a bar, on the day of his friend's funeral, and keep to his sobriety—never mind having his over-lording mother present. When we were kids, I could protect Greg from Boyd Barton or any other bully. But I never could protect him from his mother. No one could, except Marylin.

"I must say, Marylin," Bea continues, "it's very daring of you to wear such an ostentatious outfit to a funeral. Must have cost a pretty penny." Judge Bea then reaches for my gin and tonic and pours the entirety of the contents down her gullet before clapping the glass back down to the table.

Without skipping a beat, Marylin says, "And, dear, I think it's quite brave of you to sport the bitter divorcée look after so many years. You really do have it down pat." Marylin clasps her thumb and pointer finger together to make an 'okay' sign.

Bea purses her lips and shoots a look over at Greg, as if she expects him to defend her honor. Greg keeps his head buried, refusing to make eye contact, like he's suddenly a little boy again. She picks up his Pepsi to drink, but as the liquid hits her lips, she slams it down to the table, as if someone has fed her poison. "Ugh, still can't get it together enough to handle a single drink? Pathetic," she says the word so ferociously that it produces Pepsi coated spittle.

She turns her attention to the remaining drink on the table, Sawyer's Glenlivet on the rocks. Before she can reach it, Sawyer's hand clasps over the back of her wrist. For the first time that night, Sawyer stars directly into the judge's eyes. Holding both her gaze and her wrist, he uses his free hand to grab the whiskey and downs it. He places the glass back down to the table, then releases her wrist.

"Have a good night, Judge," Sawyer says, dismissing her.

Bea rolls her wrist free and then wipes down her dress. "You may be a US Marshal now, Sawyer, but I'm still a judge. Don't you forget that."

Sawyer leans in toward Bea, "Lucky for you, Judge, I don't forget anything. Ever."

Bea sends one last sneer around the table before turning on her heels.

Sawyer offers to get us new drinks and I tell him to be careful out there in the crowd, where it's easy to get sucked up. "Where is Natalee?" I ask, peering around the bar. "I haven't seen her since the funeral."

"She was a little worked up," says Grandma Marylin. "I gave her one of my special little pills and sent her home. She doesn't need to be here around all of this. Look," she motions toward the crowd with her chin, "Everyone is here to celebrate Charlie, but I doubt anyone is even talking about him. Natalee needs rest and a quiet room. Then, after some time, she will need pushing—socialization. That will help her later, but not right now. Not when it's fresh."

Grandma Marylin is speaking from experience. You don't lose the love of your life without learning something. "Every day it feels as though it happened yesterday," she would say. Charlie was her son, for all intents and purposes, and I don't know how she's managing to keep it together. To this day, I still have only seen her cry once. That was when she saw Greg, Charlie, Sawyer and me alive at the hospital after our rescue from the barn.

And Grandma Marylin's right. Everyone here at Hannigan's only came because in a small town, where there is nothing to do and no one new to meet. To them, any party is a party—even if it's acknowledging the death of one of its most beloved residents.

Charlie would have given the shirt off of his back to any random stranger on the street. We all coped in the aftermath of the abduction in our own ways, and Charlie spent every moment serving others. He was the guy that knew a guy for anything you needed, and he'd never accept a cent for lending a helping hand. My stomach turns to think that he was operating on borrowed time. The others, it seemed went two separate ways: Sawyer feels invincible. He figures if he could cheat death once, he'd surely be able to do it again. He's a cat who's used up one of his lives and lives with the confidence of eight more to spare.

Greg lives each moment in fear that he'd relive the horror, imagining it obsessively, unable to turn off the replay button in his mind. Luckily and unluckily for him, he found substances to put those thoughts on pause.

I don't know where I land on that spectrum. Some days I'm like Sawyer, with my hair and makeup in full throttle by 6:00 am, ready to take on the world, camera in hand and creative juices flowing like Niagara Falls. Those days I say yes to every invitation and seek out adventure with reckless abandon.

Other days, I'm Greg. Those days I don't want to get out of bed. I draw my black out curtains across my bedroom window and hole up under the covers. I can only stay there a few minutes before the dark becomes a backdrop for my memories and the pounding in my chest becomes too much to bear. He's in jail, I tell myself. Rick Salem can't get us anymore.

Charlie was the anomaly. He chose to see the good in others. Helping people felt like helping himself. The trick for him was to keep moving, so the ghosts that haunted him couldn't catch up. I read once that Teddy Roosevelt coped with life that way. After his mother and wife died on the same day, he dealt with his grief by never remaining still. That was Charlie, through and through.

Sawyer returns to the table, drinks in hand. Greg finally lifts his gaze from his lap. Sawyer sets each drink down, then shakes his head as he sits back down. "You can't let her get to you like that."

"Hey, I have an idea," Greg says, ignoring Sawyer. "Let's tell our favorite Charlie stories."

I can tell that Sawyer wants to press on, to force Greg to face his demons, but I shoot him a look that says 'not today.' He winks back at me. "I think that's a great idea," Sawyer concedes.

Grandma Marylin recounts her favorite story with tears of laughter streaming down her face. Prior to Charlie's parents' fatal car accident, he and his parents lived next door to Grandma Marylin. One sunny afternoon, Marylin opened her front door to find a three-year-old Charlie and his panicked mother standing before her. Charlie had his potty-training toilet seat wrapped around his neck. Charlie's mother's doe-eyes silently begged Marylin for help. After ushering them inside, Grandma Marylin did the only thing she could think to. She suckered that thing off by using every last drop of Crisco she had left in the kitchen.

'My little Charlie Chaplin' Grandma Marylin would call him. He could always make her laugh, especially when he wasn't trying.

Next, I decide to tell my favorite Charlie story. It was from our freshman year in college. Charlie and I both lived in the dorms at SUNY Binghamton University. We hadn't planned on going to the same school but, looking back, I am so happy we did. It was extra time.

Charlie studied Liberal Arts and I majored in Journalism—unaware that photography would steal my heart. We lived in the same building on campus and could usually be found together in the cafeteria or library. It was the Wednesday before winter break, which meant we were in the middle of finals and were functioning on very little sleep. A panicked Charlie showed up at my door.

"Hey, you gotta help me. I think I'm dying," he panted, as if outrunning an attacker.

I grabbed his arm and yanked him into my room, using my foot to push aside the mess my roommate had left on the floor. Rita was a nice girl but I think the Tasmanian Devil would have kicked her out of his home for being too messy. I sat down on the bed and pulled Charlie down beside me.

"What do you mean, you're dying?" I shook my head.

Charlie shot up off the bed, unbuckled his jeans and threw them down to the floor. He threw open his palms, pointing to his legs,

"See? What is that?" he yelled out.

His legs looked as if they were tinged blue. I reached out and touched the skin directly above his right knee. I rubbed my thumb and pointer finger together. No texture. No greasy feel. The color didn't transfer to my fingers.

"So? What do you think?" Charlie demanded. He was panicked, like a lost child in search of his mother.

I leaned back, laughing, putting both of his legs into my view. "I just can't believe how hairless you are."

"Maura!" he pulled up his pants. "This is serious!"

I choked down my laugh, "I'm sorry. I'm sorry." I paused. "But you're like one of those hairless cats!" I burst out in laughter again. I couldn't help myself.

"That's it! I'm going back to the campus clinic."

I jumped up, racing him to the door. "Wait, wait. I'm sorry. I really am."

Charlie looked at me, expressionless. He was pissed. "Whatever, Maura," he said, and then he reached for the door.

I grabbed his arm, "Wait, Charlie. What do you mean 'go back to the campus clinic'?"

"I went there before I came here. I saw one of the doctors and she wants to send me to get blood work done. She said she'd never seen this before and she wants to make sure it's not anything serious like Leukemia. Ok? Do you feel bad now? I could have Leukemia!"

"Wait here." I took out a box of cleaning supplies that I kept under my bed. After hearing horror stories of what dorm bathrooms were like, I came to school a little over-prepared. I took out a small green and silver canister of Ajax and sprinkled some on a washcloth. Then I poured some leftover bottled water from my nightstand over it. "Take your pants off."

"I already showered. It's not something you can clean off. Just stop."

"Just do it."

Charlie sighed and rolled his eyes as he pulled his pants back down. I rubbed the washcloth across his left thigh and watched the mysterious blue color disappear. Charlie looked on as though I was performing a magic trick.

"What? But I..." Charlie stuttered.

"Are these new jeans, Charlie?"

"Yea. I bought them last week. So?"

I realized that Charlie had never done his own laundry. Before his parents died, his mother did it for him. When he moved in with Grandma Marylin, she did our laundry the way that she did her own laundry: by paying someone else to do it. "Detergent wrinkles the fingers, dear," she would say. I'd only recently learned the ins and outs of laundry from a kind soul who took pity on me one night in my dorm's laundry room.

"You didn't wash them yet, did you?" I asked.

"No, but they're brand new. I didn't need to yet," he said, exasperated. "I've only worn them a few times."

"Well, I'm glad I caught you before you started the chemo." I stood up. "The dye from your jeans is rubbing off onto your legs. Next time wash your jeans first."

"But I—"

I put my hand on his shoulder. "I think you're going to make it, but I can get the paddles out to shock you if it'll make you feel better."

It is my favorite Charlie story. The table erupts in laughter. I realize that I hadn't told Sawyer, Greg or Marylin that story before. Charlie Chaplin he was, alright. The joy I feel in their laughter is soon overrun by the aching wish that Charlie was here to relive the memory with us.

After a couple hours, Hannigan's empties out, aside from the occasional approach from a high school classmate or old acquaintance paying their condolences. We decide that we've survived the social event reasonably unscathed.

We take the last sips of our drinks when the rush of a cool breeze draws our attention toward the front door. And in walks Boyd Barton.

CHAPTER 5:

2000

The ICE (In Case of Emergency) siren. Settlers Hill started using it in 1995, after a rare storm system called a "microburst" damaged homes, businesses, cars, and even took a few lives. The storm was so sudden and intense that its powerful winds downed a cluster of trees like dominos. People needed a warning to find shelter, and the siren was created to do exactly that. But the siren also came in handy two years later, in the summer of 1997, when several rabid coyotes came down from the mountains and went on a terroristic spree, killing cows, goats, chickens, and anything else that was in their way. There were also several reports of people escaping attacks, until finally, the coyotes were shot down.

"You think it's a pack of rabid coyotes again?" Greg's eyes widened, except he looked more excited than scared.

Maura shrugged her shoulders. "Could be, I guess."

"Let's get out of here." Charlie turned around, making a run for his backpack. He tripped over his feet, face-planting, arms and legs sprawled out like a drunken snow angel.

Greg burst out laughing.

"Why would we leave?" Sawyer walked over and picked Charlie up off the ground. "Don't you figure that if there's something dangerous down there, then we're in the right place up here?"

"Sawyer's right. Let's just wait," Maura concurred.

"You guys are pansies!" Greg said. He picked up his backpack, threw it over his shoulder, and started march back toward the trail. "I'm going down there. I want to see what's happening. Besides, we have weapons!" He thrust the tools into the air like a Medieval warrior.

"Stop, Greg. Don't be an idiot," Charlie yelled after him. There was an urgency in his voice. "Greg, stop!"

Maura looked at Sawyer. He rolled his eyes. As a group, through all of their highs and lows, they had one steadfast rule: never leave a man behind.

Maura, Sawyer and Charlie gathered their things and ran after Greg. Sawyer caught up and stopped short in front of Greg, placing a hand on his chest.

"Listen," Sawyer said. "You know we aren't going to let you go down there by yourself. Don't be stupid and get the rest of us killed. Let's just all stay together. All we've got is some shoddy, worn down hammer to defend ourselves."

Greg twisted his bottom lip downward. He patted his backpack, feeling around the edges. "Uh, yeah, about that..." he said hesitantly. "I think I left the hammer back at Odin."

A collective sigh fell from Maura, Charlie and Sawyer.

"Maybe you should have stayed in boy scouts longer than three weeks," Maura said.

Greg squinted at the dig, "Funny." He fixated back on Sawyer. "Alright. Where should we go then?"

The siren stopped. They looked in the direction of town, although at mid-trail there was nothing to see but bushes and leaf cover. Though the siren stopped, it had been so loud and constant that it could still be heard like a ghost thinning out on the breeze.

And yet it still wasn't easy to make their decision. Charlie wanted to call it a night, and Maura and Sawyer agreed with him despite Greg's tantrum-like protestations. Once they reached the very bottom of the trail, the siren resurged.

They looked to each other, waiting for someone to make the call. It could be risky to hike all the way back up. If there were rabid coyotes or ferocious animals loose in Settlers Hill, chances were they'd find the four friends. But then again, if the group went straight into town, they could still be putting themselves right into dangers path.

Maura peered around. Now they had an open view of the road. "I have an idea of where we can go," she said.

"Where's that?" asked Greg.

Maura pointed just beyond the trees to their left and said, "The barn at the old Salem Farm."

CHAPTER 6:

2018

Watching Boyd Barton walking into Hannigan's is like seeing a ghost. His black hair is parted to the side, slicked and neat. And his thick black eyelashes are a natural eyeliner to his green eyes.

He looks just like his father, Harvey, except that he's taller and must have put on at least twenty pounds since high school. Through his clothes, I can see the outline of his muscular arms and legs, and his flat stomach.

As if adding insult to injury, his clothing is exactly what makes Sawyer and I exchange surprised glances across the table. Boyd Barton is wearing a sheriff's uniform. And that means that Boyd doesn't just look like Harvey Barton, but he's taken his job, too. Could there be anything more jarring then seeing your childhood enemy in a police uniform?

I look at the time on my phone: midnight. Hannigan's usually closes that this time of night, but given the events of the day, maybe Coach Carlsen decided to leave it open for us. Aside from a few stragglers, Greg, Sawyer, Grandma Marylin and I are the only ones in here.

And now Boyd. What the hell is he doing there? And why so late? I don't remember seeing him at the funeral. He would have had some nerve showing up to Charlie's funeral.

Boyd walks straight to the bar without seeing us, thankfully.

"When were you planning on telling us this?" I say to Greg.

Greg chuckled. The shock on mine and Sawyer's faces brings the light back into his eyes. An amusement reserved only for the closest of friends. "Shit, you two have been gone a long time."

"Oh, he's as harmless as his Daddy was," Grandma Marylin cuts in. "He's still a little boy, just with a big boy badge. Charlie actually helped him sell his parents' house not too far back."

Nan Barton, Boyd's mother, died few years ago. Alzheimer's. A sweet woman. Nan and Grandma

Marylin were close friends. I think Nan was the only person she confided her fears and insecurities. Now that Nan was gone, I stood as the only other stable woman in Grandma Marylin's life. Nan was a kind woman whose voice never climbed higher than a whisper. Even during the one time I saw her reprimand Boyd, I felt like I was like watching a mouse reprimand a cat. I was sad to hear she passed away.

The bartender yells out "Last call!" and I stare at my empty glass. I thought I was done, but that was before I saw Boyd walk in. Now, I want another...or seven. The only problem is Boyd was standing at the bar, in between me and my next gin and tonic.

"Want me to go? I'm not afraid of that joker," Sawyer says.

The struggle must be written all over my face.

Grandma Marylin places her hand over Sawyer's arm and stares at me. "She's got it sweetheart. She's not afraid of him either." She stares at me while speaking to Sawyer. It's her way of indirectly telling me that I'm not afraid. And she's right. I'm not afraid of Boyd Barton. But I'm not excited to see him either.

I don't know what to expect. The man standing there at the bar is the grown-up version of the kid that used to wait outside the bathroom stall for Greg. He'd taunt him, knowing that the moment Greg decided to exit the stall, he'd shove Greg back in and dip his head into the toilet bowl. This man is the same kid that used to take Charlie's lunch and toss it in the garbage can at least three times a week. This sheriff is the same kid who used to piss in Sawyer's locker through the vent cracks. Sawyer would rotate his things between Greg's, Charlie's and my lockers to avoid it.

None of us were safe from his bullying. Not even me. I got more licks in with Boyd Barton than the others. They would tell you that it was because I'm a girl and Boyd Barton, despite his villainous ways, wouldn't actually hit me back. I don't buy it. Boyd Barton never had a chivalrous bone in his body. He was the kid who cut a three-inch chunk into my hair the one day he sat behind me in math class. The kid who would race me back to my house after school only to stand outside and prevent me from walking in the door. The kid who whistled and licked his lips at me whenever I walked by him in the hallways, making me feel like I was naked. I knew it wasn't because he liked me. He had a superpower for knowing how to taunt people. After a while, you get to know your enemies well, but the one thing that remained a mystery, to us all, was why he tortured us. Sure, he went after plenty of other kids, but none with the care and consistency that he used for Charlie, Greg, Sawyer and me.

I turn in my seat to stare at Boyd. The bartender's cleavage is resting on the bar—inches from his face.

I resolve to face him. To believe Grandma Marylin when she tells me I'm not afraid. After all, Boyd is a Sheriff now, and I doubt he walks around giving people swirlies. But before I can stand up, I hear a voice behind me. Deep and gritty. Sawyer, seated across from me, has a hard gaze pointed just over the top of my head.

"Well, well, well. Look who's here. If it isn't Mad Dog Maura," Boyd says, placing his drink on the table. My ears grow hot. "Greg, old boy, why didn't you tell me she was back?"

The way he says "she" sends a shiver up my spine. It's almost like he thinks we're old friends. Like I'm not sitting right there. Greg rolls his eyes and takes a sip of his Pepsi.

"Hi Boyd. No 'Mad Dog' here. I'd like to think, or at least hope, we've all grown up now," I say, using all my efforts to keep my tone even—pleasant but not too pleasant, and not at all welcoming.

"Nah, she's still in there somewhere. Lookin' good, by the way." Boyd smiles. Boyd could be good looking in some alternate universe. But definitely not in this one.

I see Greg's face in my peripheral. He's smirking and shaking his head at Sawyer in a 'get a load of this guy' kind of way. My ears and cheeks burn. Sawyer sits up straighter in his seat.

"Wait a minute," Boyd continues. "Aren't you dating Weston Cahill?"

"Not anymore." I attempt my best 'I would rather not talk about it' smile.

I'd met Weston Cahill just after he'd won the Oscar for Best Actor. Weston had been traveling around the country—and out of the country—celebrating his win. At the time, he was doing a spread for Smooth magazine and it was my job to photograph him. We hit it off pretty quickly and before I knew it, we were dating. It was thrilling to be with our magazine's Most Eligible Bachelor of the Year.

We went to fancy parties and flew on private jets to exclusive resorts. I couldn't walk past a newspaper stand without seeing our faces plastered on some gossip magazine. I still cringe when I see his face on a magazine or a commercial for his new movie.

"We broke up," I say.

"Oh, well, I'm sorry to hear that. Listen," Boyd places his hand on my shoulder. I want to slap it away. "You'll find someone else. Getting dumped is hard."

I laugh, well aware of the game Boyd is playing, "Reading the tabloids, are we? Well, the truth is that I dumped him. But I'm sure that your experience has been as the one getting dumped, right? I won't blame you for assuming." I pinch the tips of his fingers and remove them from my shoulder.

"How's your father, Sheriff?" Grandma Marylin asks. Her voice is a cool breeze over a dancing flame.

"Just fine, Miss Marylin." Boyd says. "Doctors told him he's got Diabetes but it's not too bad. Just has to lay off the sweets now. He wanted to be there today at the funeral and told me to offer his condolences. He was out visiting my aunt Frances. She's in a nursing home out in Ohio. Couldn't change his flight or he would've been here."

Like Jekyll and Hyde, Boyd has transformed into some kind of meek gentleman right before our very eyes. "I'm sorry about Charlie." He lowers his head. "It's a tragedy. It really is. He helped me a lot after my mom died. He was a good guy."

"Then where were you today?" I ask, unable to stop myself. It sickens me to think that he's acting like he and Charlie were friends.

"I was there. I dipped in the back for the mass. Couldn't come here until now, though. A man's gotta work," Boyd says. "Well, I'll let you all get back to visiting. I know it's been a while since the whole gang was back together again." He grabs his drink, gives us a sweeping wave and plants himself in a seat down by the cute bartender.

I wait until Boyd is out of earshot. "What the hell? You think you might have mentioned that he was the Sheriff now?" I bark at Greg.

Greg chuckles and sticks his hands in his pockets, "It's not like you'd think. Believe me, when I first heard it, I was in the same state you're in right now. And don't get me wrong, the guys still a major dick. But it's not the same. He's not hunting people down to get into a fight or taunting little kids anymore."

"Ok, whatever. But what's this about Charlie selling his Dad's house? What, were they buddies all of the sudden?" I ask.

"Who knows? You know Charlie, he's all about forgiveness," Greg says. The weight of Charlie's death wraps around us all again.

Sawyer says nothing, but I can see he's just about as done as I am. Going to Hannigan's probably wasn't the best idea for a group of people looking to avoid their past. But I'm leaving tomorrow and now all I can think about is sleep.

CHAPTER 6:

2000

Only a few years ago, the Salem farm had been a bustling farm where Henrietta and Jacob Salem worked and lived with their only son Rick. The Salem's worked tirelessly on their farm, collecting eggs from their chicken coop, milking their cows, sheering their sheep, and raising horses. There were several barns on the property, but the barn for the horses was the largest and the nicest. The Salem's made decent money from selling fresh eggs and milk to locals, but their real income came from the stables. They had a few horses of their own, but mostly rented out to local horse owners and rich kids who needed extracurriculars for their college admissions.

Henrietta and Jacob died four years ago in a car accident only a few hundred feet from their home. It was mid-May and no one had taken the storm warnings seriously. Torrential downpours left the roads slick. Roads were strewn with untended pot holes on the outskirts of town. Henrietta and Jacob had just finished a delivery of eggs to the local grocery store when their car veered off the road. It rolled three times before landing in a ditch.

Rick was in his early twenties at the time. He'd been a hard worker his whole life but had no mind for the business of farming. In his school years, kids called him slow and teachers struggled to keep him on track, but Jacob's mindset was that of his father and his father's father: school just got in the way of working. He took Rick out of school and had him work the farm full-time.

After his parent's death, the farm began to disintegrate. Rick hired some help, but didn't have any management skills. His lack of exposure to the outside world left him vulnerable to conmen, and people with only their own best interest in mind. He also didn't have his father's charisma, so one by one people pulled their horses from the rented stables. Though Rick Salem still lived in the house on the property, the Salem farm was no longer a working farm and was only referred to as "the Old Salem farm."

The four stood at the base of the trail, the siren continued to wind up and down and they wondered how much more time they had. Maura looked at the barn and realized it would be their best bet. It was shelter and it was close. That would be enough. Maura led the charge, with Sawyer, Greg and Charlie in tow, and Greg still urging them to return to the tree house. He kept saying something about coyotes not being able to climb, until Sawyer pointed out that bears still could.

They waded through the open grassy field leading to the barn. There was no telling the last time it had been mowed, and the crest of the dry blades bit at their hips as they walked.

"This is a bad idea," Greg called out at the back of the pack. He was a head shorter than the rest of them, though the oldest by a half month. He swatted the weeds from his cheeks. "What if he's home? That guy gives me the creeps!"

"Who? Rick?" Charlie bellowed over the siren. "He's harmless!" It felt good not to be the fearful one for a change.

Charlie had seen Rick Salem plenty of times over the years. They all had—at kids birthday parties at the Salem farm, filled with hay rides and pony rides. It was part of their collective childhood memory. Rick used to hold the pony's reigns for the assisted rides around the property, and each child would take their turn on a pony that wore a ridiculous miniature cowboy hat. Rick was squarely built, quiet and dirty. He smelled like the cows he milked. But he'd never been anything but polite to the children. Charlie felt bad for him in a way. They'd both lost both their parents in a single day, in a similar way. Charlie had Grandma Marylin, but Rick had only Rick.

Maura and Sawyer paid no mind to the conversation and Sawyer pointed to the old horse stables. It was the largest barn on the property and least run-down looking—at least from a distance.

The stable doors consisted of two large doors which slid from a bar at the top and met in the middle.

Sawyer and Maura jumped to one side, and Greg and Charlie ran to the other. Working together, they slid the doors open. Stale air bellowed out at them like a tidal wave. It was a smell that scraped up like razor blades through your nostrils to the center of your eyebrows. Saw dust, wet hay, fossilized manure and mold married with the scent of rotted wood. It was the type of smell that reminded you that even things that do not breathe can die.

Dry, gagging coughs rang out from the four.

Greg held his hands over his face as he doubled over. "I am not going in there," he said through his fingers.

Sawyer held the neck of his t-shirt up over his nose. "You'll get used to it. Come on." And he waved them inside.

Greg copied him and used his shirt as a mask, and then Charlie followed. Maura collected a bundle of her hair, twisted it, and brought it across her mouth and nostrils. She couldn't bring the top of her sundress up too high or it would expose her underwear. Of all the days to wear a dress. She'd only worn it because Grandma Marylin bought it for her and insisted she wear it. Maura knew the real reason Marylin wanted her to wear it. Though Marylin loved Maura's tomboyish spirit, she desperately fought as Maura's femininity advocate as the only girl among boys.

The walls of the stable muffled the siren and they were finally able to speak without screaming. Though now, because of the stench, they feared even breathing. The shutters of each individual stall had been boarded shut and the only source of light were the thin beams of dying sunlight peeking through the deteriorated wooden slats above them.

"It's empty," Charlie said. "Look at it. It's like a ghost town." He shivered. "Creepy."

"I told you that guy is weird," Greg said, referring to Rick.

"He doesn't live in here," Charlie said. "But I don't know," he looked around. "I just don't like how dark it is in here."

"There's nothing in the dark that there isn't in the light," Sawyer said.

Greg tiptoed to Charlie's back and danced his fingers lightly up his neck, "Or is there," he said. Charlie jumped an inch off the ground and slapped the back of his neck.

Greg laughed until he snorted.

"What's wrong with you today?" said Sawyer to Greg.

They always got like this, Charlie and Greg. It was usually on a day where Greg had taken a particularly grueling beating from Boyd Barton. He'd make himself feel better by picking on Charlie. Charlie always fell into the role of victim, even though both Sawyer and Maura knew deep down Charlie was tougher than that. Maybe Charlie knew Greg needed it and just played along.

But Sawyer also knew that Greg was afraid of the dark. Greg had told Sawyer one night when they had a sleepover at Sawyer's house. Greg kept turning the light on in the middle of the night. Greg had blamed it on 'ghosts' and claimed Sawyer's house was haunted. He vowed never to sleep there again.

During Greg and Charlie's scuffle, no one noticed that Maura had wandered off down the barn's long corridor lined with stable stalls on either side. Each stall had been closed and padlocked off. There were two long hallways in the barn with a connecting corridor in the middle creating an "H" shape. Just around the bend Maura spotted some light.

"Over here!" she shouted to the others. Her voice broke their trance. She waited until they caught up and pointed to the light source. They followed it through the connecting corridor and around the bend to the left. The light was coming from one of the stalls. Inside there was a worker's lamplight tied up and hanging from the ceiling at the center of the eight by eight-foot box. This stall was different from the rest because it was open and lit, and the hay looked fresher than the hay they were standing on in the hallway. But something else was different about it, though none of them could put their finger on it, just yet.

"That's weird," Sawyer said. He looked to Maura.

"Yea," Maura paused. "It is."

"Well, I'm no fool," said Greg as he pushed past the other three. He placed himself in the center of the space. "There's light, and hay that doesn't smell like shit." He spread his arms out as if presenting found treasure to his friends. "Come in!" He waved them in.

Charlie darted in on command. Maura and Sawyer hesitated for a brief moment. "He's right," Charlie said. "It's much better in here."

Maura and Sawyer, though they did not discuss it at the time, both felt their hearts thumping. It was the type of feeling you cannot decide whether to will away or pay attention to.

That was when the siren stopped. After listening to it for so long, their ears were now cavernous without it. The eerie silence settled over them like dust after a tornado. "We should go," said Maura. Sawyer nodded.

"Oh, come on, we just got here," Greg said. "Come on in, there's plenty of room! Maybe this can be our secondary club house after the treehouse, like when the weather is too shitty or something."

"No thanks," Maura said. "Let's just get out of here."

Greg reached for her playfully and grabbed her by the arm, yanking her inside. She stumbled inward and crashed into Charlie.

"That's enough, Greg." Sawyer raced forward into the stall and placed a finger to Greg's chest. His voice dropped an octave and his jaw tightened. "She should have let Boyd have you today. What's your problem? You just keep poking and poking and poking!" With each "poking" he drove his finger into Greg's chest until Greg's back pressed to the wall.

That's when they heard a sound. Not a siren this time. More like a collapse. No, a slamming. Then a clicking. Maura saw it first. "No," was all she could say.

The door to the stall had closed—it slammed shut. Something locked—it clicked into place. The four stood frozen. Even Greg stayed pressed against the wall, eyes wide.

No one could bring themselves to speak. Seconds passed like minutes. Then, the humming sizzle of the stall light disappeared and darkness fell over them.

CHAPTER 7:

2018

Sawyer and I let Grandma Marylin convince us to sleep at her house. Sawyer is an easy sell. His mother moved out of Settlers Hill when he went off to college so he has nowhere else to stay. I pretend that I don't want to inconvenience Grandma Marylin without revealing that I haven't made any hotel reservations for the night. The closest decent hotel is twenty miles outside of Settlers Hill and the closest motel is Heidi's Inn, a doppelgänger for the Bates Motel.

We say goodnight to Greg, who had only just recently moved out of Grandma Marylin's house. He'd moved in there just after he turned eighteen. Bea thought kicking him out of the nest would force him to fly, despite his broken wings. Luckily, Grandma Marylin swooped in. She does her best to sway Greg into coming along too for the night, but he refuses. He wants to sleep in the place where he's paying rent. He pretends his reasons are financial, but we all know it's pride.

"How about breakfast?" Greg cups his hand over a match lighting another cigarette.

"I know you better than to expect breakfast out of you. How about lunch? What time do you have to work?" asks Grandma Marylin, carefully lowering herself into the town-car's backseat. I can see her struggle in the clench of her jaw.

"Got tomorrow off," he says.

"Lovely," she beckons him closer then plants a kiss on his cheek.

Sawyer grips Greg by the shoulder and gives it a shake. "Get home safe, buddy. See you in the morning."

I pinch Greg on the arm and glance at the cigarette. His auburn hair burns brighter under the scrutiny of the streetlight. He's tossed that mop of his out of its mousse hold so that the waves fight one another and overlap. I consider giving him a hard time about it and remind myself that he just sat—completely sober—and watched all of us drink our grief for hours on end. I should cut him some slack.

Sitting in the back of the town car, sandwiched between Grandma Marylin and Sawyer, I can see Greg in the rear-view mirror. He's moving further and further away, getting smaller and smaller, until the only thing I can see is the flickering ember of a cigarette rising to meet his mouth and then falling to his hips.

"Is he ok? I feel like I can never tell," I say.

"I'd give every last penny of mine to know that answer, darling," says Grandma Marylin. "All four-," she winces, "Three. All three of you. I'd give it all to have a direct line to that answer. Lord knows, Charlie took the brunt of it all with Greg. He made the tough decisions...the right decisions."

Grandma Marylin settles her cheek on my shoulder. "All these years I thought I was taking care of you. Now here you are taking care of me. Where is my strength when I need it?"

Sawyer reaches for her hand and clasps it between his own. "We'll take care of him," he says. "You don't need our problems burdening you."

Grandma Marylin sits up straight and inhales deeply as though she's just woken up. "See, that's where you're wrong. You all have never been my burden. You have been my blessing."

I close my eyes to trap the tears and let the low hum of the engine lull me to sleep.

My nose wakes up first. Fresh hazelnut roast crawls through the gaps in the door frame and slithers over the plush comforter. Grandma Marylin is always up first. She says the older you get the less you sleep. For her, lying in bed wide awake is a bore.

I reach over for my phone on the nightstand and check the time—8:30 a.m. There was a time in my younger life where 8:30 a.m. felt early. Now, most mornings, I'm three coffees deep at this time, and already settled in at work.

There's a new nightlight in the corner by the door, which means that Grandma Marylin went out and bought it in preparation for our arrival. I don't need to look in the room where Sawyer is staying—Charlie's old room—to know that there is a new nightlight in there as well.

See, after three days in all but utter darkness, you need to have a little light at night. In the days after our rescue, I used to turn on the light on my nightstand as soon as Grandma Marylin left the room. I thought she would be mad that I was keeping it on all night, but then one night I found a nightlight wrapped in a silky red bow on my pillow. It was small, but bright enough to do the trick. We never talked about it, but when I passed Charlie's room at night to go to the bathroom, I could see the soft glow beneath his door, too.

My room is the same as it was when I lived here. The crystals that hang from the ceiling at the center of the room catch the morning light. I touch my mouth, my cheeks, my eyelashes. The makeup, the layers of mascara and foundation, blush, bronzer, have all been lifted and my skin feels fresh. Grandma Marylin. "There is no greater sin than sleeping in your makeup," she always insisted.

I smile. I must have fallen asleep in the car. That means that Sawyer carried me in and Grandma Marylin took off my makeup. I stretch my arms over my head and for a brief moment I am happy. Pressure begins to build when I remember why I'm here.

What if I just had a dream within a dream? That's it. I close my eyes and attempt to bend the laws of the universe to my will. Wake up to the real world where Charlie is alive. He will run into the room any minute and rip the covers from me and tell me to get my lazy ass up. He wants to go hiking. No, not to that mountain. To the other one. He wants to get a croissant with cream cheese at the Rolling Pin Bakery on the corner of Main Street. He'll finish it before we get out the door and order another for the road.

That haze before my eyes isn't the cloudiness of a dream. It's my inability to accept my new reality. It kind of seems like a memory, because I'm ready for it to be one. I'm ready to find the universe's remote and hit fast forward to a time where I can miss Charlie without feeling the full weight of it.

I sit straight up. Keep it moving so I don't dwell on the pain. I throw on a pair of blue jeans, but don't change out of the shirt I slept in. It's mine, from another life: a white tee with "Go Team Blue!" written in blue paint across the front with the number eight on the back. Senior Year Spirit Day. Charlie was on Team Blue with me.

Grandma Marylin and Sawyer are already sitting at the kitchen table when I walk in. There's fresh lavender in a crystal vase between them and the scent of Chanel number five in the morning air. Sawyer is sipping a large cup of coffee with the newspaper rolled up tightly in his lap. Grandma Marylin sits down with her delicate ceramic tea cup. It's white with thin, blue intertwining flowers—a gift from her engagement party. Coffee has never so much as touched her lips and she wears that fact like a badge of honor. 'Addicted...all of you,' she would say as she'd sip her thirteenth cup of Lipton tea for the day.

She clocks my entrance and points to the pot. "It's a serve yourself kind of morning, dear."

"Good Afternoon. Nice shirt." Sawyer peers over his cup at me.

I look at the oven clock. 9:00 am. Not too bad for being hungover. I wonder if Sawyer is as hungover as I am. If he is, he's hiding it well. His hair is carefully messy, in way that probably takes fifteen minutes to get right. And there aren't any bags under his eyes.

"I thought maybe it would make me look eighteen again," I say, pouring myself a cup. I plop down into my seat and slink to a withered "J". Grandma Marylin raises an eyebrow and I sit up straight with my elbows off the table. I take a sip from my mug and the sweet bitter liquid cruises over my tongue and jumpstarts my every nerve ending, from hair to heel.

"Weren't we supposed to meet Greg for breakfast or something? I don't know. I drank a lot. I could have just imagined it," I say.

Sawyer nearly snorts coffee out of his nose. "A lot is an understatement."

"We changed it to lunch," Grandma Marylin says. She stirs her tea and the clanking of spoon against porcelain rattles my brain.

"Oh, thank God. And please, Sawyer, you were right along there with me. Drink for drink, shot for shot." I jiggle my coffee cup at him and he winks back at me. I only let myself give him half a smile.

"Noon. At Empress," Grandma Marylin says, ignoring our banter and pouring herself a second cup.

There's knock at the door. Grandma Marylin dabs at her lip with a napkin then hurries to the door the best she can. She's leaning as if there's an invisible string running through the left side of her body, pulling her to the floor. I hadn't noticed how bad her condition had gotten until this moment. Whenever I speak to her on the phone about it, she says that its fine. That she's fine. That she barely notices it, and that if some doctor hadn't cursed her with a diagnosis, she would never know the difference.

I don't need to turn around to know who just walked in the door. I know those heavy footsteps, that deep chuckle responding to anything Grandma

Marylin says. It's Phil Cooper. Phil the Plumber. Cooper the Pooper Scooper. He was a friend of Grandma Marylin's late husband and after she'd been widowed, Phil took over as her resident plumber slash personal handyman. On the evenings that she would invite him to stay for dinner after he fixed something, Charlie and I would roll our eyes at each other and brace ourselves for the second-hand embarrassment that came with Phil's shameless and unrequited flirting with her. We were young but it didn't take an adult mind to know he was interested in her money. Phil always managed to "casually" mention a story about not getting paid in full for a job he completed, or how the hospital was robbing him blind for a medical bill. Then he'd slip in how if he and Marylin met first she would have married him. There was a new sob story every day, followed by a flirtation and Grandma Marylin fell for it every time, taking financial pity on him.

Sawyer's taking his last sip of coffee when he catches my 'it's too early for this guy' look. He spit-laughs his coffee back into his cup.

"Look at this guy, Marylin!" Phil booms behind me. I turn to see him squinting at Sawyer. "Never thought

I'd see the day where little Sawyer Swenson was taller than me."

"Good to see you, Phil." Sawyer sits back down.

"And look what we have here! Is this a movie star?" He slaps his palm to his forehead. "Maura, my mistake." He rubs his greasy palm over the top of my head, matting my hair into a static mess.

'Phony baloney Phil,' Greg used to call him.

"Hi, Phil, how are you?"

"Phil? You hear this Marylin?" He plops down in her seat after she gets up to get him a cup of coffee. He's wearing grease-stained jeans and a grey t-shirt that's been washed one too many times so I can see the impression of his belly button through the fabric. He was never exactly a slim man but the years have shown no mercy to his beer belly. "Calling me Phil," he chuckles. "Whatever happened to Mr. Cooper?"

Grandma Marylin places his coffee in front of him. "Hush, Phil, they're adults now. They can call you whatever they want."

Sawyer gets up from his seat and offers it to Grandma Marylin. He moves down one, glaring at Phil. None of us could ever quite understand why she put up with him.

"So, what are you doing here?" I ask. "Didn't see you at the funeral yesterday."

Grandma Marylin chimes in. "There's a leaky faucet in the master bathroom."

"Should be an easy fix." Phil takes a sip of the coffee and lets out an exasperated 'Ah' before shifting his eyebrow up at me. "As for Charlie, I paid my respects here and to Natalee before the funeral. See, I don't like churches. Legend has it I go up in flames when I walk through the door." He widens his eyes like a magician mid-reveal. Was this supposed to be funny?

"Right," I say.

"Charlie was a good boy," he continues, "Never got himself into trouble, never gave Marylin here any grief. It's a damn shame what happened to him up there in those mountains."

The coffee climbs back up into my throat.

He lets out a burp into his closed fist and the smell of a half-regurgitated egg sandwich permeates the air. "I swear, Marylin, I've been up in those woods every chance I get looking for the fuc—" he searches for a more delicate word, "shithead that did this."

"Phil!" Grandma Marylin says. "The kids."

Phil roars with laughter. "You just told me they were grown!"

And that was Phil in a nutshell. "Shit-head" was as about as delicate as it ever got with him.

"Still hunting, I guess?" Sawyer says.

"Oh, I'll stop when I'm dead," says Phil, going on to recount in full bloodied detail the last doe he bagged. Most men in Settlers Hill, especially the ones in Phil's age bracket, grew up hunting in the surrounding woods. They'd claim it was for food, that they'd make use of every part of the animal, but for someone like Phil, he hunted for pure sport. "If you're lucky, I'll take you with me while you're here."

I swear I see Sawyer shiver. Grandma Marylin places her hand gently on Sawyer's forearm and I can't tell if it's to calm him, or to prevent him from clocking Phil across the cheek.

One time, prior to our abduction, Phil insisted on taking Sawyer, Charlie, and Greg out hunting with him. I wasn't allowed to go because I'm a girl, and apparently having a vagina impairs your ability to hold a gun or track an animal. Long story short: it didn't go well. Phil gave them all guns—which I'm not sure is legal—and after a long afternoon of tracking and missed shots, Phil shot a doe. Charlie had begged him not to. Phil, for all his bragging, was a shit shot. The poor animal was still alive when they got up to it. He told the boys one of them had to finish it off right between the eyes. He said it would make them men. Apparently, his dad made him do the same when he was their age.

Charlie was too busy puking, so it came down to Sawyer and Greg. When they couldn't decide, Phil put his hand over Greg's on the gun to make him take the shot. Greg struggled and yelled for him to stop. The sound of a shot interrupted their scuffle. Sawyer had shot the doe between the eyes so Greg didn't have to. Grandma Marylin didn't talk to Phil for a while after that. Not until after our rescue from the barn. Not until after he'd sent flowers and cards and offered to do any house work for her for free until the end of time. Even then, she was always wary of him.

"Let's not drag up old wounds, shall we?" Grandma Marylin says. "These two are too busy to hunt. Sawyer is a Marshal now, and my Maura here is a big-time photographer for a successful magazine in New York City."

"All right, all right," Phil threw his hands up in the air. "I give! Well, let me get to fixing this leaky sink of yours—although, Marylin, I'm starting to think that you go around this house breaking stuff just so you can call me up." He winks.

"Not even in your dreams," I say, smiling too widely to be sincere.

"Oh, she knows I'm just playing around with her, don't you, Marylin? Besides, I better not mess around with this lady. Her husband was real tough, you know? I don't want him hauntin' my ass!" Phil pushes the table away, sliding himself back and leaves his coffee cup behind. "I should get started. This should only take a few minutes and I'll be on my way. Got a few jobs today. Gotta make my rent!"

Phil makes his way back to the bathroom, the floor boards creaking under his feet.

Sawyer and I clear the table, insisting that Grandma Marylin sit and relax.

"Why do you like that guy?" I ask, cupping crumbs off the table and tossing them in the garbage.

"He was a good friend of George's since childhood. He's been very kind to me over the years since I've been widowed. And, yes, he's a few crayons short of a full box and doesn't always make the best decisions, but he's not a bad man. He's what I like to call a 'left over caveman'."

"The guy's a creep," says Sawyer sitting back down.

I nod. "He would always cozy up to us, act like he liked us, when you were around and then when you weren't around, he was just...ugh I don't know. It's just like Sawyer said: he's a creep. Grouchy and bossy."

Sawyer cut in. "I think he's in love with you."

"I think he's in love with your money," I say.

"Now, hush," she says. "He's only in the next room. I won't embarrass a guest in my home. It isn't polite to talk about someone when they're in earshot. Just wait until he leaves." She sips at her tea, winks, and gives Sawyer a pinch on the cheek.

"Perfect, we can talk about him at the diner," I laugh. "Then Greg can join in." Greg loves himself a good shit talking session, especially when it's about Phil Cooper.

"That reminds me," says Grandma Marylin. "We are going to go see Natalee this morning after Phil finishes up here."

Charlie and Natalee's house is on the other side of town. It has some property to it, three acres or so, which isn't so unusual on the outskirts of town, even though the zoning laws keep properties at a minimum of two acres. Charlie loved it there. He had a green thumb and said that working outside helped to clear his head.

Grandma Marylin insists we have her driver escort us. She claims it's Sawyer and me who are in no state to drive. We play along.

The driver snakes around the bend into Charlie's "S" shaped driveway. We had seen his wife Natalee at the funeral, but only from afar. As the widow, she was bombarded with condolences, hugs, kisses on the cheek and pelted with phrases like 'If you need anything don't hesitate to ask' and 'A young woman like you? You are going to be just fine.' Truthfully, I don't know Natalee all that well, so when Grandma Marylin suggested that we give her some space yesterday, I was fit to give it to her.

Charlie and Natalee only dated for six months before they tied the knot. There was no engagement party or bridal shower. Greg was convinced it was a shot gun wedding given the haste and lack of fuss. We all took bets on the due date.

But no baby ever came. And Natalee is all alone now. Was it worse to be a young widow? To have a fighting chance at starting over? Or does it feel like being tortured for nothing? Maybe only having a short time with the person you thought you'd grow old with makes you weary for anyone else who comes after. I wonder if that's something Grandma Marylin will talk about with her. Maybe widows can speak frankly and openly to each other, in a way that the rest of us couldn't possibly understand.

"What do I say to her?" I asked Grandma Marylin as the car rolled to a stop.

"What do you mean? You say that you are sorry for her loss," she says.

"But it's our loss, too," I say.

"You never were too keen on sharing, dear," she says. "I can see that not much has changed." And just like that, I'm checked back into place.

The property dwarfs the house. Ivy has taken over much of the brick edifice, reaching its arms up toward the shingles of the roof. I step up to the door and the scent of the lilacs lining the three simple front steps wraps around my head like a rubber band and pulls. Florals always give me a headache, and now, all I can smell are the flowers from Charlie's funeral. There were lilacs there too, right? Or were they magnolias?

I'm digging through my purse for an aspirin when the door opens. I straighten up, expecting to see

Natalee with a tissue in hand, but instead in the doorway stands Harvey Barton, Boyd's father and former town Sheriff.

Suddenly, I'm eleven years old again, staring at a man who at six foot two, might as well be twenty feet tall. His graying hair and the crow's feet that sprawl from the corners of his eyes only make him more handsome. His structured jaw and cheekbones are like that of an actor from the forties, the kind that twirls a leading lady towards him before kissing her.

My mind forks itself away from my body and I find myself lunging towards him, propping myself up on my tippy toes and sweeping my arms around his neck. My chest presses to his sternum and I feel his arms bustle at my lower back, accepting my embrace. I am eleven and he's just opened the door to the stable all over again. His is the first face we have seen in the three days since the doors shut.

I've seen Harvey Barton plenty of times since he found us in that barn. Throughout the years, he was always there, looming, watching, and protecting. And yet, I've never had this type of reaction to his presence before. I suddenly become self-aware and embarrassed by my overwhelming and unwarranted emotion. I loosen my grip around his neck and he lowers me softly back to the ground.

My cheeks are wet but it doesn't feel like I'm crying. Harvey is staring down at me.

"I...I'm so sorry," I stammer.

He smiles. It's the type of smile that can light up a whole room. He looks at you and you might as well be the only person there. How could Boyd come from a man like this?

"That's all right. It's good to see you. I'm glad you're here," he says and his gaze shifts to Sawyer. His smile grows. "Marshal." He winks and tips an imaginary hat. They shake hands with a strong clap. Sawyer is no longer the little boy Harvey helped out of the barn. Harvey greets him like a man and Sawyer does his best to hide his glee. "My God, would you look at you two," he says like a proud father before turning to Grandma Marylin. He kisses her on the cheek. "Marylin, you look radiant as always."

"Thank you." She's fallen victim to his charm as Sawyer and I have. "Although I must be honest, I didn't expect to see you here. Boyd said you were out of town."

"Just got back this morning. Came straight here." Harvey's eyebrows knit together. "Tore me to pieces that I couldn't be there for the funeral. I got the call from Boyd about Charlie right after I landed in Chicago. It's a moment I don't care to relive. Would have cost me an arm and a leg to switch my flight and you know how it is, I'm retired now."

Marylin leans in and drops her voice to a whisper. "I could have helped you, you know."

Harvey takes her by the hand. "I know you would have, Marylin. But I would never ask that of you."

"How is she?" Marylin asks of Natalee.

Harvey nods. "She's ok. Sad. Still in shock, I imagine. I think we both know that once the visitors stop coming around as often—when life goes back to normal for everyone else—that's when things will get rocky."

"You're very right about that," she says. From widower to widow they come to an understanding.

"Come on in," he says and shifts aside to let us through the door. "I'm sure she'll be very happy you're here."

The floral smell only intensifies as he leads us through the entryway into the living room. There are dozens of condolence flowers lining the walls.

The house is a little different than I remembered it. I'd only seen it when Charlie was about to purchase it, so it had been empty and still had the previous owner's paint on the walls—canary yellows mixed with what Charlie called "duck shit green." Now, its colors are muted beiges and taupe-greens, rustic with a touch of Mediterranean.

Natalee is sitting on the couch, looking at her phone, when we walk in. She sees us and places the phone face down on the glass coffee table. The clink echoes into the cathedral ceilings. Her blonde hair is wet like she's just taken a shower and the moisture makes it look brown. It takes me a minute to realize that she doesn't have any makeup on. I've never seen her without makeup before.

"Marylin," she throws herself into Grandma Marylin's arms. Grandma Marylin stumbles backward slightly before catching herself. "Thank you for coming."

She proceeds down the line, hugging Sawyer and then me. It feels foreign. Forced. Charlie had been the buffer between us. And truthfully, I'd never tried to get to know Natalee. I guess I always figured there was time, and now, here we are, without Charlie to make conversation. Alone.

Natalee welcomes us to sit on the couch and offers us something to drink. "That's all right, dear. We won't stay too long. We don't want to exhaust you," Marylin says.

"Well, I should get going," Harvey says. He looks down at his watch and taps the glass with his pointer finger. "Darn thing never says the right time." He chuckles.

I want to jump out of my seat and beg him to stay. The more people in the room the less awkward it will feel. He leans down to give Natalee a hug and tells her to call him if she needs anything. He tells her he's right down the street.

Natalee thanks him and gets up to see him out. When she sits back down, I notice how frail she looks. She was always thin, but right now, there's a frailness to her. Her muscles protrude through her skin with each small movement.

Sawyer is seated next to me on the couch, leaning forward with his elbows on his knees. His hands are folded together like he is a cop breaking bad news to a loved one. He's just as uncomfortable as I am. "So, how are you holding up?" he asks.

Natalee crosses her legs and folds her hands over her knees. Now that we are at eye level, I can see the glassiness in her eyes, the brownish hue circling them.

I know that look. She's hopped up on something. Probably for the pain. Anti-depressant? Anti-anxiety? Maybe both. I kind of wish she'd share some of whatever she's on.

"Oh, I'm ok," she says to Sawyer. "It's not really real yet, you know?" She glances over my shoulder toward the entryway. "I just keep thinking, 'Oh, he'll be home any minute now. Just another late night or an open house that went too long.'" She twiddles her thumbs.

"Well, I know that we," I motion between Sawyer and me, "aren't exactly nearby, but if you need anything, don't be afraid to call." I'm doing it now. I'm echoing the relentless loop of the same three or four condolences she's been getting this whole week. I want to say something else. Something with meaning, but the words just won't come.

Natalee says, "That's so kind of you, Maura. I know we never really got to know each other. You guys were just so close. It was so sweet the way Charlie would talk about you all. And especially you, Maura. You were like his sister. I should be offering you my condolences, too."

I'm taken aback by her compassion and graciousness. Maybe I had it all wrong with Natalee. Maybe she wasn't the snotty cheerleader I thought I knew in high school. Or she's simply changed. After all, who is the exact same person they were when they were sixteen?

Grandma Marylin raises an eyebrow and pats my knee. "I have a feeling you two have more in common than you may think." Natalee's shoulders drop. I guess she felt as awkward with me as I did with her.

"I'm really so happy you all came by," Natalee says and swallows hard.

"Charlie never shut up about you," Sawyer says like a shot out of a cannon. Like he'd been holding it in and looking for the right time to say it.

Natalee's eyes light up and for the first time since we arrived, she looks as though she might break into tears. "Really?"

Sawyer nods. It was news he was happy to deliver. "Never shut up about that lemon chicken you made. Said you were the coolest chick he ever met and that he couldn't believe he got you."

Natalee let out a puff of air that was equal parts cry and laughter. A release of tightly held emotion. "Can I be honest?" she asks. "I was the lucky one to have him. No one I dated had ever been so nice to me. Put me first. Checked on me when I was having a bad day."

She turns to Grandma Marylin and a tear streams down her cheek. "You raised him right. He was my best friend."

Grandma Marylin's teeth clench in her closed mouth. She chokes back tears that are begging to come through. "My sweet, sweet boy."

"He was so stressed lately." Natalee says, looking in her lap. "I hate to even say this. To bring it up. Charlie was so open with me about it, but I know it's not my place. He was...he was set to sell the Old..." she chokes on the words, "to sell the Old Salem farm. And I just think that going there, being back there...I don't know. Maybe I should have stopped him. It was too much for him. He probably went out hiking to clear his head. Maybe if I'd just been more supportive this never would have happened. She breaks down in tears, burying her face in her palms, bent over on the couch. Grandma Marylin staggers over to comfort her.

We stay strong as we wait until Natalee calms down. Tell her it wasn't her fault. That there was nothing she could have done. It is only once we are back in Grandma Marylin's town car that the walls break down between us.

"Did you know about this?" Sawyer asks in a low growl.

Grandma Marylin shakes her head and I let out a demonstrative 'No'.

"Why would he do that?" Sawyer is angry with Charlie. I can tell. Like an older brother mad at his younger brother for being so reckless.

"Maybe he wanted to sell it to someone who would tear it down. I mean, I don't know why the town didn't demolish that thing years ago." I wish we'd heard the plan from Charlie. For a moment, I'm angry with Natalee for laying the burden of that information on us.

Grandma Marylin stares out the window. "It doesn't matter anymore..."

We get to the Empress diner just before noon. Sawyer is still reeling from what Natalee told us. But Grandma Marylin is right. It doesn't matter now.

The Empress Diner is the best diner in town. Well, it's the only diner in town. Locals blabber on and on about the time it was on that Food Network show with the guy with the funny hair whose name I can never remember. That guy hemmed and hawed over Empress, giving everyone here something to talk about until the end of time. The hash browns. It's all about the hash browns. Diced up, crisp potatoes with sautéed onion. The secret, we all came to learn on the show, was bacon grease. That's what I need right now. Nothing cures a hangover quite like potatoes and bacon grease.

The waitress, an attractive middle-aged woman with more red lipstick on her teeth than her lips and a haircut that went out of style in the 80s, tries to seat us in a booth at the center of the diner. Before we sit, Sawyer politely insists that we move to the open table at the very back. He sits with his back to the wall and his eyes on the front door. His Marshal's reflex to have his eye on every inch of the place. It's a habit he picked up in law enforcement, and Grandma Marylin and I have both grown used to his request.

He's taken the window seat and sunlight shines warmly on his right cheek. He's grown a little stubble overnight. It looks good on him.

"I just don't understand..." Sawyer begins again.

Grandma Marylin raises a hand. "I only get you for the next few hours before you leave me again. We are tabling this discussion for now, do I make myself clear? I'm sure Charlie had his reasons and was going to tell us. We have the rest of our lives to mull over this.

I just want to have a nice lunch with you three." And that was the end of that.

The previous diner had left their newspaper on the seat. Grandma Marylin thumbs through it. She squints at the headline. "Settlers Hill Seahorses Set to Slaughter Carville Crocodiles." She chuckles. "Now, I love alliteration, but when have you ever seen an aggressive seahorse?" She hisses an "s" in search of a better option. "What about snakes?"

"Scorpions?" Sawyer teases.

"Sabretooth tigers," I say.

Grandma Marylin's done the trick. We're now running through a list of every animal starting with an "s," and by the time our waters make it to the table, we've temporarily forgotten our dizzying upset over Charlie's secret.

I'm dying to order lunch, or even just an appetizer, but Marylin insists that we wait for Greg. "He'll be here any minute." She thumbs through the menu even though she knows she's getting what she always gets—banana pancakes with peanut butter chips. Elvis pancakes.

It's a Monday so the diner is filled with retirees and octogenarians tapping the sides of their hard-boiled eggs and chit chatting about which garage sale had the best loot.

Everyone here knew Charlie, but I don't overhear his name on anyone's tongue. Maybe that was just my stilly notion, though—that everyone should still be mourning, still be talking about him. A small part of me feels like the moment we stop talking about him will be the moment he's truly gone.

"So, tell me about this new girlfriend of yours." Marylin smirks at Sawyer.

"Girlfriend?" I hear myself say and I do my best to control the shock in my voice.

Sawyer leans against the back of the booth and he cracks his knuckles. "Not a girlfriend. My friend just set me up on a blind date."

I want to ask if he likes her. If they had more than one date. Does he have a picture? These are questions I might normally ask him or Greg or Charlie, but considering what happened the last time I saw Sawyer— the thing I haven't told anyone yet—I feel like I can't ask him.

Grandma Marylin slaps her hand to the table playfully. "Don't make me call your mothers to get the scoop. Tell me, do you like her? Let's see a picture.

When are we seeing her again? What does she do for a living? She does have a job, doesn't she? Not another one of those vapid models again, I hope? That stage of yours was infuriating. I've had better conversations with my tea pot than that Lacey something or other you brought to meet me that one time."

I'm unable to stifle my cackle and Sawyer's chuckle bursts through the seam of his lips. I don't know why I worried—Grandma Marylin would never let him get away with half-hearted information.

"Laney," Sawyer corrects. The dimple on his left cheek deepens.

"Oh, whatever." Grandma Marylin waves him off. "All I know is she couldn't figure out how to flush my toilet."

To be fair to the poor girl, Grandma Marylin's toilet has a rope pull dangling above the tank to flush, which isn't common nowadays, but that doesn't stop water from coming out of my nose. The waitress sees me in passing and drops me a few extra napkins.

Once we all calm down Sawyer adds, "It was just one date two months ago. It was nothing."

It was always 'nothing' with Sawyer, or so he claims. Even Lacey, or Laney, or whatever her name was, was the longest run he's ever had and that relationship lasted just under six months. Grandma Marylin and I have discussed our theories at length over tea—okay, okay, martini's—and my theory is that he's picky. Between Grandma Marylin and his mothers, he grew up with three strong, capable women in his life, and that's hard to compete with. What woman could live up to all three of them?

She was two martinis in when she spat back, 'Pff, no. I'll tell you what he needs. He needs to quit messing around with these twenty-two-year-old model nobrains who want diamond earrings for blow jobs so he can find a real woman. One who challenges him. Keeps him on his toes. A real partner.' Then the conversation shifted to the other bullet points on our boozy gossip list, like Greg and Charlie, and because I was lucky, some hush-hush scandal in town. It was juicy enough to make us both nurse two-day hangovers the next day.

"And what about you, miss?" Grandma Marylin holds up her menu and coyly peers her eyes over the top at me. "You've gone pretty quiet since your breakup with Weston. Paparazzi still following you around?"

She knows we broke up, but not why. Here, with Sawyer—who knows why—is not the place where I want to discuss it for the first time openly. So, I concentrate on the question at hand. "Ugh, they were the worst. They followed me a little bit after we broke up, but they've kind of fizzled out. Bloodsuckers."

Sawyer shifts in his seat and looks at me. "Wait, wait, wait a minute. You, a photographer, hate other photographers? A little hypocritical, don't you think?"

"Not at all." I flick his ear. He laughs and withers back. "I get permission from the people I photograph. They get hair, makeup, and the works. Paparazzi wait outside your door so they can catch you with bed head and smeared mascara. They lurk outside restaurants to catch you three drinks in, hoping you might trip off the curb and flash come cooch to make for a good story."

"Yeah, yeah, yeah," Sawyer pinches my leg under the table. I yelp and smack his chest with the back of my hand.

"All right, all right! Enough you two. We're in a public place," Grandma Marylin chastises.

A few more minutes pass and the waitress circles back around. She pulls out her notepad and pen. "We ready? Or are we still waiting on someone?"

I pull out my phone to check the time. It's 12:30. Thirty minutes late.

"Just another minute and he'll be here, I'm sure," Marylin says.

A few more moments pass by. Sawyer's pumps his heel to the floor over and over again. The booth seat shakes with him. I nudge him to stop and he does for a moment, only to start up again. "What's with the earthquake?" I ask.

His lids are heavy as he looks past me through the diner window. Then he checks his watch. "I've got to get on the road today sooner rather than later," he says.

"He'll be here," Grandma Marylin says. She and Sawyer exchange worrisome glances.

I can't help but feel as though I'm watching a conversation through a one-way mirror. "Is there something I should know?"

CHAPTER 8:

2000

G reg bum-rushed through the pitch black toward the stable stall door. "No, no, no," he muttered.

"What's happening?" Sawyer said. He, Charlie, and Maura stood frozen.

"Hello?" Maura called out and the echo of the roomy barn disappeared. Now, her voice was stifled in a vacuum.

"Someone locked us in here. Open! Open up!" Greg pounded his fists, each word escalating into a frantic begging.

It was nearly pitch black. A sliver of sun peeking through the gapped slats of wood made just enough light to make the four were shadowy silhouettes to one another.

Maura reached blindly for Greg through the darkness, following the sound of his voice.

Greg threw Maura's hand off his shoulder and pulled on the door, throwing his hips backward for leverage. Sawyer could hear the movement and joined in, grasping the wood and yanking as hard as he could.

"Air," Charlie's voice boomed from the back of the stall. He was still unable to unfreeze himself from where he stood. "We're going to run out of air!"

"No, we're not. We'll be out of here in two minutes. It was probably the wind that shut the door. And now it's just jammed," Maura snapped, her words shaky. Not even she believed what she was saying. There was no wind that could slide, let alone lock, a heavy barn stall door like that.

Greg whips around to face Maura, or at least the direction of her voice. "Wind? Wind can't lock a door."

"He's right," said Sawyer. "It's got to be the owner. That Rick guy."

"Why would he do that?" said Charlie.

Greg paced around like a caged animal. "He's a psycho. Why else would he lock kids in a barn? We have to get out of here."

"Here, I have an idea," said Maura. "Greg, you stand here near the door, and I'll get on your shoulders. Maybe there's a way out over the top."

"There's nothing up there! It's boarded shut," he protested. "Plus, we'll never reach just the two of us."

"We have to try. This is crazy. Who does that?" She reached into the darkness until she found his shirt sleeve and dragged him closer to the door. He knelt down and she used the stall door to steady herself as she climbed her feet atop his shoulders. Greg groaned under the added weight and forced himself up until his knees locked into a standing position.

Maura used her hands to feel around. Wood. Wood. And more wood where it shouldn't be. That part of the stable stall should be open, like it is in each of the neighboring stalls. Why is this one boarded up?

There's nothing. No light. No one would even keep a horse in here, let alone four people.

"Ugh," she muttered.

"What?" Charlie asked, panicked.

"Let me down, Greg. It's all closed up here," she said.

Greg lowered himself to the ground but lost balance, bringing both him and Maura tumbling down into the hay. "I told you guys this was a bad idea."

Maura opened her mouth to speak when she was interrupted. The sound is harsh. Indeterminable at first. Sharp. Slish. Slash. Like metal scraping against metal. Like the sharp edge of a knife running along the other side of the stall door. The four stood breathless, listening. Waiting.

The door rattled as something slammed against the it. Something stabbed into it, over and over again, until the four friends found themselves with their backs pressed to the wall on the other side of the stall.

CHAPTER 9:

2018

Sawyer's eyes dart to Marylin's. It's a questioning look. She signals her permission with a nod.

Sawyer shifts in his seat to face me, like a parent breaking bad news to a child. "Greg had a little relapse right after Charlie died."

"What do you mean 'after'? Charlie just..." I can't bring myself to say the word.

"The day after," Sawyer continues. His arm is laying on the table in front of me and I can see the muscles of his forearm tensing. Is he nervous to tell me this? Is he angry with Greg? There is some emotion begging to break through his calm façade, but I can't pinpoint it.

"What happened? And why didn't anyone tell me about this?" I ask.

"You've had enough on your plate," Grandma Marylin cuts in. I know she's referring to my recent breakup. I resent the weakness it implies. That I'm so delicate that people are counting the straws one by one as they place them on my back, so as not to break it.

"What happened?" I press on.

Sawyer glances around to make sure no one is eavesdropping. Small towns equal big gossip. "The day after Charlie died, Greg didn't show up for work," he starts before Grandma Marylin cuts in.

"His boss at the gas station, knows about Greg's past struggles. He was the only person who would hire him." Grandma Marylin leans across table, closer to me. "He called me when Greg didn't come in. He had a feeling something was wrong."

My heart is racing.

Sawyer picks up. "Grandma Marylin found Greg in his new apartment. He took enough Xanax to knock out a horse and there was cocaine on his dresser."

Grandma Marylin's voice grows softer. "Luckily, he hadn't gotten to the cocaine yet. I called an ambulance when I couldn't wake him and they were able to pump his stomach."

"I came down that day," Sawyer confessed.

"You've been here since last week?" I say, betrayed by the exclusion.

Sawyer nods.

Grandma Marylin raises a finger. "Now, don't go blaming him. Talk to me. I was the one who called him in and insisted he not tell you."

"That's why you're so antsy," I say to Sawyer. "Greg is late and you think he's messed up again."

"Listen, I'm sorry we didn't tell you," he says and his expression softens. "We didn't want him to go to the bar last night, but he insisted. Besides, alcohol was never his problem as much as the other stuff. We figured it would be worse if he missed out or felt ostracized."

I'm antsy too, now. I reach for my phone and dial Greg. The phone trills until I hear his voice on the other end—but it's just his voicemail. I hang up without leaving a message and try again. Sawyer raises a finger to get the attention of the waitress as she passes our table and he asks for the check. I get Greg's voicemail again, Sawyer is already at the front of the diner paying for our coffees and Grandma Marylin's tea. He returns and throws a few dollars on the table. "Let's go," he says.

On the steps outside the Empress Diner, we devise our plan. Divide and conquer. Grandma Marylin decides she will check for Greg at her house, in case there was confusion about where they were to meet. It's a comforting thought, but the more likely reality is that Greg is lying somewhere face down in a puddle of his own puke, nose bloodied from too much cocaine and his heart in need of a jumpstart. That or he is blue lipped on his back with needles sticking out of his arm. Luck, unlike cocaine, Xanax or heroine, eventually runs out.

Sawyer and I volunteer to go to Greg's new apartment. Sawyer insists that Grandma Marylin takes the town car back to her house. Greg's place is within walking distance from the diner.

We part ways and the tension in the air is palpable. Sawyer and I still haven't spoken about what happened when we saw each other last, that night in my apartment. What he said. What we did.

This is the first time we've been alone since then, but it's hardly the time to hash things out. So instead, I focus on the betrayal at hand.

"I can't believe you didn't tell me about all this," I pant. I'm doing my best to keep in step with him. Back in the day, I could outrun him easily, but now he has eight inches of height on me, and from the looks of it, he probably spends more time at the gym than I do.

"What would be the use in telling you? There was enough going on and it wouldn't have made a difference if you had been here. You should be thanking me," he says over his shoulder.

If he were to turn around and look at me, he'd see my flamed cheeks. "That's not your call to make."

"You're right. It was Grandma Marylin's. She told me not to say anything and I did as I was told. You would have done the same thing in my position."

I want to kick him in the heels. Trip him and then race ahead of him. 'Mad Dog Maura,' I hear his voice in my head from the day before. No. I'm not that person anymore. And besides, he's right. I would have done the same thing. Protected him. But I'm not about to tell him that. Betrayal and anger are easier and more manageable than worry, so I let myself stay angry as we sprint forward.

I haven't been to Greg's new place yet, so I keep in toe with Sawyer, following his lead. We round the corner of Flamingo Street onto Blackbird Road and stop in front of number 39. Greg's car, a 2018 Hyundai Elantra, is parked out front.

The house is a small white cape with blue shutters and an ivy-covered mailbox. Thorny rosebushes sit beneath the bay window at the front of the house, guarded by ceramic garden gnomes. Stone fairies hold out bowls of water for birds to bathe in and drink from. There are steps along the western side of the house leading to Greg's apartment.

"He rents the upstairs." Sawyer opens the latch on the gate.

"Who lives downstairs?" I follow him through the backyard over a stone path leading to the wooden stairway.

"Miss Winters," he says as we begin our ascent. I'm taken aback by this. Greg lives above Joanne Winters? As in, our old English teacher—the lush of a woman I spoke to just last night? Why didn't either of them mention this?

I'm immediately aware of what a bad idea it is to have a recovering drug addict living upstairs from a desperate divorcee with a drinking problem. We reach the top step and I shake my head. 'Don't judge until you have all the facts' I remind myself.

Sawyer balls his fist and bangs on the door. No answer. There aren't any windows to peek through.

I press my ear to the door. "Nothing," I say. No TV chatter or music or shuffling of feet headed for the door.

Sawyers jaw is clenched so tightly it looks as if his teeth might turn to dust.

"Did you see if it's locked?" I reach forward to check it myself. The door opens without so much as a creak.

"Some Marshal I am," he quips. We bump shoulders, stuck in the doorway as we rush through like two stooges.

I power through and enter first into what I assume is Greg's living room. It's a ten foot by ten foot room with slanted ceilings made of an unpainted knotty pine. A faded forest green rug cover the floor and an Ikea couch sits across from a single flat screen tv mounted on a coffee table. Its empty and soundless, aside from the whirring ceiling fan.

"Greg?" I call out. No answer.

My phone rings. It's Grandma Marylin. She tells me that Greg isn't at her house and asks if we've reached his apartment yet. I say not quite and tell her I'll call her back. Sawyer shoots me a confused look. I shrug. I don't know why I lied.

Through the living room there is a small hallway and to the left, a small bathroom. To the right, there's a boarded-up door that must have once led to the stairs before the house was split as a two family. Across the small hallway is Greg's bedroom. Neither of us bother to knock on this door.

The bedroom is not much bigger than the living room, except there is a brick chimney that cuts through the center of the room. The fireplace must be downstairs where Miss Winter's lives. Sawyer flicks on the light.

"Greg?" I say again, in vain. It's clear he isn't in here.

"Do you smell that?" Sawyer says; his face is contorted like he's about to sneeze.

I hadn't noticed until he said something. It was as if my nose had been turned off so my eyes could work over time. I take a whiff and choke on the stale musty scent.

Sawyer and I stare at each other a moment. The answer is at the tip of our tongues, but it's blocked. We break our gaze and slowly pace around the room. "His car is out front," I remind him.

"It is, isn't it." Sawyer is sniffing around the room like a bloodhound and I realize that I am too.

The space is neater than I thought it would be. 'An organized mess', Greg would call his system. Only he knew where everything was in his room as a kid.

My back is turned—I'm glancing over the volumes of self-help books stacked above his dresser—when Sawyer calls out, "Maura. You need to come see this." His voice is straight as a line. Yet there is a seriousness to it. An urgency.

I walk over and find him standing over Greg's bed. A twin-size mattress sits cocooned between the chimney and the wall. Saying nothing, Sawyer keeps his eyes fixed on the bed. Now I see what he sees. My knees wobble and I grip the chimney behind me.

The comforter is peeled down halfway over the bed and in between the fitted and top sheets, poking out from the pillow cover is hay.

Sawyer and I stare at the dry, split strands bunched and piercing the blue gray cotton sheets until one of us has the courage to move. Sawyer shifts first and his movement breaks my trance. We float like voiceless zombies to the front door, close it behind us and stand on the landing that overlooks the neighborhood.

There's a lump in my throat and my limbs tingle numbly, swollen and heavy. My feet feel like cement blocks as I descend the stairs. Sawyer is moving with the same heaviness. He hasn't blinked yet.

I grab his arm when we reach the bottom and pull him back to face me. "He's playing a joke on us," I say but the words are a lie. Though we both know that there are virtually no limits to the lengths old friends will go to pick at or on each other, this is...this is different. Even Greg wouldn't use a trigger point that sensitive, that damaging, for the sake of a few laughs.

Sawyer shakes his head. He can see that I'm still grappling with my own words.

"What does it mean? Where is he?" My thoughts are screaming inside my head but the words come out as a dry, cracking whisper. "Do we call the police?

"Who is the police around here, Maura?" he says pointedly.

He continues, "Besides, what would we say? 'Oh, hi, I want to report hay on a mattress?'"

"No. We'd report him missing."

"He's been missing for all of an hour as far as we know. No one is going to care until he's been gone at least 24 hours. Even then, considering his history with drugs, they'll probably phone it in. Say that he's overdosed somewhere and that it's probably too late to help him. A waste of time."

"So, correct me if I'm wrong, but what you're saying is if we call now it's too early, but if we wait until its considered urgent then it's too late?

Sawyer gives a single nod.

My phone rings in my pocket. Grandma Marylin again. I toss the cell to Sawyer to answer. I can't bring myself to be the one to tell her what we saw in there.

And Sawyer is right. We have nothing to tell the police right now. Greg hasn't been missing for that long. We could be getting worked up for nothing. But the hay. I can feel it on my skin still, sticking my thighs. I remember breathing it in for days on end, the micro dust it sheds as it wears down, floats into the air and down the nostrils. You can't stop breathing it when you have no window to open and no door to poke your head out of. Three days of standing, sitting, and sleeping on hay. Ever since we were discovered—freed—the sight of hay is like nails on a chalkboard. Maybe that's why I moved to the city. Not much hay in Manhattan.

Sawyer hangs up the phone and hands it back to me.

"What did she say?" I ask.

"Keep looking. That's what she said. She's going to make some calls but said we should talk to Miss Winters, see if she's home. She might have seen him, or maybe she knows something."

We swing around to the front yard and ring the doorbell. The door is painted a red similar to the lipstick that ran over Miss Winter's teeth the night before. It's hard to tell in the daylight, but there doesn't appear to be any lights on inside. I check my watch. "Sawyer, we're morons. It's a school day."

"She's still teaching?" Sawyer asks.

I'm antsy again, tapping on my heels side to side. "How much time could we possibly have to find him? It'll take at least an hour for us to walk back to Grandma Marylin's, get a car, drive over to the school."

Sawyer takes his phone out. "Welcome to the twenty-first century, kid." He does a quick google search for the administration office's number and then dials. He does his best US Marshal voice and asks to speak to Miss Winters. He says that its urgent and that someone needs to collect her from her classroom at once.

I find myself pacing around him, circling him like a shark. "Miss Winters?" he says when she's finally on the phone. I stop in front of him and wildly motion for him to put it on speaker phone so I can listen in.

He continues, "Miss Winters. Hi, this is Sawyer Swenson. I'm not sure if you remember me..."

She cuts him off, "Sawyer, why of course I remember you!" Her slur has disappeared. And she doesn't exactly sound hungover either. "To what do I owe the pleasure?" There's a flirtatious snap to her tone.

"Have you seen Greg at all this morning? Before you left for work?"

"I haven't," she says, "But I mean, I usually don't see him in the mornings. He leaves for work after I do. I think he works the afternoon or evening shifts at the gas station now. Why? Is everything all right?"

"To be honest, we're not sure. That's why I'm calling. Can I give you my cell and you'll call me if you see him? Or if you hear anything?"

"Actually, now that I think of it, I did see his mother this morning. She arrived just as I was leaving, so, around eight. Maybe she came to see him for breakfast?" Her voice grew high in that hopeful way, when you want someone to feel relief from your words.

"Thank you, Miss Winters." He hangs up.

"As if the judge would ever bring breakfast," I say.

Greg's mom had never been a doting mother, the kind to 'drop in' and check on her son—let alone come by for a mid-week breakfast. And running into her last night at the bar proved she hadn't changed one bit.

She still lives in the house Greg was born in. The house his father left behind even though Greg was begging to go with him. Instead, Greg was left to live—survive, rather—Bea's tough love approach to motherhood. Sure, she provided a safe home stocked with food and a first aid kit, but the warmth and protection ended there. It was clear that she wanted the best for her only son, who insultingly looked more like her estranged husband than herself.

Once, Greg made the mistake of clinging to his mother's leg in a childhood moment of insecurity and was told that 'nobody likes a ginger kid, let alone a soft ginger kid.' She'd sent him away like a horse shoeing a fly.

"What would she be doing at Greg's?" I wonder as we pace down the sidewalk. "You think she did that? She put the hay in his bed? I know she's cold, but is she out and out cruel?"

"I think if there is one thing that we've learned, it's not to put anything past anybody."

He's right. When quiet, simple, Rick Salem was taken in, tried, and convicted, there wasn't one person in town who believed it at first. Poor, orphaned, destitute Rick. But the evidence spoke for itself. It appeared he wasn't so simple after all and now he's rotting away in Yates Federal Prison. My skin crawls, just considering that he is only forty miles away.

We arrive at the courthouse, looking for Judge Bea in her chambers. The brick building is one of the oldest in the town, dating back to when the size of Settlers Hill's population was only a quarter of what it is now—back when pigs and cattle outnumbered people. Judge Bea's car, the same black Bronco she buys every time the previous one dies, is in the parking lot. There is no security guard at the door, waiting by a metal detector to check my purse with a flashlight or asking Sawyer to empty his pockets. Not in Settlers Hill.

"It's so strange being back here," Sawyer whispers to me as he opens the door.

Until he said that, I hadn't considered that the last time we'd been at the courthouse was for Rick Salem's trial. We'd been dressed up in our Sunday's best. On the outside, we were shined and primed for the press and cameras, but our insides were hollow, itchy, and frozen with fear.

"Looks the same," is all I can say.

The hallways smell like mothballs and cleaning fluid, as if the janitor tried—and failed—to cover up the mustiness with bleach. Chemicals can only do so much. We follow the signs to Bea's chambers and arrive at the large oak door with her name plate. I knock three times.

There's a grunt from the other side. "You may enter."

Sawyer and I look at each other before my hand turns the knob. We aren't looking at each other as two adults, but as the children we once were. We'd seen Bea the night before and the interaction was less than pleasant. I take a second to collect myself. The door opens and I jolt forward into the room, landing right at Judge Bea's feet. I hear Sawyer's stifled snort behind me as I gather myself to stand, Bea's nose inches from mine.

She's wearing a navy-blue pantsuit with a slick white button down underneath, snapped tight to the top. There are Botoxed women with more expression lines than Bea. She stares down her nose at me as though I'm a stranger. "Can I help you?"

I think of Grandma Marylin and what she would say to me. What she would do. I force myself to drop my shoulders and cock my chin to meet her gaze. "Were you at Greg's this morning?"

"Excuse me?" she says.

Sawyer steps forward. "What time did you arrive at Greg's apartment this morning?"

Bea shifts her gaze between Sawyer and myself. "Why do you ask?"

"Because we can't find him and it seems you were the last person to see him," I say.

Bea shakes her head and walks back to her desk. "Is that what this is about?" Her heels clap against the hardwood floors. She sits in her leather high back chair and clasps her hands over her lap. "Well, I'm sure he is off on another one of his infamous benders."

Sawyer chimes in, "No, not this time. We think—"

She throws her hands up in the air, cutting him off. "All that money I poured into renowned rehab centers and this is where it gets you, huh?" She plants her pointer finger on her temple. "The problem is that he's got a weak mind. He's all fine and dandy until life doesn't go the way he wants it to go, then it's down the tubes for him."

"Money *you* poured into rehab?" I crouch toward her like a cat stalking a pigeon. "We," I motion to Sawyer, "Sawyer, Charlie, Grandma Marylin, and I—we fronted him the money for rehab." My ears run hot. "You've done nothing for him. You haven't helped him one bit. What? You threw him a bone once—a few bucks—and you want to act like you were carrying all the weight?!"

Bea places her elbows on the desk and leans forward. "My money. Your money. What does it matter?

It was wasted and you know it. You can't find him now, can you?"

"There was hay in his bed," Sawyer says.

Bea's expression switches gears. Her cocked smile gets wiped from her face. Her eyes stop blinking and she is staring a hole into Sawyer. "Excuse me?" The veil has dropped.

"Hay," Sawyer repeats. I hadn't expected him to reveal that bit of information. I figured we'd been on the same page. That we would hold back information to see where Bea led us. What she'd admit to. I'm intrigued by her visceral reaction, now glad he said something.

"So?" she says, flippantly. I can see her throat muscles tightening beneath the loose skin of her neck.

"So, we think something funny is going on," I say. "Maybe it's someone's idea of a cruel joke but—"

"I am sure that is all it is," she says.

"What time were you there this morning?" Sawyer asks again.

Without hesitation, Bea answers, "8:30 am."

"And what time did you leave?" Sawyer says.

"I stayed no longer than five minutes," she says. Her answers are as stern and quick as Sawyer's questions.

"Why?" he asks.

Bea stands up and brushes the wrinkles out of her pants. "It wasn't a social call. I had to drop something off. I put an envelope in his mailbox and then I left." She rounds the desk. "Now, I think it's time for the two of you to leave." She opens the door to her chambers.

Neither Sawyer or I move.

"What was in the envelope, Bea?" Sawyer says. I've never heard him call her by her first name-to her face.

"That's private," she says and sweeps her hand, motioning us out the door.

"Not anymore it isn't," I say. I hope I don't look as nervous as I feel.

She takes a deep breath and lets it out. "Fine, I'll tell you. But after I do, I don't want any other part in this. He is a big boy and he's on his own. How you two choose to waste your time is up to you. Agreed?"

Sawyer and I nod. Bea continues. "Greg and I had a shared account from when he was younger. Money that I held onto and saved for him. I assumed he would go to college one day," she chuckles. "What a fool I was. Anyway, I'd forgotten about it and he came to me a few weeks ago asking for money. He said he owed Coach Carlsen money. Swore it was legitimate. I didn't believe him, but I followed up with Coach Carlsen and he assured me that it was legitimate. Carlsen loaned Greg money for suits for interviews a while back. Greg wanted to reimburse him now that he's working a steady job at the gas station, but he didn't have quite enough money. I took what he owed him from the account and put it in that envelope. Now please get out of my office before I throw you both in a cell for trespassing."

We say nothing and trek by her. Once we cross the threshold, she slams the door.

Once we're out front on the sidewalk out, I say, "Something isn't right. I don't think Coach Carlsen is the type who would be loaning out money for suits for interviews."

"You know he used to sell his players steroids in high school, right?" Sawyer says. We're walking now. Though we haven't discussed it, we both know where we are headed: Coach Carlsen's bar, Hannigan's.

"Maybe Greg is hiding out from Carlsen. He owes him money, so he just decides to ghost everyone to protect himself."

"But what about the hay?" Sawyer asks.

I consider the disturbing, albeit important, detail. "Maybe it's not at all related to..." Even after all these years, I can't talk about it freely. I shake my head to clear my thoughts. "Maybe it's not what we think it is. What if Greg just put the hay in his bed so it would look like someone was in the bed? "

"You think someone came looking for Greg, and he happened to have hay on hand to stuff into his bed? You think he'd go through all that just to buy time before he made a break for it?"

"Well, not when you say it like that. And hey, at least I'm coming up with ideas."

We walk a few blocks in silence. We stop at the corner before the bar and wait for a car to pass, Sawyer's hand reaches for mine, almost reflexively. Without looking at me, he says, "Are we ever going to talk about it?"

I know what he means. He's not talking about Greg. Or the barn. He's talking about that night at my apartment. The night Weston left me.

I open my mouth to speak but then close it before any words can escape. "I...let's just find Greg first."

He gives my hand one last squeeze and then releases it before we cross the street.

Hannigan's, in the scrutiny of daylight, isn't the bustling bar it was last night after Charlie's funeral. I wince. Was that only yesterday? How many days can you fit into 24 hours?

CHAPTER 10:

2000

The sound was like the sharpening of tools. Long and drawn out like a blade against blade or the clanging of metal. The sound filled the small space. Minutes felt like hours. It seemed like it would never stop.

Charlie, Maura, Sawyer and Greg sat in the lightless hay-stacked space, sound filling the empty spaces between them. It was all they could hear, sending each of them into further isolation.

Then the sounds stopped. And when it stopped, its harsh notes hung in the air like dust settling after a tornado. For a while, they said nothing. They just observed the looming threat that the sound would return, wondering what would follow.

It was Greg who broke the silence. He was sitting now, hugging his knees rocking back and forth staring arbitrarily into the dark. "This isn't good. This isn't good."

"We're gonna get chopped into little pieces. I don't want to die." Charlie broke into a sob.

"We shouldn't've come here. I knew it," said Greg.

"No one's chopping any of us up. There has to be a way out of here," Maura said, getting to her feet.

That's when it occurred to Maura that she hadn't heard Sawyer's voice. "Sawyer?" she called out and squinted to align her eyes with the few spots the light kissed.

No one answered, but Maura could see she wasn't the only one standing.

"Over here," called Charlie, sniffling.

When Maura called for Sawyer, Charlie had reached into the space beside him. Sawyer sat hunched over his knees with his palms pressed to his ears. Charlie dug the tips of his fingers beneath Sawyer's palm and pulled it away from his ear. He shouted, "Sawyer! Are you ok? Are you hurt?"

Greg leapt from where he sat and followed Charlie's voice to Sawyer's side. Sawyer still said nothing.

Greg was the only one who knew why Sawyer had frozen up. It was like that day in the school's elevator.

He and Sawyer were riding up from the cafeteria in the school's basement to the third floor, late for Math class. The elevator stopped. A quick power outage in the school, rectified in fifteen minutes. But for those fifteen minutes, Sawyer scratched at the doors, panted, his lungs grasping for air. The nurse said it was a panic attack. Sawyer made Greg take an oath of secrecy about it.

"Hey, buddy," Greg's tone shifted. It was no longer angry or resentful, but calm, like nothing was wrong. "Just open your eyes, okay? Breathe. We're gonna be okay." He placed a hand on Sawyer's back. His breath was heavy and fast. Panting.

The three surrounded Sawyer, a trinity of protectors and for a brief moment, they forgot their own fears of being trapped. They only thought about Sawyer.

"Is he hurt?" Maura said

"No," said Greg, "He doesn't like small spaces."

"This isn't that small," said Charlie. "He can stand up and walk around."

Greg shook his head, though he wasn't sure if any of them could see it. "He's...what's that word? I can never remember it. Something with a "C". I've heard it on TV before or something. He doesn't like to feel trapped. It makes him freak."

"Claustrophobic," Maura said.

"We have to get him out of here, fast," said Greg.

CHAPTER 11:

2018

Coach Carlsen was the richest man in town, back in the day. He made his money as a quarterback in the NFL and returned home to Settlers Hill after being fired for "sexual misconduct." He never officially came clean, but everyone knew what "sexual misconduct" meant. It meant that he was messing around on his wife and got caught in bed with one of the young, bouncy-bosomed cheerleaders. And what's more is that multiple cheerleaders came forward saying he'd not only pursued them, but became aggressive when he was rejected.

But not even that could tarnish his fame in the small town where he made his name. The high school quarterback turned pro returned like the Prodigal son. All in all, the NFL didn't take a big hit with that loss. He was second string and got tossed around to different teams because no one really wanted to deal with him for all that long.

When he'd returned home at the ripe old age of twenty-nine, he had thick brown hair and grey eyes that sparkled as bright as his professionally whitened teeth. At twenty-nine, the downward spiral begins for professional athletes, but as far as the people of Settlers Hill were concerned, Patrick Carlsen was in his prime. Newly divorced and ready for the taking.

He never did marry again, though. Instead, he had a string of girlfriends, some long-term, others short-term, and all of them overlapping. But of course, I didn't experience that side of him. He was far outside my generation and my only interaction with him had been at a distance. He was the football coach for everyone from pee-wees all the way up to the Varsity team. There used to be other coaches in town, fathers who would take the job to get involved in the town and stay close to their sons, but Carlsen methodically got each of them out of his way. He didn't just want to coach football in Settlers Hill, he wanted to own football in Settlers Hill.

And so, he did, handing out harsh criticisms to pimpled players. He picked favorites—like Boyd

Barton. He'd coached Boyd from little league through to high school and chose Boyd as his star quarterback. Carlsen's specialty was culling the weakness out of the team like a scythe through summer grass.

Sawyer and I stand before the brick building, gazing up at the sign. With only a few cars in the parking lot, it seems to have lost its charm from the night before.

Inside Hannigan's, there is an older couple dining to the far left with club sandwiches and oversized pickles stuffed in baskets between them. At the bar is an older man with graying hair who's leaning over the edge of the bar so tightly that his shirt has lifted. I can see more of his butt crack than any of his distinguishable facial features.

Sawyer nudges me. He's spotted the coach behind the bar with his hands in the cash register and his back to us. There's a mirror just beyond the liquor bottles and I can see his face—his scrunched brow making deep valleys on his forehead. Except for a few extra grooves near the corner of his eyes and above his brow, his face has been untouched by time. I'd seen him in passing last night but right now, he seems larger.

Maybe it's because now, there are less people in the bar, or maybe it's because I'll always feel like a child in his presence. But there's no use in feeling small. I'm here for information. I'm here to find Greg, I remind myself and push forward.

Coach Carlsen sees Sawyer and my reflection moving toward him. Before we have the chance to announce ourselves, he turns around to greet us.

Much to my surprise, he's smiling at us, shifting his gaze between Sawyer and me as if we are old friends who've come by for a visit or new patrons ready to be liquored up.

"How are ya?" he says, laying two napkins out on the bar top. "What can I get you two?"

The old man seated at the bar interjects. "Bartender now, Patty old boy?" He says with a deep-throated chuckle.

Carlsen cocks a smile. "When you own the place, you got to jump in every so often." He raises eyebrows to repeat the request for our order. It's clear he doesn't recognize us.

"We're not here for drinks. We just have some questions," Sawyer says.

Carlsen juts his chin back and stacks the napkins back to their pile. The smile on his face has worn down a bit. "What, are you cops or something? You talk like a cop."

"Not exactly," I say. "We were here last night. We're friends of Charlie's."

"Well, I'm sorry for your loss. Charlie was good kid. Always was." He looks between Sawyer and me a few times. With each shift of his gaze, the recognition in his eyes burns a little brighter. "Hey, you're those kids," he says. "Marylin's kids. The one that looney put in the barn."

The words send an unexpected electrical shock from my toes to my temples. The scars on my back itch. Sawyer stiffens. It's the casual nature of Carlsen's voice that stings so acutely, as if what happened to us was just some trivial piece of town gossip.

"That's us," I say, determined not to flinch.

Carlsen folds his arms over his chest and leans back as if there is an invisible chair back to hold him up. "What can I do for you? You got a bill from last night that needs settling or something?"

"Have you seen Greg since last night?" Sawyer asks.

"Who?" Carlsen says.

"You know, that other kid from the barn," I say.

Carlsen shakes his head. "Greggy? Didn't even see him last night to be honest. I don't know if you could tell, but it was pretty busy in here. Didn't really get a chance to chat. Your boy go off the rails again?" I wish everybody would stop saying it like that.

"We just paid a visit to the judge," says Sawyer. "She says you got some business with Greg. Something about you loaning him money to buy suits for interviews?"

A bartender, a blonde, hourglass shaped girl in tight black pants with her cleavage pressed to her chin, passes through the mini saloon doors that separate the restaurant from the back of the bar. Carlsen shifts back to give her some room to move around.

Carlsen nods. "Uh, sure. You here to pay his debt?"

"Maybe you tell us what the money was really for?" Sawyer says.

"Is this an interrogation or something? Should I call my lawyer?" Carlsen's voice gets louder, catching the attention of his employee. She's clearly pretending to clean behind the bar while she keeps an ear cocked to our conversation. She leans down to break up ice in the bin and I can see clear down her shirt. I wonder how many tips that move gets her in a night. I feel the sudden urge to see if Sawyer is looking too, but I force my eyes forward.

"Maybe it is, and maybe you should," says Sawyer.

Carlsen squints. "You a cop?" he asks again.

"US Marshal," Sawyer says.

This catches the busty bartender's attention. No longer pretending to clean, she stands straight up and watches our conversation as though she's behind a two-way mirror.

"Well, in that case, I think our conversation is over. If I want to sit and talk to a cop, I'll call Boyd," Carlsen snaps. Is that a veiled threat?

It seems we've pressed too hard, and that only makes me want to push further. Carlsen's defensiveness grates on me and for a moment, I feel reckless. "You still selling steroids to kids or are you strictly in the bar business now?"

Carlsen's cheeks go crimson. It's not due to embarrassment, but rage. The bell that hangs over the entrance to the bar alerts us that it's been opened. It's Harvey Barton.

Harvey smiles when he sees us.

Sawyer leans into my side, and just out of Carlsen's earshot, he whispers, "Don't say anything about Greg.

I think Carlsen is doing something illegal and I think Greg is a part of it. He'll never tell us anything in front of Harvey."

Finally, something we agree on. I nod and wave to Harvey.

Harvey takes off his ragged grey baseball cap and waves it at us. "Twice in one day, huh? I must be one lucky guy." He gives me a kiss on the cheek and shakes Sawyer's hand.

Was that only this morning that I saw him at Charlie...I mean, Natalee's house?

"Normally I would say it's a little early for you to be drinking, but given the circumstances, I guess you deserve one," he says.

"Thanks." I laugh. "So, what are you doing here?"

"I always used to say 'only drink on the weekends'." He pulls out a chair from the bar and sets himself down. Without so much as a word, the young pretty bartender places an open Heineken in front of him. He takes a sip, exhales, and his shoulders drop. "Except every day is a weekend when you're retired."

Carlsen slips down to the other end of the bar.

"You just get here? Or are you leaving?" Harvey asks.

In tandem, Sawyer and I reply, "Leaving."

"Shucks," he says. "Thought I was going to get some more time with you guys." His eyes settle sweetly on mine and I feel that urge, that childish hunger for the father I never really had. I want to reach out and hug him again. I know he wouldn't reject me, but I hold back anyway. I wonder if Boyd has ever appreciated how good he has it.

I turn back to Carlsen, but it seems he's used Harvey as his distraction to escape. If Carlsen is running some sort of gambit around here with drugs, steroids, or whatever, he definitely wouldn't want Harvey knowing about it. Back in the day, when Harvey was Sheriff, he had zero tolerance for drug abuse and was even harsher on those who sold them. He and Judge Bea were an unstoppable force on that front, for a very long time. I wonder how Carlsen slipped under his radar if we knew all about it even as kids.

"I wish we could stay, too," I say to Harvey, and I mean it. I was dreading coming back to Settlers Hill, but leaving means it's all real. It'll mean that Charlie is really dead and buried. "We just have to wrap up some things before we head out of town. I'm hoping to come back for Christmas, though."

"Well, I won't keep you," he says. "You two stay out of trouble."

We say our goodbyes and step back into the daylight.

"You see where Carlsen went?" Sawyer asks.

"No, but he went running when Harvey came in. That means something is definitely up. It might have nothing to do with Greg's disappearance, but there's no way Carlsen is a legitimate businessman."

A hissing sound slithers on the wind from somewhere at the end of the side walk. Peeking around the side of the building is the busty bartender.

Her shoulders are hunched like she's caught a chill in the warm Spring air. She waves us over while taking a tiny step back. She looks distraught, almost. Once we're within ear shot, I whisper, "Are you OK?"

"I really don't want my boss to know I'm out here talking to you, okay? So, I'll make it quick," she says. Her voice is reedier than I'd expected. It's as if she's trying to match her pitch to the whistling wind.

I nod and she continues, "I overheard that you guys are looking for Greg?"

"Do you know where he is? Have you seen him today?" Sawyer cranes toward her.

"No, but I do know that he doesn't owe my boss money for suits or anything like that. I don't know exactly what Greg was doing for him, but he was always around the bar when Carlsen was here. I would see them exchanging envelopes filled with cash all the time. Then, last night after everyone was leaving, they got into an argument over something out on the street. I couldn't really hear what they said, but Greg flicked his cigarette in Carlsen's face and Carlsen tried to punch him."

"Tried?" I ask.

"Boyd...the sheriff," she corrects herself, "stopped him before anything happened. He broke up the fight. After that Greg left. And that's all I know."

"Why are you telling us this?" asks Sawyer.

"Greg is a really nice guy. He comes in during the afternoons a few days a week for lunch. There are only a few guys that come in here who actually look me in the eye and talk to me like a person and not like some piece of meat. Greg was one of those guys. I saw you guys sitting with him last night, so I figured you're his friends. And if his friends are looking for him, then I should try to help out. Plus, Carlsen is a creep, so it wouldn't be the end of the world if I got fired."

"Creep how?" I say.

She rolls her eyes and tucks her hair behind her ear and looks to Sawyer while she answers my question. "He's not handsy or anything like that. But when he hands you your paycheck, you've got to count out each dollar to make sure he hasn't shorted you. That's what kind of boss he is. And he runs some funky business on the side. I don't want to get anyone in trouble or anything but," she pauses, bites her lip and looks around, "like, this town has a lot of drugs in it. A lot. Especially at the high school and stuff, you know? Not much for kids to do around here. But I've heard rumors about him," she nods toward the building, implicating Carlsen, "being involved. I don't know how much he's involved or even if it's true. He's a pretty private guy but I've seen some pretty sketchy people come in here and he takes them into the office then they leave without buying a drink or anything. I don't know, it's just shady."

"Well, thanks for telling us all of that," I say trying to steal her gaze from Sawyer.

Still looking at him, she runs her fingers over his arm and says, "A friend of Greg is a friend of mine."

It takes everything inside me not to break into laughter. I can tell she thinks she's being subtle, stroking his arm and leaning in with her baby doll eyes strewn open wide. There was a point in Sawyer's life where this kind of attention from a girl would have sent him into a stutter. Frankly, I'm shocked to see just how cool he keeps it.

He smirks. "Thank you very much. We'll let you get back so you don't get in trouble."

"Promise me you'll call me when you find him? I just worry." She bites her lip and slips her phone from her back pocket looking up at Sawyer.

I smile big and snatch her phone from her manicured fingers. "Oh, sure doll, here," I go to her contacts, add my number in and give myself a quick call so I can have her number. "Look, now I have your number. So sweet of you to be concerned. I'll be sure to give you a call. And um, what's your name?"

"Oh, yeah, that's great. It's Jessica," she says and puts the phone back in her pocket.

She disappears around the corner and I hear the slam of the backdoor.

"Well, that was interesting," says Sawyer.

CHAPTER 12:

2000

Sawyer felt his friends swarming around him, but he couldn't hear anything they were saying. Like they were using the voices of the adults in Peanuts cartoons, they spoke to him in wavering tones without any real words.

Blood thumped so heavily in his ears that he thought his head might explode. There was a pain at the center of his chest and his jaw hurt. He held his teeth together so tightly that it was a wonder they didn't turn to dust. His breath was shallow and quick, then absent. Can't get out. Can't get out. The only words in his head. The only words that mattered.

He opened his eyes for a moment and was met with darkness. He shut his lids quicker than he'd lifted them. There was a certain level of denial he could reserve for himself if he couldn't see the space in front of him.

Sawyer only recently found out he was claustrophobic—in the elevator that day with Greg. The halting of the steel machine sent him into a panic, and he was just as surprised with himself as Greg was. He went home that day and told his mothers. They sat him down and did their best to convince him that it wasn't all that uncommon to feel that way. They said he shouldn't be ashamed and offered to take him to someone, like a therapist, who might be able to help him work through it. He'd given it some thought, but ultimately rebuked the idea when he thought about what other kids might say if they found out he was seeing a therapist. They would think he was crazy.

He felt a hand on the back of his neck. It wasn't Maura's. It was too big. It must have belonged to Greg or Charlie. Next, there were fingers on his cheeks—just below his eyes. They were trying to get him to open his eyes. To talk. To say anything.

Sawyer managed to open his mouth, his tongue dry and cracking against the roof of his mouth. "Stop!" he yelled.

The hands lifted from his neck and the fingers left his cheeks. The air in front of him cooled slightly. They'd inched back. Sawyer was never much of a yeller, not even in moments where it was warranted. Sure, he cursed and used other foul language like the rest of the kids his age, but he rarely ever raised his voice.

He swallowed hard and forced himself to open his eyes. If he was going to snap out of this trance, he knew he was going to have to do it on his own.

Still feverish with fear, the world wavered in and out of focus, although there wasn't much to see. He could make out Maura, her floral dress so yellow and bright that it clung the last drops of light the stable had to offer. His eyes landed on a single flower, on that was crooked and folded in half over her lap. The thumping in his ears softened. The banging in his chest slowed. It was only once his episode had settled that he thought about how strange it was that she was in that dress. Maura didn't even wear shorts in the summer time, yet here she was, in the girliest dress he could imagine. She would punch him right in the nose for sure if he tried to rag on her for it. And for that brief moment, lost in that trivial thought, he'd almost forgotten where he was.

A voice broke through. "Don't worry. We're getting out of here. I promise." It was Greg.

"That opening," Maura chimed in. "Where the light is coming through. Do you think we can jimmy the board free? Even if one of us can squeeze out, then that person can swing around to the doors and unlock them."

"Or they can run and get help," Charlie said excitedly.

Sawyer's throat remained tight as his other symptoms subsided to a manageable level. Something had changed in the last few minutes. Panic turned to planning. No longer stagnant, they worked together.

CHAPTER 13:

2018

We decide to head back to Grandma Marylin's house to talk to her and regroup. At this point, I feel like I need a pen and paper to keep track of everything that's happened. Yet somehow, we're no closer to finding Greg than we were a few hours ago.

Sure, Carlsen may have had something to do with Greg's disappearance...which is what we seem to be calling it now. Greg's disappeared once before, we all did, but I've never been on this end of a disappearance before. It occurs to me that Grandma Marylin, Sawyer's mothers, and hell, even Bea, must have felt this cavernous pit in their bellies all those years ago. When you're the one trapped in a box, you feel helpless. But it never occurs to you that the people trying to free you from that box feel just as helpless.

It's the not knowing that's the worst part. All I need is a call or a text from Greg— something that says "hey, I'm ok, just messed up". That would be preferable to this complete loss of contact. Radio silence.

How dare Bea talk about Greg's stints in rehab as if she had anything to do with them? The only thing she ever did was act as a driving force toward the substances that landed him there. It's believable that she could have thrown a dime or two at the enterprise, but I know she never visited him. Not once during the three times he'd gone in.

Each of our visits to Greg in rehab was different. One was completely voluntary—it happened after Greg had gone missing for a full week before he turned back up at Grandma Marylin's. He'd watched a friend die of a heroin overdose and it scared him enough to make him check himself into the closest rehab. The only problem with that place was that it was too close to home. There were some people in there that he knew—people we went to high school with. Once out of rehab it didn't take long for them to fall back into trouble.

Greg's second visit to rehab was court ordered. He blew through a red light and drove his car straight into a tree. Thankfully, no one was hurt but Greg was promptly arrested for driving under the influence. It wasn't his first, or even second, strike. Since Greg's mother was the judge, another judge did the sentencing. Fortunately, that judge was a friend of Bea's, and sent Greg to rehab instead of jail.

The second visit to rehab seemed to have a stronger impact than the first. It was out of state—Grandma Marylin made sure of that—and Sawyer, Charlie, Grandma Marylin and I visited him on every visiting day available to us when he was there. I wish I could say that I liked who Greg was off of drugs, but the truth is, he was cranky and snapped at us whenever we came to visit. 'It's the withdrawal,' his therapist assured us after our first visit. She told us our visits would help, so we kept coming back no matter how terrible he was. And for six months, Greg stayed clean.

His third stay wasn't court ordered, but it certainly wasn't voluntary. He nearly overdosed. I remember being so angry with him. I paced around Grandma Marylin's kitchen, because I couldn't watch him breathe through a ventilator in the hospital anymore. I screamed and cried and cursed his girlfriend at the time. She was the one who brought him back to square one, or negative square one.

Grandma Marylin stopped my pacing and placed her icy hands on my burning cheeks. "You know more than anyone, dear, that when you go to hell and come back, the devil always keeps one hand wrapped around your ankle so he can pull you back whenever he likes. Some people are better at fighting it off, staying above ground. You are one of those people, though you may not feel so. Sawyer and Charlie too. But not Greg... not yet. We'll get him there, dear, but not by blame or tears. It will take compassion and example."

Sawyer and I walk into Grandma Marylin's. I smell paint. She'd spent her younger years in Manhattan attending prestigious art shows with famous artists. She fell in love with paintings and began making her own. She never planned to sell anything, and instead, just wanted them for her own walls—and mine, Sawyer's, Charlie's and Greg's.

But I know what she's doing right now. She's not painting to relax or because she's feeling particularly inspired. She's painting because she has to stay busy. Painting is one of the few physical activities she can do without complete exhaustion or someone else's helping hand. I do the same thing any time I'm anxious—I keep busy, but in other ways besides painting. For Grandma Marylin and me, our demons are like mosquitos—they are less likely to bite if we keep moving.

Sawyer and I collapse onto the couch. Grandma Marylin gingerly sits in the love seat across the coffee table. And then we tell her everything—recounting our trip to Greg's, the call to our old English teacher, our visit to Bea's office and our conversation with Carlsen and his loose-lipped bartender.

"Well, Bea acted like we were trying to rob her when we showed up there. At the end, she threatened to have us thrown in jail if we didn't get out." Sawyer picks at a hangnail on his thumb. "I don't know what her problem has always been with us. She needs to get laid." As the words left his mouth, I could tell he regretted them, remembering the company sitting before him.

"Sawyer, dear," Marylin cranes forward. She smiles like a cat with a mouse beneath its claws. "Do you find women to be so simple as to be driven mad by the absence of a man's penis? Do you know something we don't? Does the male anatomy serve as a panacea for all that ails us?"

"That's not what I..." Sawyer chokes on each word.

"Do not forget your roots, little boy," she cuts him off. "Bea's actual problem is two-fold. Firstly, it all stems from the simple fact that she chooses to be miserable. For her, to be miserable is to be happy. Second, she demands respect based only on her title, and does little to nothing to deserve it. Then she resents those of us who refuse to give it to her."

"I'm sorry. You're right." Sawyer bites at his cuticle. It's his version of waving the white flag.

Sawyer lost that fight before it even began.

"Carlsen's not going to tell us anything. That much we learned," I say to change the subject.

"Do you know if he's doing anything illegal?" Sawyer asks Grandma Marylin. "One of his bartenders stopped us as we were leaving. She didn't really give us much detail but she seems to think that he might be dealing drugs on the side."

Grandma Marylin shakes her head. "Patrick Carlsen isn't doing anything illegal that I know of, but I wouldn't be surprised if he was. I'll make some calls. Georgina Rappaport knows everything that goes on in this town. I'll have to butter her up a little for it, but if there is anything to know, she'll know it.

"I think we should go talk to Boyd," Sawyer says. He stands up, already settled on the decision.

I shoot out of my seat. "Not so fast. Didn't we just talk about not telling Harvey when we saw him. Isn't that how we'll keep Greg out of trouble?"

"That was before we talked to the bartender, Maura. It's getting to the point where this doesn't feel like one of his normal benders. For one thing, we didn't know about Greg and Carlsen's argument after we left the bar. Also, Greg usually calls or texts us to tell us off or to say how much he loves us or hates us through his highs and lows, but this...this is different. And I think you know it is, too."

"I'm just not there yet. I'm not ready to jeopardize Greg's life. If he's been messing around in dirty business with Carlsen, he could be in way bigger trouble than he's ever been in before. And I don't trust Boyd. Do you?"

"As a person, no. But there are a lot of guys I work with who I don't want to be best friends with, and that doesn't mean they're bad at their job. Boyd broke up that fight between Carlsen and Greg. That means he was one of the last people to see Greg."

"I don't trust Boyd and I won't put Greg on his radar. Boyd is the same jerk he's always been," I say, dizzy with disbelief. "How are we even having this conversation right now?"

Sawyer opens the front door and turns back to me one more time. "Just come with me."

I glare back at him and say nothing. He waits a beat longer for me to answer, then turns and closes the door behind him.

"Why does he do that?" I sink back to the couch in the spot where Sawyer had been sitting. I can feel the heat he's left behind on my skin.

"Earlier today, he didn't want to involve Boyd in this any more than I did, but now he wants to run to the police. And apparently, what I say doesn't matter."

Grandma Marylin drapes her tan alpaca shawl over her left shoulder. "Do you want me to give you the long answer or the short answer?"

"Short."

"He's a man," she says.

I raise my eyebrow at her.

"Fine," she says. "The long answer. He's a man, and no matter how good of a person a man may be, he has the innate need to do the opposite of what you tell him to do."

"Charlie isn't," I catch myself, "wasn't like that."

"The hell he wasn't," she cracks. She walks to the kitchen. Her knees look like they might give out beneath her. I race up to meet her side and she swats the help away. She puts the kettle on for tea and points for me to sit down at the kitchen table. "Let's not waste time talking about what goes on inside the heads of men."

She sits across from me and lights a cigarette. She offers me one and I decline. How many hours did I spend in my youth surrounded by the dim grey smoke that jumped off her words? I found myself disinterested in the concept of smoking when everyone else my age seemed to be experimenting with it.

When we were younger, Grandma Marylin stopped smoking for a while. She saw a hypnotist a few towns over and deemed herself cured. But once we all moved out, she took it up again. Said she was bored as hell and that everyone needs at least one vice to be considered normal. This was hers.

"Maybe I should just go with Sawyer. I can't just sit here and do nothing," I say. "But I really don't want to see Boyd again."

"You're not going to. You are going to sit here and clear your head for a minute while I make some calls.

Besides, I think you made the right choice, but I'm not worried that Boyd will throw Greg in jail. I'm worried you would be much too much of a distraction for him. You always have been."

I roll my eyes.

Grandma Marylin gives me the age-old line: "Roll your eyes some more and maybe you'll find some brains back there, little girl."

CHAPTER 14:

2000

She didn't want to just sit around. He was going to come back and who knows what plans he has for them. No one who locks kids up is going to be up to any good. Every brush of hay, every knock of wind against the wall, makes them jump. Is it him? Then silence.

Maura had been in this particular stall before—she been in all of them—back when Rick Salem's parents were alive and the farm was up and running.

Grandma Marylin had set up some horseback riding lessons for her a few summers back. Maura was dying to play football with the rest of the boys, but they wouldn't allow a girl on the team. They said she was too small and that she would get hurt. After all, girls "can't handle a sport like that."

Horseback riding treated her just fine. It wasn't quite the contact sport she'd been looking for, but there was something freeing about climbing atop that massive animal and guiding it wherever you pleased. Sometimes she would pretend she was Joan of Arc riding off into battle, arm high and steeled to the wind, fist clenched and shouting into the imaginary battle line that lay before her.

But back then, the stable didn't look the way it does now. Each stall its own window, but here the window had been boarded up from the outside.

Maura shuffled away from Sawyer and the boys and ran her fingers over the window. The glass was still intact, so Maura knew it hadn't been boarded up because the glass had broken. So why was it boarded up?

On the wall to the outside of the barn, there was a slip of light coming in between two warped boards of wood. Maura tried to peeked through it, but the opening was so thin that she couldn't even make out what lay on the other side. If she remembered correctly, they were angled towards the open pasture facing town.

"Nothing is going to fit through here," she said.

Greg met her side and also tried, in vain, to look through the slit between the two wood planks. "Anyone have a pocket knife? Maybe we can try to shave down the wood and make a hole to get out."

"I have a pen," Charlie said. He sprang up, leaving Sawyer seated silent and motionless on the floor. Charlie handed his pen over to Maura, their not-so-fearless leader.

She took the pen and scraped the point over the corner of the gaps in the wood. She reared her elbow back-and-forth scraping and shearing, but making no real headway. The only result was a barely visible divot.

"It won't work. And even if it does it'll take years to carve a hole big enough to fit through," said Greg.

"Stop. You're not helping at all. You're just complaining. Do something!" Charlie said.

"Wait," said Maura. Hope fluttered in her chest. "Where is the backpack? With all the tools? For the treehouse, for Odin. There's a hammer in there."

The word hammer sent them into a tizzy. They dropped to their hands and knees. They scanned the floor for the backpack and squinting their eyes to see if it was hidden in any of the deeply shaded corners. It was no use. The backpack wasn't in the stable.

"We must've dropped it," said Charlie, panting.

This somehow felt worse to Maura—the feeling of gaining hope for a moment, only to be let down instantaneously. The backpack with the hammer had never been in the room. It must have been lost in the scuffle on the other side of the door. And that meant they were back to square one.

She walked back over to Sawyer and knelt before him. "It's ok, we're going to get out of here." Lying to him felt like lying to herself.

Then there was a loud creaking. The barn doors, she thought. Maura wanted to scream out for help, but chances were that the person going into the barn right now was the same person who locked them in there in the first place. None of them could get a good look, but she knew it was Rick. Who else could it be?

In the times that she come to the Salem farm for her horseback riding lessons, Maura had only seen Rick handful of times. He was helpful to his parents and a hard worker, but he was often out somewhere else there wasn't any people. In the few times she did run into Rick, he never made eye contact with her. He simply he grunted heavy breaths as he walked.

"You never really know someone...even when you do," Grandma Marylin would say.

Footsteps now. Maura stayed by Sawyers side. Charlie and Greg shuffled through the hay and away from the light, staying far away from the door. She wondered if they were thinking the same thing she was. The footsteps grew closer, louder. The four didn't move and they didn't breathe.

The footsteps stopped right in front of the door. The sound of a key entering a padlock pierced the room. But then came something none of them could have expected. The door rattled back-and-forth like there was a wild, ferocious animal on the other side. Maura, Greg, Sawyer, and Charlie shot back in unison. Their spines dug into the pine wall furthest from the stall door.

The door slid open. A flash of light stabbed the dark. And then there was a sound—the sound of something dropping—that thumped onto the hay. The light disappeared and the door slammed shut. They could hear the sound of the key locking a padlock once more. Footsteps moved away again. And just like that, he was gone.

Maura was the first to act. When she was sure he was gone, she crept forward to discover what had caused the thumping sound on the hay. When she was in from of the stall door she reached down, her hands shaking on descent. And there they were. Four large water bottles.

CHAPTER 15:

2018

Grandma Marylin is on the phone in the kitchen and I'm sitting on the couch where she left me. Clear my head, she said. How, exactly, am I supposed to do that? My stomach growls but I don't want food. I try to think what I can do while she makes her calls and Sawyer talks to Boyd. Who else can I talk to? Where else could Greg possibly be?

It occurs to me that even though I'm under the impression that I know Greg inside and out, I really don't know much about his day to day life. Whenever we talk on the phone or see each other, we cover all the important things: work, love interests, and his struggle with sobriety. Then the conversation often diverts to discussing old times. The fun times. The times where we just felt like kids. The times before those three days in the stable.

But, if you were to ask me any of the everyday stuff, like what Greg eats for breakfast, how he takes his coffee, or what he does to wind down after work, I would have to admit that I didn't know. And what did it ever matter? It wasn't important. Whereas now, having play by play of his day might take us to him. Instead, I'm just sitting here like a fool while everyone else around me does the work.

Not even Grandma Marylin would really know about Greg's daily life. She's spent more time with him than I have in the past ten years, but lately, Greg's kept her at an arm's length. She was more of a mother to him than his own mother, and so he treated her like many men treat their mothers: with love and respect, and a little bit of distance.

Of course, the person who would know what to do next is Charlie. Charlie never let Greg get away with being cagey. He never let any of us get away with it. That's why he was the glue that held us together when our adult lives threatened to tear us apart.

But Charlie isn't here to help us. We are all Greg has now. I get up from my seat. I resolve to take some sort of action. Though I don't know what said action will be yet. All I know is that setting myself in motion will be inspiration enough to drive me forward into a new idea.

Grandma Marylin hangs up the phone and returns to the living room to find me standing motionless in the center of the room. She raises an eyebrow. "Are you ok, dear?" she asks delicately, as if the force of her breath might knock me over.

"What did Georgina Rappaport say?"

Grandma Marylin sighs. "That woman can talk. I had to listen to thirty minutes about her grandchildren's piano recital before she'd spill anything." She walks over to the miniature bar in the far-right corner of the living room and pours two fingers of gin into a glass and adds a splash of tonic. My eyes shift to the clock. It was five o'clock already. Grandma Marylin always mixes herself a gin and tonic at five, come hell or highwater. "Now, remember, whatever Georgina says is not to be taken as scripture. She's got large ears and loose lips so she's only repeating what she hears. Not everything one hears is the truth."

"I understand."

She takes a sip and turns to me, leaning on the bar. "According to Georgina, Patrick Carlsen was selling steroids to his players back when you kids were in high school. But when Harvey caught wind of it, he shut Carlsen down immediately and told him that he wouldn't arrest him as long as he stepped down from coaching. Carlsen must have been smart enough to agree to the deal, because that's when he opened Hannigan's Bar. It was supposed to be Carlsen's show of legitimacy."

"So, that's it? Now he's a legitimate businessman?"

Grandma Marylin purses her lips and cocks her head. I know that look. I've interrupted her. "May I finish?" I nod and she continues. "Now, the bar has been open for a few years, but word has it that since Harvey retired a few years ago that Carlsen has been dipping his toes back into some muddied waters. According to Georgina, a few months back, he'd been seen getting a little too cozy with an underage girl. She was one of the seniors over at the high school, and he got in a fist fight with the girl's father when her father found out they'd been seeing each other. So like I said, I do not know what is fact or fiction, but that's all I have on Patrick Carlsen."

I wipe my palm over my eye, exhausted. "So, it's possible what the bartender told us, then. It's possible that Greg could be working with Carlsen. It would make sense given Greg's history, added with them exchanging money and then getting in a fight last night. I can't think of another scenario that makes sense. Why else would Greg and Carlsen be involved?

Grandma Marylin takes the last sip of her drink and sets the glass on the bar with a clank. "We don't know that yet."

"Maybe that's why Harvey was there in the middle of the day. He never was a big drinker so I can't imagine retirement made him one. The bartender handed him his drink without him even ordering. Maybe that's what he's been doing—keeping an eye on Carlsen."

Grandma Marylin shrugged. "It's possible. Harvey Barton may not be Sheriff anymore, but he keeps a close eye on this town nonetheless. I wouldn't be surprised."

"I should call Sawyer." I look at the clock to confirm the time again. Just after five. "He's been gone for over an hour."

When I call, I get Sawyer's voicemail. I don't leave a message and decide to text him to call me ASAP. Twenty minutes go by. I call again, this time leaving a voicemail. Service could be shoddy in Settlers Hill, I tell myself.

"Maybe try calling him from your landline," I say to Grandma Marylin.

"I don't think that will make a difference, but okay," she says and makes the call.

But there's still no answer.

It's now been forty-five minutes since I first called Sawyer. He's been gone for almost two hours. My chest tightens and my mouth runs dry. It wasn't like Sawyer to not answer his phone. Even when I've called him during work or even a date, he would at least text me that he'd call back later. It was one of the things I liked about Sawyer—that he was always present even when he wasn't.

I go into the foyer and slip my shoes back on. "I can't just sit here," I say. "I'm going to the police station."

I wonder if something happened with Boyd. Maybe they got in some sort of argument like old times, and instead of stuffing Sawyer in his locker, Boyd one-upped himself and stuffed him in a holding cell.

Anger bubbles in my throat. I knew going to see Boyd would end badly. Why didn't Sawyer just listen to me?

I drive the rental car to the station. Clouds overhead threaten to burst. I crack the window for air and spittles of rain tickle my arm. I love it. Something about the way the cold hits my worry-warm skin cools my nerves.

As I'm stopped at a light on the corner by the dollar store, another thought occurs to me. What if Sawyer's lack of response has nothing to do with Boyd? What if Sawyer found Greg and has bad news to report and doesn't want to tell us? Images of an overdosed Greg face down in some crack den carpet flash through my mind like one of those cartoon flip books. I grip the steering wheel harder as if it will get me to the police station faster. Whether I like it or not, that's where I have to go. That's where Sawyer said he would be.

I lower the window to let more air in. By now, the raindrops have gone from beads to gum drops, and my whole left shoulder is soaked but I don't care. I need to breathe.

In the station parking lot, there are patrol cars staggered throughout parking spots along the north side of the building. Boyd's car, the one with the word "Sheriff" along its side, is nearest to the front door. I look for Sawyer's car, driving a second loop around the building. Nothing.

I call him one more time before I park the car. Voicemail. I check my texts and refresh my messages.

I glance back at Boyd's car and then look at the front doors to the station. Breathe, I say aloud.

"Walk in like you own the place," Grandma Marylin always told me. "If you look nervous or seem like you don't belong, people will take the opportunity to treat you that way." So, I do my best to follow her advice. It's only once I am inside the door that I realize how ridiculous I must look. The left side of my body drenched and the right is bone dry. I imagine that it isn't water, that I'm Joan of Arc once more, riding into battle with the weight of a shield of armor along my left arm. Lord knows I've always needed armor with Boyd.

The station has been updated since I've last seen it. Since it's a small town, we have a small station. It seems to have lost its "Andy Griffith Show" vibe and traded up for dark wooden desks topped with computers, each with a glistening name plate. The walls are decorated with American flags and plaques. There's also a plant on every desk, adding a touch of greenery to the space.

There's a woman seated at a desk to the front of the station. She isn't a cop, and I can tell by her monochromatic beige button-down dress and the depths of her crow's feet that she's nearing her seventies. She's plump and has a large round face, but her tiny features are crowded to the center, making her look like some early Renaissance painting of a baby. The name plate on her desk reads "Midge."

Midge greets me with a smile. "How can I help you?" She lowers her fire engine red reading glasses and folds her hands on the desk in front of her. Her voice is a soft tweet.

"Hi." I step forward, looking around more anxiously than I'd hoped. "I'm looking for Boy—um—Sheriff Barton." That's going to take a hell of a lot of practice to get used to. I had a hard enough time trying not to call Harvey "Sheriff" anymore.

"Oh, sure, and your name is?" she asks. Her cheeks look like two perfectly round plums staring up at me.

"Maura, Maura Bennett," I say in more of a "Bond, James Bond" way than I intended to.

Midge's smile drops. She swallows hard and drops her hands to her thighs. "Oh, my," she says. "I...I'm so sorry."

My heart drops. Sawyer. Was he here? Did something happen? What does she know that I don't? My vision grows fuzzy and I have to remind myself to blink. "Why? What? What happened?"

She shakes her head. "Charlie. His passing. I know you were close. I...I remember when you were kids... what happened...on the Salem farm...and I just, I just..." She stops and looks as though she's about to cry. She stands and rounds the desk. She's shorter than I thought she would be, so short I could rest my chin on the top of her head. She takes my hands and holds them tightly in her own near my belly button.

Midge rambles on, "My Lord, this town used to be as safe as it got when I was a girl. Now...well, I'm not going to say it's going downhill, but we've been struck by tragedy one too many times. Oh dear, even with all that awfulness at the cemetery. Can you believe it? Teenagers raiding graves for fun. Apparently, it was part of a dare or something. A fascination with the occult has found its way into our sleepy little town, it seems." She raises a finger in the air. "Peer pressure! That must be the cause of it." She gives my hand an extra squeeze. "I prayed for you, you know? While you were missing, and then after you were found too. And then when I heard about...about Charlie."

Midge just reminded me why I left Settlers Hill. In New York, I could be anyone. Maura Bennet is a nobody there, anybody. But here I was marked. It wasn't concern I saw in her eyes, but pity. Like a spark to gas, my name, along with Sawyer's, Charlie's and Greg's, ignited something in people. We've talked about it all together before, many times before I left for good. And Greg put it perfectly: "They look at us like damaged goods."

"Thank you," I say to Midge in an attempt to conceal my discontent. And then I continue on. "Sorry, but I really need to speak with the Sheriff."

"Of course. Wait here." She scurries off into an office at the back and emerges with Boyd. He's wearing a half-cocked smile.

"Well, well, well, Miss Bennett," he says when he reaches the front.

"Miss Bennett." Showing off for Midge, maybe?

"Sawyer," I say back, blankly.

Boyd raises an eyebrow and chuckles, pointing at himself. "No. I'm Boyd."

"No." say. "I'm looking for Sawyer. Was he here?"

Boyd looks to Midge, who is seated back at her desk, typing away at the computer. She shrugs and shakes her head.

"Haven't seen your boy," Boyd says. He leans back and adjusts his belt.

I stare at him like he's a statue in a museum. He looks different now than he did last night, but I can't pinpoint why. He's wearing the same thing, his uniform, and his hair is styled the same way. He's clean shaven, but he wasn't sporting much stubble last night either. Not as far as I can remember, anyway.

Could it be the way he's standing? Maybe that's it. Cocky still, but more relaxed. It isn't lost on me how odd it feels to be standing feet away from my childhood nemesis, while he's wearing a sheriff's uniform.

"Hey, Midge, look at this." Boyd turns to the little woman and smiles big with his finger on his front tooth. "See that? That's fake. You know why?" He turns to me with a smirk. "This little lady right here knocked my tooth square out when we were in middle school. She was pretty tough back in the day. Folks called her Mad Dog Maura."

I frown. Boyd's leaving out a key part of the story—the fact that he'd started the fight. He started every fight. I have a vivid memory of him ruthlessly pummeling Greg like some bootleg MMA fighter for the third time that week.

"Sawyer," I continue. "He said he was coming to see you."

"What would Sawyer Swenson need from me? I thought he was some big US Marshal hotshot now." Boyd sits on the edge of Midge's desk.

Shit. I didn't consider this scenario—the one where Sawyer hasn't been here at all. Not only does that mean that I have no idea where the hell Sawyer is, but that now, I have to be the one to tell Boyd about Greg. I grit my teeth and force the words out. "Greg is missing."

Boyd nearly laughs in my face. "I thought you said you were looking for Sawyer."

My Joan of Arc armor has slipped down my shoulder entirely. I feel naked and foolish. "I am looking for Sawyer. Sawyer came here to talk to you because we can't find Greg. He wanted to talk to you because you saw Greg and Carlsen fight last night at Hannigan's. That means that you might have been the last one to see him."

Boyd stands up and takes a step toward me. "Fight? That 'fight' was nothing. In this town, ninety percent of my job is breaking up tiny little drunken bar brawls like that."

Greg wasn't drunk, but I decide not to push it further just yet. "Well, we haven't been able to contact

Greg all day. No one has seen him anywhere. And now I can't find Sawyer." My voice cracks.

Don't cry in front of Boyd. Don't cry in front of Boyd.

I'm not feeling steady enough to tell him the part about the hay. It feels private somehow, like telling Boyd and Midge would be exposing some wound I don't want touched. A wave of embarrassment washes over me.

Boyd takes a step backward and directs me to follow him into his office. Midge gives me a casual, 'Hope you find your friends,' and I do my best to smile back.

I can smell the full strength of Boyd's cologne as I follow in his wake. It's spicy and cheap like one of those dollar store candles marked "In the Woods". Maybe I'm making a mistake coming to him about Greg and Sawyer. Just because he's the Sheriff now doesn't mean that he's a good person all of the sudden. Who knows, maybe Carlsen's got Boyd in his pocket. I don't know who to trust, and I'm not going to take a chance on trusting Boyd Barton of all people. But I am here because I need something, I remind myself, just be careful.

"Take a seat," says Boyd. He closes the door. "So, they've only been missing since this morning?"

"Greg since this morning and Sawyer for a few hours."

"That hardly seems like something worth panicking over, to be honest. Protocol is to wait twenty-four hours before I can file a Missing Persons' report for an adult. Maybe they just went off together to have some time without you. You know, some guy time."

"I don't think that's it." Why is he diminishing this?

"You know, Maura, I know you've only ever had guys as friends, but sometimes guys just need time without women around," he says like he's teaching me a lesson.

My cheeks are getting hotter by the second. I wonder if it's visible. "Boyd. Something isn't right, okay?" I realize I just have to tell him. "This morning, when Sawyer and I went to look for Greg at his apartment there was…"

"What?"

"There was hay in his bed."

"Hay?" He considers it a moment. "I mean, that's pretty strange, but hardly worth worrying about."

I want to scream. His ignorance is begging me to explain what that means. For three days, Greg,

Sawyer, Charlie and I spent lying on that hay under our feet. We even draped it over us at night to keep off the cold. It didn't matter that it was stained in our piss and vomit and blood. Even now, there are some nights where—even though I lay in my Egyptian cotton sheets—I can still feel it stabbing against my skin.

"The barn," I choke up and his expression drops. "It just seems like a cruel thing for someone to do. I know Greg wouldn't have done it."

Boyd nods and focuses on a small wooden clock. After a few ticks of the second hand he says, "I understand. But still, that isn't really enough to launch an all-out investigation."

"I'm not asking you to do that," I snap. I stand up. "Whatever. I'll find them on my own. I don't need your help."

Boyd gets up and walks around the desk. He's so calm, it's unnerving. He reaches for my arm and I jerk it back.

"What are you doing?" I say and inch to the door, my muscles tensing.

"I was trying to calm you down. Just take a breath. I was going to offer to help you find them. I'm sure there is a perfectly reasonable explanation for all of this." His encouraging words don't match the condescension in his face. Is he just placating me?

I don't trust a word out of his mouth. He might be a grown man standing before me in a Sheriff's uniform, but all I see is a bully in a Halloween costume, lifted from his daddy's drawers. Nothing about this man's demeanor suggests that I'm talking to the Boyd I know. It's like he's doing his best Harvey imitation.

"What do you have to lose by letting me help you?" He asks.

I don't say what I want to: Everything.

CHAPTER 16:

2000

C harlie finished his water first. There were only four bottles, one for each of them, thrown into the barn through the stable door. He didn't intend to finish his water that quickly and hadn't realized his mistake until he'd taken his last gulp.

Charlie hadn't realized how thirsty he was until he swallowed his first mouthful. He'd always been a fast eater and drinker, and often finished his dinner before Grandma Marylin and Maura. He was always forced to wait until they were done. He didn't mind, though. Dinner was his favorite meal of the day. And breakfast for dinner was even better. In fact, Grandma Marylin made a special point to make sure Charlie had breakfast for dinner for his birthday every year since she adopted him. Bacon, eggs—usually in the form of an omelet—sausage, pancakes, and scones. The works, as he liked to call it.

Dinner. The light from the crack in the wood was fading quickly. They'd been given water, but would they get dinner? Even prisoners get three meals a day. Charlie's stomach quaked at the thought of food.

"Wait." Charlie flicked his empty water bottle from his fingers. It landed soundlessly in the hay.

"What?" asked Greg. "Something wrong with your water?"

"Yes," said Charlie.

"Just tastes like regular water to me," said Maura, moving her hands around the outside of the bottle, inspecting it.

"The bottles were sealed," Sawyer's voice croaked from the corner. He stood for the first time since they'd been in there.

Charlie considers this. Sawyer was right. The cap snapped from its plastic hinges upon opening. But even more reassuring was the fact that Sawyer was standing. "Are you okay?" Charlie asked.

"Yeah, as long as everyone stops asking if I'm okay," Sawyer said. He made his way over to the small opening, attempting to look through it. "Someone will look for us. My moms, Grandma Marylin, the police. Someone. We won't be in here long." His voice begged the fates.

Sawyer's confidence rippled through Charlie, sending electricity through his veins. If Sawyer could be that confident and positive, then so could Charlie. Greg may have been the loudest and Maura may have been the bravest, but it was Sawyer that Charlie saw as their unofficial group leader. Later in life, looking back, Charlie would come to realize that Sawyer was a great leader because he made decisions based on rational thought and not impulsive emotion. But that was something Charlie always sensed about him from the beginning.

"We need to conserve the water, Maura said. "What if no one finds us?"

Charlie hoped no one noticed that he'd already drank all of his.

"He could kill us before we even need more water," Greg argued.

"That doesn't make any sense," said Maura. "Why would he give us water just to kill us?"

"You ever see a cat play with a mouse before it kills it?" said Sawyer.

The thought makes Charlie sick to his stomach. Water sloshes around in his empty belly threatening to come back up.

Greg paced for a time, occasionally bumping into the other three, until Maura told him to sit down or she was going to break his legs if he bumped into her one more time. There would be no sleeping.

Complete darkness came quickly. Exhaustion, mental and physical, set in. Fear kept them awake. Charlie leaned against the wall, shifting his weight from one leg to the other to stave off stiffness. He tried to occupy his mind with happy thoughts, but none would stick. Instead, all roads led to Rick Salem.

Charlie kept circling back to one memory, even though it was different than one would expect. It's not the thought of the shadowy figure locking them into the stable. It's not that of the young man on his lonesome, riding the tractor while Mr. and Mrs. Salem taught all of the party-goers at Stacey George's seventh birthday party how to milk a cow. No. The memory was from about two years ago.

Back then, Grandma Marylin faithfully ran all of her errands on Saturday mornings with Maura and Charlie in tow. If they were well behaved, Marylin would swing by to collect Sawyer and Greg on their way home and they would all have a fun-filled movie night complete with popcorn and sweets. But it was one Saturday morning, a year ago, that stood out to Charlie.

Wandering around the pharmacy while Grandma Marylin filled her prescription, Charlie stumbled upon Rick Salem and the cashier—a short, round woman with curly hair—in an embrace. They were standing just off to the left of the register and Rick, much taller than the woman, was hunched over with his eyes pressed into the side of her neck. From the slight convulsions of his body and the sympathetic look on the woman's face, it was easy to see that Rick was crying. Rick's parents had died only a few weeks earlier. Charlie saw that losing your parents hurts no matter what age you are. Charlie had Grandma Marylin. Rick had no one.

It wasn't long after that, Rick let the farm fall to pieces. He sold away all of the livestock in order to get by until he was only living by himself up in that house. It was just Rick, his house and his barns.

Charlie ran his fingers over his empty water bottle once more. The waterless vessel crinkled under the weight of his fingertips.

"Shit," said Maura from somewhere in the blackness.

"What's wrong?" they all seemed to ask her at once.

"I have to pee," she said.

"So, pee," Sawyer said.

"It's going to be gross. One of us is going to step in it or something. I can't even see where I'm going in here," she argued.

Greg snickered. "So, what? I just went a little while ago."

"Ugh, Greg!" Maura yelled, half laughing.

"Just go," said Sawyer. "Besides, it's not only pee we're going to have to worry about if we don't get out of here soon..."

"No way! I'm holding my shit until we get out of here and the three of you better, too!" Charlie said.

"Ok," said Maura in concession. "I can't go if you're listening though. Just talk. About something. Anything. And talk loudly."

"Maybe we should talk about a plan. You know, how to get out of here," said Greg.

"Good idea," Charlie said. "Any ideas?"

"What if we did it the next time he opens the door?" Greg said. "We could bum rush him."

"Okay, yeah. One of us can hold the door while the other three run out and tackle him. Then, we'll run," Sawyer finished the thought.

"Exactly," said Greg. "Hey, Mad Dog! You in?"

Maura grunted in frustration. "What part of leave me alone while I try to pee can't you understand? Ugh, I have to start all over again now."

Greg, Sawyer and Charlie laughed amongst themselves until a loud noise silenced them. The siren wailed from the center of town.

"What's that for?" said Greg.

That electricity in Charlie's veins recharged. "That's the emergency siren again," he said. "Maybe they know we're missing. Maybe they're coming for us."

CHAPTER 17:

2018

By the time Boyd and I step out of the police station, the drizzle is gone—but so is the light. Greg and Sawyer are missing, yet the universe has moved on as it would if they were standing right beside me. In a way, it feels like a betrayal. We step outside. The rain has gone and so has the light.

"Got dark," says Boyd.

"Yup." I make a beeline for my car and open the driver's side door.

"I think it's best if I drive," says Boyd, feet still planted on the sidewalk.

"What? A little girl like me can't drive her own car?"

Boyd points toward his police car, the denim blue Ford with SHERIFF written in gold lettering on both doors. "It's common to use a police car for police work."

"I thought this wasn't official police work," I say and close my car door.

Nevertheless, I climb into the passenger seat of Boyd's car. There are four air fresheners hanging from the rearview mirror but there isn't much of a scent left in any of them. His car is surprisingly neat. From what I remember of Boyd from grade school, middle school and high school—jeez, I've known this guy almost my entire life—he usually kept things grimy and smelly. Even though most boys that age keep their personal space messy, Boyd took it to a whole new level. But now, he keeps his car so clean that it could be a lesson in neatness. I survey the floor beneath my feet and cannot find so much as a single crumb. I peek over my shoulder into the back seat, which is tidy minus a few tufts of dog hair.

Boyd catches me checking out his car. "Sorry about the hair," he says. "It's from Cosmo, my dad's dog. I was watching him when my dad went to see my aunt. Old Cosmo left some of himself behind, I guess."

"I guess so."

Boyd starts the engine. "So, did Sawyer walk or drive here?"

"Drove," I say.

"I'm guessing you didn't see his car anywhere on the way here, right? Did you drive around, or did you just come straight here?"

"Just straight here." I say, looking out the window.

I know I'm being short with him, but I can't help it. He's being more pleasant than I'd anticipated, but I still don't trust it. My jaw is clenched so tightly my back molars hurt. Maybe I still was Mad Dog Maura. But right now, when I need to find my friend, what does that matter anyway?

"Alright," Boyd clears his throat. "Then I think it makes sense that we do some loops around town and search for his car. After that, maybe we can make some calls."

"There's no one to call. Everyone who he would see or talk to is sitting right next to you in this car. I mean, beside Grandma Marylin."

"So," he says, focusing on the road as he rounds the corner out of the police station parking lot. "What was it actually like, dating a celebrity?"

I look out the passenger side window, wishing I had a cigarette. I don't even smoke, but jeez, it would be a nice distraction from Boyd. And hey, maybe it would calm my nerves too. They're so jittery that the last thing I want to do is talk. I would prefer it if we sat in silence.

"It was...interesting," I say.

"You know, even though we don't have a whole lot of those celebrity gossip magazines down at the pharmacy, I've seen your face on a few of them. How long did you date for?"

"Too long."

"How'd you meet?"

"At work."

I keep scanning the streets for Sawyer's car. Nothing.

"Hmm," he says. "Well, I haven't had any relationships quite as high profile. Me and Tammy Gresham dated for a few years after high school, but that kind of fell apart. She moved away and got married to some electrical engineer. I only know that from online. Social media's a hell of a thing, isn't it?"

"Guess so."

He sighs. "Listen, Maura, I'm just trying to make conversation here, okay? I'm not trying to make you uncomfortable," he says. His voice is even, soft, like he's talking down a child who's in the middle of a tantrum.

He continues, "I know we didn't get along as kids, but a lot of time has passed since then."

"Didn't get along?" This time, my words aren't short; they're indignant. "That's hardly accurate. You were horrible, Boyd. You basically made a living off of tormenting the four of us."

An image of twelve-year-old Boyd chasing Sawyer with a firecracker launcher on the dark summer streets flashes in my head. And there's another one, of Boyd stealing all of Greg's clothes when Greg was in the gym and then whipping off Greg's towel from his body. Greg had to walk all the way down to the gym teacher's office naked—hand clutched over his privates—as the rest of the sixth-grade class cackled on like hyenas. And I remember the endless times Boyd taunted Charlie, calling him an orphan, and leaving notes in his locker saying that said that Charlie's parents faked their own deaths just to get away from him.

"We were kids," he says awfully forgiving of himself. "There are two sides to every story."

"Watching Oprah, are we?" I snap. The memories bring my anger front and center. "And while we're still on the subject of "catching up": last night, you acted like you and Charlie were friends or something. There is no way you two were friends. He would have told me if you were. And he would have never forgiven you for everything you put us through. You were a terrorist, Boyd. Plain and simple."

Boyd slams on the breaks.

My body jolts forward but the seatbelt catches me. "What the hell?" I shout.

He shifts in his seat to face me, one hand still on the wheel. His voice is calm. His eyes are daggers. "Charlie was able to step outside of that little club, that little world you four had, and meet me as a man. He came over and helped care for my mom when she was sick. He was my friend. We were in a good place before he died. And if he didn't tell you that, then maybe it shouldn't be my friendship with him that you're questioning."

I want to knock that tooth of his out a second time. Questioning my friendship with Charlie? That's a new low, even for Boyd. Charlie is dead, so what did Boyd have to gain from pouring salt on my wound?

Boyd keeps his eyes on me. I catch movement in my peripheral. A car is approaching behind us. Boyd sees it too and shifts back to continue on driving. For ten minutes, we sit in silence, both huffing out anger out through our noses like dragons. We focus on scanning for Sawyer's car.

A few moments of silence and my anger runs its course quicker than I expect. Boyd is still staring out the window. I try to imagine that he isn't the sniveling little asshole he was for all those years on end. Can people really change? I guess I have, right? And supposedly, Charlie was able to put the past behind him and foster a relationship with Boyd. Maybe it something I could do too.

The idea feels strange. Boyd notices I'm staring a hole through the side of his cheek and snaps his neck to look at me. He looks sadder now, more than anything.

"Listen," he says. "I was a little shit when we were younger. I know that. All I'm saying is that you four weren't angels either. But, for what it's worth, I'm sorry. I'm not that kid anymore. And I'm sorry for what I said about you and Charlie before. I was dumb to belittle your friendship or whatever. I guess the old me still comes through once in a while. But I do want to be better. And I do want to help you. I hope we can be on better terms one day, like Charlie and I were."

I let his words hang in the air for a moment. The honest truth is that I'm too tired to hold onto any grudge right now. I have bigger fish to fry. And whether I like to admit it or not, I need Boyd's help. "Thank you, Boyd. Sorry I'm so...defensive. I appreciate you helping me."

Boyd breaks a smile, but it's nothing more than a sad concession. "You know, I was there that day when they found Charlie in the woods like that, all torn up from that animal."

My stomach churns. "Please, Boyd, I don't want to hear about it." Maybe one day I might want the details of what my friends mangled, half-eaten body in the woods looked like, but today is not that day.

"Sorry," he says. "I don't mean to upset you. I just...I don't know. I hadn't really talked to anyone about it."

"It's ok. I just can't think about it right now."

"I understand," Boyd says and for a moment, he almost becomes human to me.

And that's when I see it. "Boyd, Boyd, Boyd. There." I point out the passenger side window, smacking his arm with my other hand. "It's Sawyer's rental car. Right there." He can't pull over fast enough. I'm gripping the handle, ready to jump out.

Sawyer's rental car is a bright blue Hyundai Elantra on the corner of Rhododendron street and

Mum drive. What would he be doing all the way over here? This is nearly the edge of town. There aren't even houses over here, just some small abandoned farm homes from before suburbanization and a three-story brick apartment building. Settlers Hill doesn't have a sketchy part of town, but this is the closest thing to it.

This is where Phil Cooper lives. I've only been there once—Grandma Marylin had an appointment that ran late, so she asked Phil to watch us. If I close my eyes I can still smell the stench of mothballs and clove cigarette ashes that filled his apartment. Afterwards, when Charlie and I complained to Grandma Marylin about the stench and the mess, she never dropped us off there again. Come to think of it, I wonder if Phil even lives here anymore. But then again, I'd be okay with never seeing the inside of his house again.

Boyd is going too slow. I can't wait. I jump of the passenger side door before the car comes to a full stop.

"Hey, hey! What are you doing? Trying to get yourself killed?" Boyd yells after me.

I ignore him and charge forward. There's no one's inside. I press my nose against the driver's side glass as if Sawyer's six-foot frame might be hiding somewhere beneath the seat.

Nothing.

I see Boyd's reflection approaching. "Nothing?" he asks.

"Nothing."

I try the door anyway. It swings open.

There's nothing inside. No trace of Sawyer. No wallet. No phone. Not so much as a gum wrapper left behind.

"Empty," I say, my breath quickening.

I find myself pacing around the car, like Sawyer might jump out of it at any moment. This must all be a bad dream. I thought finding his car would bring me to Sawyer. He feels even further away now.

"Hey, over here," shouts Boyd. He's standing on the passenger side, waving a piece of paper in the air.

I run over and snatch the paper from his fingers. It's difficult to see in the dark. Boyd takes a flashlight from his belt and shines it on the paper for me. Pasted on the inside fold of the paper is a patch of cloth. And the sight of it sends all of my blood rushing to my head.

I recognize that cloth immediately. It's the same bright yellow floral pattern of the dress I wore in the barn. My hands hover over it, almost afraid to touch it.

I'm dizzy. My fingers go limp. The cloth dances all the way down to the pavement.

CHAPTER 18:

2000

Silence.

The siren was gone. The sound of it rang in the friends' ears like smoke left behind after a fire has been put out.

"Everyone ok?" Sawyer asked in a shaky voice.

Intermingled "yeah" s echoed through the stable. No one wanted to talk.

Sawyer had been able to rein in his panic from earlier in the stable, but his limbs still felt both heavy and weak. There was a knot in his stomach, that same feeling he got right before a teacher handed a test back.

He wanted to throw up.

"The siren," Maura whispered. "Do you really think it could be for us?"

"It has to be," said Charlie. "Grandma Marylin would definitely have noticed that we're missing by now."

"My moms, too," Sawyer said. His stomach tightened even more at the thought of his mothers.

Vera would have been the one to realize Sawyer was missing first. Those first hours home from chemo were the roughest on Ramona with all the nausea, puking and fatigue. Those were the nights that Vera ordered pizza and told Sawyer he could eat his dinner in front of the TV. It was a novelty, because Ramona and Vera enforced strict 'family time dinners' as a way for them to stay close. But Sawyer didn't mind those family time dinners. He kind of liked them. Ramona and Vera were funny, especially when they were together, bouncing jokes and one-liners off of each other. It was like having front row seats at a comedy club.

Tonight's a chemo night, Sawyer thought. He shouldn't be standing here, trapped in a dark stable. He should be cuddled up on the couch watching reruns and eating pizza with his moms. The thought of pizza made him realize how hungry he was.

"Then it won't be long before someone finds us. There are only so many places to check in this town," said Greg.

"That's only if that's really what the siren was for," said Maura. "He could kill us before anyone gets here."

"Stop that," Sawyer said.

"Stop what? Being realistic?" Maura fired back.

Sawyer sighed and sat down in defeat. What was the point in arguing? It wouldn't change anything.

"We need to try to get out of here," said Maura, "We can't just sit around and wait for someone to find us."

"Someone will find us," Charlie said assuredly.

Sawyer thought again of Vera. He hoped she wouldn't tell Ramona that he was missing. He'd heard of people dropping dead from bad news or dying of a broken heart. What would happen to his sick mother if she heard her only son had gone missing? Her energy was already drained from the hours of chemo. Would this scare take her very last drop?

He shook his head. No. He couldn't wait this out.

"Maura's right," Sawyer said. "We need to do something."

"Any ideas?" asked Greg, skeptically.

"Let's wait until he comes back. Bum rush the door," said Greg.

Sawyer had forgotten all about that conversation which now felt like a lifetime ago.

"If he gave us water, maybe he will give us food," Charlie said.

Sawyer wonders how Charlie is able to keep even an ounce of that childish positivity he's clinging to.

Charlie kept on chattering. "I'm sure he'll come back. I'm sure he'll come back."

"Okay," said Maura. "But even if he does, that could be a really long time from now."

Sawyer closed his eyes. "We don't know. But what other choice do we have?"

Hours passed in dreadful silence. By the time the light shone through the thin gap in the stable wall, Sawyer had stopped drifting in and out of a restless sleep. His heart had been pumping too fast to ever fully release his consciousness—even though his body had been begging and pleading for the sleep.

Throughout the long hours of complete darkness, there had been the occasional rumblings amongst his friends, but Sawyer kept his thoughts and his words tight to his chest. Talking was painful. And just being here was painful enough.

Sawyer couldn't stop thinking of how he felt in those first moments that they were locked in the stable. He was so mad at Greg for talking shit and yanking Maura around like some rag-doll. When the stall door shut behind him, he hadn't fully understood what was happening. Certainly not right away.

But once he saw that they'd been caged like animals, that was when the voices of his friends slipped away from him. He knew his friends were still there, but their words were muffled. The room seemed to sway around their heads like they were all on some dizzying carnival ride.

That smell. Few things smell more rank than pee that's' been sitting out. He brought the neck of his shirt over his nose.

That was when it hit him. "Why is the hay in this stall fresh?"

"What?" Maura called back.

"The hay," Sawyer repeated. "In all of the other stalls we passed before we came in here, the hay was used, trampled, and dirty. But this," he reached down and ran his fingers through the rough strands, "this is new."

"I don't know," Maura said. "I haven't really thought about it. I'm glad it is, though."

"You don't think it's strange?" said Sawyer.

"Strange how? I think it's lucky," said Charlie.

"It's almost like someone put the hay down knowing we'd be here," Greg says.

Exactly what Sawyer was thinking.

Sawyer opened his mouth to agree when Maura cut in. "But how? Or, I mean, why?"

The creaking the heavy doors to the barn silenced them. Sawyer's heart beat against his chest so roughly he thought it might break skin and jump out.

Then, footsteps from beyond their caged stable stall slapped casually against the cement barn floor. They grew louder as they got closer.

Sawyer forced out a whisper. "The plan."

They tensed into position as the sound of a key entering the padlock whispered through the stall door. Sawyer's hands shook in anticipation. Like tackling in football, he told himself.

His heart was pounding. He didn't want Maura to face this guy head on. He wanted it to be Greg or Charlie. The person charging their captor was in the riskiest position.

Maura would never agree to take a back seat. So he told himself that he was going to take the brunt of the attack. He was going to be the one to throw himself at the man so Maura could run past, get out, and get help.

The lock clicked open. Silence. No movement. Not yet.

Then door moved, rattling open slightly and quickly. Greg and Charlie threw their bodies forward. The man pushed back, trying to shut the door again in a panicked frenzy. Greg and Charlie were losing ground. The door was shutting.

Sawyer's legs had turned to stone. He gritted his teeth harder and ripped his feet from the ground. He ran forward and shouldered the door alongside his friends. With his help, they were able to pull the door open against the man's force—just by a few inches. Maura kept her eyes focused hard on her target- the opening.

Sawyer screamed out "Maura, no!"

He didn't want her to go out there alone. He had planned to grab the door, but he didn't think it through when he did it. And now, it was too late.

Maura launched her body forward and gripped her hands on either side of the opening. Sawyer saw the man's hand reach through and grip Maura's hair at the crown of her head.

He yanked on her hair and like water down a drain, Maura disappeared through that gap and out of the stable.

CHAPTER 19:

2018

"Where did you get this?" I cry out, darting down to the ground to pick up the scrap from my childhood dress.

"It was on the front seat." Boyd says.

My throat tightens. It's like breathing through a straw. "Did you put this in Sawyer's car? Is this some kind of sick joke?"

Boyd's cheeks scrunch up like he's genuinely confused. "What are you talking about? A joke about what?"

"First the hay in Greg's bed, now this," I say.

"Now what?" Boyd examines the cloth, turning it over in his hand as if that might help him figure out what he's missed.

A bug lands on my right arm and I slap it off. The sound echoes into the still night air. There isn't going to be an easy way around this. "When we were..." I never could find an easy descriptive phrase for what happened, "When we were in the stable, in that barn, this was the dress I was wearing. They threw it out at the hospital." I stare at Sawyer's car. "Why would someone leave this in his car? Who would leave this in his car?"

"Well, maybe we should start with 'What was Sawyer doing over on this side of town'?" said Boyd.

The houses out here on the outskirts of town were sparingly filled. Beyond the building, there was only grassland backing up to a rocky forest that wasn't even all that suitable for hiking.

"He must have been looking for Greg. Maybe he knew something I didn't," I say. "But this," I take the cloth back. "This isn't right. Whoever put that hay in Greg's bed put this note in Sawyer's car. I'm sure of it."

Boyd reaches for the note. "I've got a bag in the car I'm going to put this in. Evidence, you know?"

Boyd walks back to his car and rifles through a bag in his center console.

I stare at Sawyer's car in the lamplight. The glimmer of hope I carried with me during our tour around

Settlers Hill in search of Sawyer has disappeared. Sawyer's disappearance has other implications. It means that Greg isn't on some bender. It means that the hay in Greg's bed was as purposeful as the note in Sawyer's car. There's no practical joke being played here. Somehow, both Greg and Sawyer have gone missing in the last twenty-four hours and some sicko is sending a message.

Is the message for me?

"So, what now?" I ask Boyd.

"Let's go down to the station. I really should wait twenty-four hours to file a Missing Persons' report, but there are some other things I can do in the meantime to keep things moving along."

I climb into the passenger side. Boyd is willing to investigate this case officially now. This should come as a relief, but it doesn't. I know that true relief will only come when I know where Greg and Sawyer are.

How was I going to tell Grandma Marylin about the cloth? She was already sick with worry, no matter how difficult it was to see from the outside. Her stiff upper lip always carries her through the roughest waters. But still, there was something so painful about the idea of being the person who has to break every ounce of bad news to her. Our nightmare was being trapped in that stable. Grandma Marylin's was not being able to find us, not knowing if we'd ever come back, imagining the terrible things that could be happening to us. And now that Greg and Sawyer have dropped off all radar, I have an inkling into how she must have felt all those years ago. Which was worse? Being the victim or loving the victim?

"We're going to find them," Boyd says. He starts the car and I watch as Sawyer's car drifts away from me in the side mirror.

"Maybe."

I want to feel strong. I want to stand up and feel powerful. I want to drive forward with the force of a thousand winds and knock down every door—scale the town like a one-woman SWAT team. But instead, I feel weaker than before.

Boyd is eerily calm. Honestly, I can't decide if his serene nature pisses me off or soothes my own building anxiety.

Sawyer's car was about as far away from the police station as possible, so it takes lightyears for us to get back. We stop at a light and Boyd opens his mouth to speak. But then he closes it before any words get out.

"What?" I say.

"I didn't say anything," he says without looking at me.

"I know, but you were going to say something. Just say it."

Boyd tightens his lips and then folds to my request. "I don't want to make you more upset you than you already are."

"Like that's ever stopped you before. Just say it."

Boyd sighs. "It's just that, that whole thing with the hay and now with this piece of the dress, it makes me think about what happened to you all in that barn. I can't believe Rick Salem did that to you. Back then, I didn't really understand. Back then, I was just thankful it wasn't me and my friends." He raises his hand. "Now, I know that was selfish of me, but I was a kid. And now, being a cop and all, I think about what that did to my dad."

"What do you mean?" I crack the window. The cool air helps loosen the knot of pain between my eyebrows.

"Listen, when you're in law enforcement you pray to God you never have to deal with anything with kids. There's just something different about it. And, I don't know, but after he found you there in that barn, even though you were...you were alive. It just changed my dad.

"He was just sadder after that. He covered it up in public, but he was always sad at home. I've never really talked to him about it. My mom said he wouldn't talk to her about it either. She thought that finding you all there in that barn broke his faith in humanity.

"He thought Rick was a good guy. Well, maybe not a good guy, but not a kidnapper or a child abuser, like he turned out to be." Boyd pauses as if he's reaching out for a memory just within his grasp. "Actually, the only thing he really said was 'Can you believe this happened? How did this happen?' He kept asking, almost like he felt responsible. Like he couldn't protect you. But maybe I only say that because that's how I would feel now, as Sheriff."

"I guess I never really thought about how it affected him," I say. Is it selfish that I'd never considered how our disappearance and even our discovery affected others in its wake?

"Growin' up, huh?" Boyd laughs.

We're a few blocks away from the station when Boyd's radio buzzes to life. A woman's voice echoes through.

"Sheriff, a call came through. Drunk driver. No crash—she just pulled over and wants some assistance going home," the dispatcher says.

Boyd leans forward. "Yup, I'm a little tied up right now."

"Boyd," the woman says and her tone loses all semblance of dry professionalism. "It's Natalee."

My neck snaps at Boyd.

Without meeting my gaze, he grunts, "Location?"

"She's on the corner of Honeysuckle and Perrywinkle," she says then signs off.

Boyd slows the car. "You mind if we go take care of this?"

"Yes. I mean, no. I mean, of course not, yes we can go."

Boyd does a U-turn without acknowledging my mangled sentence.

We find Natalee's car on the side of the road on Periwinkle Lane, which is a good three miles from her house. Boyd parks behind her. Her lights are off and the shadow alignment suggests she's tilted her seat back.

I trail behind Boyd to the driver's side window. He taps on the glass to get her attention. The rapping startles her, and her hands fly up to her chest. She quickly realizes it's Boyd and smiles that tired, drunken, sad smile.

She cracks open the door and pours out of the car, leaning hard against the frame to stand. "I'm so sorry. I'm so embarrassed," she says, her pale hair tangling over the tip of her nose. This morning she had managed to keep her appearance together, but I've never seen her look more human than in this moment.

She smiles to me as if to extend the apology.

Boyd wipes the strands of hair from her face. "It's okay, Nat."

At first, I'm thrown by his familiarity with her, but then I remember that Boyd said he and Charlie had become close. Still, why Charlie hadn't mentioned that. Maybe he thought I would never understand. Maybe he was right. I guess I'm jealous, resentful, that Boyd knows Charlie's wife more than I ever did. But maybe that's my fault more than anyone's. I don't come here often. But who could blame me?

Natalee's voice brings me back to the conversation. "I just went over to Hannigan's. I thought I wanted to be alone, but then everyone left and it was just me in that big empty house." Her words are slow and exaggerated from the alcohol. I can smell it on her breath. Whiskey. Not what I would have expected from the head cheerleader turned housewife.

"That's understandable," I say. And I do understand. I get to go back to the city after all this, where I have my job and my other friends. Even though I'll be grieving everything else in my life will stay the same. I'll miss Charlie, of course. I'll feel the pain of not being able to call him or speak to him, but for Natalee, she is alone. She's starting over, but isn't starting fresh. I know something about what that's like.

"Thank you for coming," she says. "I hope I didn't interrupt your date."

"No!" I say.

Boyd smiles coyly at me. "Oh, come on, we could have at least had her going for a minute."

I laugh. This is all fun and games, but we need to focus on our actual emergency. Where are Sawyer and Greg? I know I should wait before I interrogate Natalee. But I can't. If there's a chance someone has information on my friend, I need to get it out of them immediately. "Have you seen Greg or Sawyer today?"

Natalee tucks her chin back. Her glassy eyes shift between mine like she's watching a pin ball bouncing.

"I saw Sawyer and Marylin with you this morning. Not Greg. Why do you ask?"

"No, reason," Boyd answers. He shoots me a stern look to stop. He takes Natalee by the arm and pulls her over to walk with him, supporting her weight on his arm. "You've been through enough. It's good that you called instead of driving the rest of the way home. Charlie would want you home safe, so let's get you there. Okay?"

Where was this Boyd when we were kids?

He puts Natalee in the passenger seat of his car, right where I had been sitting. Her head floats back to the head rest and her eyes turn to tired half-moons. He fishes through her purse, pulls out her car keys and tosses them to me. "Drive her car home, would you? Then we can be on our way with our other thing from before?" He raises his eyebrows. He clearly doesn't want to say anything in front of Natalee.

Natalee slurs out, "Be careful, that's Charlie's car."

I agree and get in. It still smells like Charlie, like cinnamon. I lift the center console and tears prickle my eyes. There's a small bottle of the cinnamon mouthwash Charlie used every day. It was his favorite. The tears threaten to drop, so I slam the top of the console shut.

Focus.

I adjust the seat to sit closer. Natalee has at least four inches on me. It's a keyless ignition which takes me a minute to figure out. By the time I'm ready, Boyd has already swept off down the road, completely out of sight. Shit. I don't know how to get to Charlie's house from here. It's been a while since I navigated these roads in the dark. Not a lot of street lights around here.

There is a GPS in the left-hand corner of the windshield. I open it up, hoping there's a 'home' destination saved. Nope. Maybe it's in the recent destinations?

I don't get very far. My stomach drops and the scars on my back burn like they did when I first drove into town.

Staring back at me, just four addresses from the top of the list of recent destinations, is Yates Federal Prison. My mouth runs dry. I squint at the lettering as though it might change or reveal something new. Yates Prison is where Rick Salem was sentenced to life imprisonment. What was Charlie doing there?

CHAPTER 20:

2000

For Maura, crossing through the threshold of the stable stall door was like emerging from water—only to be smacked down by another wave. There was a searing pain on the crown of her head where he grabbed her hair, so sharp it made her eyes close.

She never saw his face. For years after her rescue, in the waking hours of the morning and in the misty fog of nightmares, Maura would see flashes of his belt buckle, but never any other image of him. And the memories change so often that she couldn't trust it.

When he grabbed her, his hand was over her eyes. His palm reached across her face, ear to ear. His hand was smooth—sickeningly soft—and strong

He wrapped his other arm around her waist. Her heels dug into the cement as he dragged her backward.

She screamed, but couldn't even hear herself. She only felt the vibration of her voice through the bones of her skull. Her body wriggled, but it was no use. He was bigger and stronger than her.

Her breath staggered and during each short inhale, she smelled food. Something hot, something savory—like a gravy, gravy with onions. Her stomach roared painfully.

His hands stayed tightly clasped over her eyes as he swung her to the ground. A weight pressed against her rib cage, making it hard for her to breathe. He'd pinned her to the ground. Her arms were pinned under his knees. His hand slipped away from her eyes and was seamlessly replaced by a sort of cloth. He tied it in a knot behind her head.

Once she was blindfolded, he lifted his body from hers. She drew the full breath her body had been begging her for.

Then he took her hands and tied them together at her belly with a thin, plastic rope. The frayed fibers dug into her wrists so deeply her fingertips throbbed. He sat her down to the floor, no hay, just cold hard cement.

"What is he going to do with me?" she said to herself, over and over again. She longed for that stable stall where her friends were.

For a long time, there was nothing. No movement. Was he sitting there, just staring? Or had he left? The uncertainty was almost too much to bear.

Was this her punishment for trying to escape? This separation...or he do something worse? The blindfold grew wet with tears. Soon, she couldn't breathe through the congestion in her nose. Her chest heaved with each uncontrollable sob.

Where were the screams and protests of her friends? Had he separated each one of them too?

Footsteps methodically echoed toward her. The muscles in her shoulders tensed so tightly the bone behind her ears vibrated with pain. Every inch of her body waited in fearful anticipation of his touch.

His even palm stroked her cheek and she whipped her face away, that same hand coming back around to slap her back to sit up straight. Acidic vomit spewed out of her mouth.

She couldn't see where it landed but the severe grunt of the man let her know that it'd gotten on him. He sighed in disgust and then grabbed her by the back of the hair once more.

He dragged her across the ground as her feet tumbled and trailed behind, her weak legs unable to keep up. Then she heard the sound of a key entering a lock.

A flutter of excitement surged through her. She'd be back with her friends again! Funny what perspective can do—she wanted nothing more than to go back to that cramped stall. But then the man flung her body into an open space. She tumbled forward, colliding into something hard—metal or iron. The door slammed behind her.

She pushed the blindfold up over her eyebrows so she could see. She wasn't in the stable stall where her friends were. She felt around with her hands still tied together. Metal tools. She was in the storage closet of the barn. She'd seen it many times when she come to the Salem farm for horseback riding. Her body ached to rage against the door or use the tools to break it down. But he would be waiting on the other side and she had no doubt that would make her punishment much worse. She collapsed to the floor and buried her face into the back of her hands. Her back stung like a thousand bee stings. The pain kept her breath shallow and short. And for the first time since her mother abandoned her, she prayed.

Back at the stable stall, Greg sat on the floor in the corner where Maura had just been snatched. His left hand was bleeding, a piece of wood splintered into the thin-skinned space between his thumb and pointer finger. The wood had slid into his skin like a needle through fabric when the man on the other side shut the door. Greg, along with Sawyer and Charlie, had been holding on tightly, but it hadn't been enough. The force of the door closing had thrown them all to the ground.

In those first moments, where Maura's disappearance had been so fresh it was barely believable, all of the air seemed to have been sucked from the room. He remembered how the words leaving his mouth: *No! Stop! Maura! No!*

No. He said it over and over again, as if it were a response to a question. May I take your friend? *No.* Like reprimanding a dog who took a bone. *No.* Shouting out to God that you hate what He is allowing to transpire. The answer is *No.* Or was it the answer to another type of question: Can you believe this is happening? *No.* I refuse these terms.

Greg kicked the door. He punched it and the blood from his fresh wound sprayed on the wood and hay. The door answered back to him: *No.*

A paper slid through that single opening below the stall door. Charlie had found it first. Greg raged tirelessly on that door, until the feeling of Charlie's hand on his shoulder gave him pause.

Charlie unfolded the paper in the darkness and brought it towards the light. He squinted and read the blue ink. The man had written in half print, half cursive writing that read: Make one sound and she's dead.

The three boys stared at the paper. Sawyer took it from Charlie. He turned it over to see if there had been anything else written there. No words, but blood. Panic rippled through them. Greg ran over to the opening to see if he could get a look at the man walking away.

Greg kicked through the thick hay to the center of the stable stall. Charlie and Sawyer stood beside him, their mouths sewn tightly shut.

Greg stopped. If they made a sound, he would kill Maura. That note meant she was still alive, right?

Greg sat where he'd been standing and Charlie and Sawyer followed suit. The threat had shaped their submission. Unable to talk, Greg was left only with his thoughts, worries and guilt.

He was the one who pulled Maura into this stall to begin with. He had been joking around—in fact, if they hadn't been captured, he would have thought nothing of it. But a tiny part of him had known he was being a jerk. Something about those days, where he had to face the cruelty of a school bully only to go home to the Judge, always made him sour.

Greg closed his eyes and willed his mind to go further back through time. If he had only done a better job at convincing them to stay at the treehouse, they would never be in this position. He knew that's what his mother would say: 'You are responsible for the things that happen to you.' Grandma Marylin said it was half-truth, half bullshit and that growing up means knowing the difference.

He knew what everyone thought of his mother—that she was some cold-hearted, bitter divorcee with one of the most powerful positions in law enforcement in a small town. She was self-righteous and acted like she was the fairest representation of the law—as long as you didn't get on her bad side, because she was easily slighted and morally corrupt.

He knew what his mother thought of him—that he was a ginger headed, chubby wimp who attracted bullies like flies to honey. His torment was an embarrassment and an inconvenience to her, and she would neither thwart his enemies nor lick his wounds.

But Maura always helped him, he thought and the corners of his lips turned downward and his eyes welled with tears. Sure, Charlie and Sawyer jumped in when they could, but they were often too busy fighting Boyd off of themselves. Maura was the only one who wasn't afraid. She never was. But Greg was sure she was afraid now.

Maura was his gladiator, and now she's at the center of the colosseum beneath the paw of the lion. There was nothing he could do to help her, not unless he could go back in time. Even if he had a plan to help her now, he'd never be able to communicate it with Charlie or Sawyer. His head pulsated with helplessness.

He looked down at his bleeding hand. He could feel the blood spreading, encompassing his entire hand. The phrase "caught red handed" played in his head. He wiped the blood on his shirt.

He wished an adult was here. Grandma Marylin would know what to do. He always found his solace in her house. He would never forget his first visit there. The garden gnomes and flowered fairies stared back at him from the stone path leading to her front door. And when he entered her house, it was like he was inside some sort of Victorian time-warp.

He knew Grandma Marilyn's place was different—it was a home from some old world that no longer existed outside pictures in books and historical TV dramas. Her New York accent was as foreign as a British accent, and he often longed to hear her pronounce words like "coffee" and "all" and "dog". Walk awl the dawgs and get the cawfee. She was eccentric, exciting, and compassionate. It was her Band-Aids he wore after a beating. It was her calls to the Principal that bought Boyd time in detention. And when Boyd gave Greg another beating shortly after, Grandma Marilyn bought Greg self-defense classes at a karate studio in the next town over. The only problem was that even with all of the moves, Greg lacked the confidence to use them. The beatings continued. Greg sighed. *It should be Boyd in this stable stall and not us,* he thought. *If anyone deserved this it was him. Could it be him doing this? Was Boyd strong enough to yank the door away from all three of us and grab Maura at the same time? No, no. It had to be Rick. But why?*

His stomach quaked in hunger. Greg wanted to talk to Sawyer and Charlie to figure out a plan. They couldn't risk making even the tiniest sound. The man could be listening, waiting for them to slip up. If only they could do something instead of just sitting around waiting to die of starvation, not knowing what was happening to Maura on the other side. He looks around at the small, dark space before him. At the young age of eleven, Greg already knew there are things worse than death.

CHAPTER 21:

2018

What had Charlie been doing at Yates Federal Prison? I rattle my brain on the drive over to his house. I try to think of anyone Charlie might have mentioned—a friend, a coworker, a client, anyone who might be in that prison. Was it possible he'd mentioned it to me and I just didn't listen?

No. Had the word "Yates" left his mouth, every alarm in my body—the ones that are ringing right now—would have gone off. I never would have let him go there. Rick Salem is there. I've never been to a prison like that—one that's filled to the brim with murderers, rapists, and the criminally deranged.

When I arrive at Charlie's house, Boyd is escorting Natalee from the dark steps of the front porch into the warmly lit foyer. Their backs are to me. I can see

Natalee's shoulder dropping and pressing into Boyd's side as he props her up. Her cheek nestles against his shoulder and he draws her in tighter. Was something going on between them?

I park in the driveway. Circular step-stones lead to the porch. Each step echoes into the soundless night air. Natalie is tired, drunk, and grieving but I need to know why Charlie was at Yates federal prison. The question burns a hole in my stomach.

The front door is closed but unlocked. I let myself in. That same smell, the overpowering scent of funeral flowers brings my headache back. Boyd meets me in the foyer.

"I just tucked her into bed in her day clothes. Figure it's not best I go undressing anyone," he says.

"Yea, I would say so." I answer him, but my mind is elsewhere. I'm calculating how I can weasel my way into Natalee's bedroom to ask her about the prison.

Boyd catches my longing gaze and dips his face into its path. "What's wrong?"

I take a micro-step forward. "I just have to ask Natalee something really quickly."

Boyd pivots left to stop me and raises a hand. "I don't think that's such a good idea right now. She's in rough shape. Why don't we wait until morning?"

We? Does he expect we'll be together still in the morning? Out on the town looking for Greg and Sawyer, still without success? Or is he just placating me like an eager child?

"It'll just take a second." My nerves sizzle like fireworks. One question is all I need.

Boyd ushers me over to the door. "I don't want to wake her. Let's talk about this outside."

Once on the porch, Boyd leans in. I can smell the spearmint on his breath. "Did something happen? You're pretty jumpy."

"It could be because my friends are missing, only hours after my other friend's funeral? I can't imagine why I'm not relaxed."

Boyd purses his lips. "Fine. Jumpier, I should have said. You seem jumpier." He emphasizes the word as if he's teaching it to me.

I steady myself against the railing, my exhaustion hitting me in waves.

"It's Charlie's car. When I drove it over here, I had to use his GPS because I couldn't remember the address..."

Boyd smirked and moonlight glimmered off his teeth. "You have been gone a while, huh?"

"Shut up. I found the address, but also noticed that Yates Federal Prison was in there."

Boyd's smile drops. His Adam's apple move up and down as he swallows.

"You already knew about this, didn't you?" I say, my eyes dry as they widen.

He stuffs his hands in his pockets, stares down at his feet, and picks at the floorboard with the toe of his shoe. "I guess the statute of limitations on secrets ends when the person dies, right?" He lifts his gaze to mine. His eyes intensify in the moonlight.

My stomach tightens. My limbs stiffen. My breath shortens. "What do you mean?" I want him to get the point and tell me what the hell he's talking about.

Boyd looks to the door and then cocks his head over to his car. "Let's go talk in the car."

Boyd takes his time, as if he's intentionally trying to draw this out. I consider kicking at his heels to speed him up but I'm too tired even for that.

Boyd settles into his seat. Natalee's perfume permeates the air. It stayed behind, fruity and strong like something a high schooler might wear.

I open my mouth to speak, but he beats me to it. "Listen, Maura, before Charlie died, he'd been set to sell the Salem farm. He said he didn't talk to any of you about it because he thought you would try to stop him."

Another betrayal. After I'd learned that Charlie was selling the Salem place, I was able to accept that he didn't want to tell Greg or Sawyer or Grandma Marylin or me about it. We'd all had a traumatic experience there. But then for him to go and use Boyd as his confidant? No. I can't bring myself to accept that just yet.

Boyd continues, "I don't know if selling that place just sparked something in Charlie, but right around then, he told me that he wanted to go talk to Rick Salem."

"About what?!" I snap as if Boyd is responsible. I catch myself. "Sorry, continue."

"I guess Charlie never really believed..."

"He never believed that it was Rick Salem who took us," I finish.

Boyd nods. "He said that you guys never got a clear look at him, not once in the whole time you were in there. That even though Rick Salem was a full-grown man, his mind wasn't all that grown."

"I don't know. Charlie isn't...wasn't the only person to think that. So, what happened when he went to talk to him?"

Boyd shakes his head and puts the key in the ignition. The engine turns over in a roar. "I honestly don't know. He went there about a week before he died, and he and I weren't the kind to talk every day. I figured I'd ask him the next time I saw him, but I never got the chance."

"But what did he ask him? Did he say?"

"No. He just said he was going there to find some clarity. Some closure." Boyd shifted the car into drive.

"Listen, about Greg...you said he went missing this morning, right? That I was pretty much last person to see him with Carlsen last night?"

"Yes," I say, relieved Boyd is focused on finding Greg and Sawyer.

Boyd points to the time on the console—10:00pm. "Looking at the time, I think I can get away with filing a missing-persons for him now. I won't be able to write one up for Sawyer just yet though, you understand?"

I lean back against the head rest. "Yeah....Thank you. What about..." my throat swells, "What about the barn?"

Boyd looks confused. "What about it?"

"I mean, there's that note, the hay, Greg and Sawyer missing...Should we check the barn? Maybe this is all some person's version of a cruel prank."

"You think Greg and Sawyer are holed up in that barn again?"

I keep my eyes locked out the window so Boyd won't see the tears pooling in my eyes. "Not necessarily. But if all roads are leading back to what happened to us...there...it's probably worth checking out, right?"

"Can't hurt," he says and dials into the station.

"What are you doing?"

"What does it look like? You're sure as hell not going over there to check it out. I'll have some of my guys go to the barn."

He puts the phone on speaker. The voice on the other side sounds less like a man and more like a little boy who isn't old enough to hold a badge and a gun. "Yes, Sheriff?"

Boyd says, "Pedinski, I need you and Evans to go down to the Salem farm. Take a look around the barns, especially the one meant for stables. We've got two people missing, and I wanna just check in there to make sure they aren't hiding out."

I sigh. I appreciate that the limited details that Boyd gives this guy. I know it's completely within Boyd's jurisdiction to tell his team all the facts, but if he'd released them, it would have made me feel exposed.

"Uh...what are we...uh," Pedinski stammers, "You maybe want us to wait until the morning?"

Boyd's voice deepens. "Somethin' the matter, Pedinski?"

"No, no," Pedinski jumps to say. "It's just that...that place...people say its haunted."

"People? Pedinski, you've got to be kidding me right now. You're telling me you can't perform your police duties because of some local bull shit ghost stories?" Impatience gives way to rage in Boyd's voice.

"Sorry, sir. No, of course not. We'll get right over there."

Boyd hangs up and tosses his phone into the cupholder. It smacks the plastic like a rock rolling around in a tin can. "Sorry about that," Boyd breathes. "Pedinski's not a bad guy. Pain in my butt, though."

"Haunted?" I say with a tinge of amusement.

"Pedinski and some of the other guys were still in diapers when...you know, when it happened. So to them, it's just some story that gets them all excited in this boring old town."

It's surreal of think of my story as someone else's folklore. "I guess I never thought of it that way."

"Listen, I'll drop you back at your car at the station. I think you should go back to Marylin's to try to get some rest. I'll give you any and all updates as I get them. I promise." I can tell he thinks his words are going to give me peace. He's wrong.

But I agree with Boyd anyway. We spend the rest of the ride in silence, during which I hatch out my plan.

Because sure, I told Boyd that I will go back to Grandma Marylin's. I told him I'd wait for his word. But really, once I get back to my car, I'm going directly to Yates Federal Prison.

2000

Maura prayed in the broom closet. Her first prayer since her mother left. She'd been too young to remember much about her father's death. She was only four, so it wasn't so much a memory as an image she pasted together from other people's memories. She knew it was an overdose. Her mother found him face down on the living room carpet.

She remembered only two things vividly: the lights and Grandma Marylin. She had thought the lights had looked like Christmas. Her father died in the wet, mosquito-heavy heat of summer, but when she saw the red and blue lights of the ambulance and police cars, she'd thought Christmas had come early.

It didn't take long for her to realize that the lights outside were no sparkling Christmas tree. Maura's mother called 911 and wept beside her husband's lifeless body. She dug her fingers into his shoulders, unable to let go. Grandma Marylin lived around the corner. She came over when she saw the lights and heard the sirens of paramedics and policemen. She walked into that chaotic living room and spotted Maura, doe-eyed and frozen in the corner. Marylin stomped over to the child, scooped her up, and turned to one of the policemen at the scene. Then she scolded him in a low growl, "You are useless, the lot of you, letting this little girl sit in the corner by herself. You should be ashamed of yourselves."

She took Maura home and cleaned her up. She dressed her in one of her t-shirts, which hung on Maura like an oversized dress. Maura slept there that night and for three days, Marylin watched after her until Maura's mother came to collect her. It pained Marylin to give the little girl back. The drugs that killed her father were probably still crawling through her mother's veins. Marylin even went to Harvey about it, but there was little he could do without proof that the child was in danger with her mother.

And so, for the next two years, Marylin kept a close eye on Maura and her mother. Maura wanted to stay with Marylin, especially after Marylin took Charlie in after his parent's accident But Maura's mother wouldn't give. It was only when she met her new boyfriend—a man who went by "J" with track marked veins and droopy eyes—that things changed. J wanted out of Settlers Hill.

The last time Maura prayed, it was just before her mother dropped her at Marylin's doorstep. Maura overheard J telling her mother that they couldn't have any fun with Maura around. He said that her mother should quit her secretary job so they could travel the road like Gypsies in love. That another mouth to feed would do nothing but weigh them down. Maura prayed that night, not for her mother to refuse the offer, but rather that she'd take him up on it. Maura knew that her mother's absence would be better for her. That she would get to live with Grandma Marylin and Charlie. There, she'd have her own room with clean sheets and warm meals, and she'd never have to worry about her mother's handsy boyfriend. Maura's mother was happy to drop the dead weight that was her daughter at Grandma Marylin's doorstep.

Those prayers worked then, so why wouldn't these prayers work now? Seated in that dark closet with her hands tied together, Maura wiggled her fingers so she could interlace them into prayer position. She kept her mouth shut and moved her tongue along with each Hail Mary, and every Our Father.

The space outside the door was eerily quiet. No footsteps. No clanking. No sharpening of tools. Not a peep from her friends. Maura tried to imagine which was worse, noise—or the absence of it.

But then the footsteps came. The door swung open and light poured into the closet like a flash before it disappearing again. Something has hit the floor. When the door opened, Maura unclasped her hands and felt around on the floor, hesitation shook her fingertips. What could he have thrown in here? More water? Yes! Her fingers grazed a water bottle. And beside it, there was something spongey. Bread. A roll, maybe. The tension in her chest released slightly. She tried to remember the last time she ate. It was at lunch at school, the day before. How long someone could go without eating?

She scooted the roll and water onto her lap then used her teeth to twist off the water bottle top. Water spilled down her chin as she drank. It was only after the third gulp that she felt the moisture return to her tongue. The water sloshed around in her empty belly. Plain, white bread had never tasted so delicious. She didn't even care that it was stale. She tore through most of the fist sized roll before stopping herself. Because she didn't know how long she was going to be in here, or if the boys hadn't had anything to eat, she forced herself to save it, for herself. Save some for them.

Maybe it was her prayer that brought the food. She would have much preferred if God had hand delivered her home but this would have to do. She was grateful all the same. But again, it made her wonder... if this man wasn't planning on killing them, what was he planning to do? She longed to know what was happening with Greg, Sawyer and Charlie. She longed for that sliver of light in the stable. Waiting here in isolation was torture. But she had no other choice. So she set down her water and bread, laced up her fingers, and again, she prayed.

CHAPTER 22:

2018

Boyd and I exchange numbers when he drops me off at my car so he can keep me updated. I wonder if he can see the dishonesty on my face. I'm not really going to Grandma Marylin's like I said I would.

After Boyd leaves, I start to think through my plan. Yates Federal Prison is an hour away. It'll be nearly eleven by the time we get back to the station. There is no way the prison has visiting hours in the middle of the night. And with the amount I'm worrying, there's also no way I'm going to be able to sleep.

I decide that I will head over to the prison and camp out in my car. That way, I'll be able get in there as soon as I see daylight. Maybe there are better uses of my time—driving around town some more looking for Greg and Sawyer, making calls, knocking on doors to gather information. But then I think of the hay and the note with the patch of my dress. Their disappearance has to be connected to Rick Salem.

Now that I know Charlie had met with our tormentor only a week before his death, I have an uneasy feeling that nothing is what it seems.

Someone is heckling us with that hay, that note, and the dress. Though it pains me to leave anything in Boyd Barton's hands, I have to trust that he is going to do what he can to find Sawyer at Greg. But I really wish Harvey Barton was still Sheriff.

What should I tell Grandma Marylin? She'll think it's strange when I don't come home tonight. And besides, I can't leave her in the dark, not when I'm the only one in the group who isn't missing or dead.

I type Yates Federal Prison into my GPS and decide to call her on the way.

She answers. "Hello?"

"Hi. Nothing yet," I say.

I hear her sigh through the phone. "Sawyer, too?"

"Yeah."

"Come home. Now," she says sternly.

"I can't. I...I'm going to keep looking," I say.

"Bull shit," she says. "You were always a terrible liar, Maura. Tell me what you're really doing."

The car drives the length of a football field before I can muster the courage to answer. "I'm going to Yates."

"The prison?" I can hear the panic rising in her voice. "For what?" The receiver vibrates at the harshness of the word.

It doesn't take much for the dam to burst. I tell her everything—about the note, Boyd and Charlie's friendship and the GPS. I tell her I kept quiet because I'm worried she would panic the way I've been panicking.

She pauses before responding. Her voice is cold. "Turn the car around."

"I...I can't. I'm sorry. I love you and I don't want to worry you more but I...I just can't. I have to see this through."

"Right." She pauses for a few breaths—and takes a few pulls at her cigarette. "This is my fault. I realize that."

"What do you mean?"

"I raised you not to let yourself be swayed by anyone else when you think you are right. Not by anyone— not even me. But you realize what's going to happen, right? When you see that man, you are going to lose every ounce of gumption you feel right now."

"I..."

"Well, you should know that. I'm only telling you this so you aren't caught off guard. It's easy to feel confident when you aren't face to face with a monster. Now, I don't like that you'll even be in his presence, but I respect that you're sticking to your guns. And that's exactly what you're going to have to do in there. Don't let him convince you that he's a different man. That he isn't the same man from all those years ago. Men in prison always claiming that they've found salvation. Oh, and I'm sure there will be a guard there with you. You don't let him out of your sight, you hear me?"

"Yes."

"I don't like this," she huffed. "You call me as soon as you leave that place, you hear me? I don't want to be calling your phone without getting an answer. Now, I'm going to wake Bea the hell up because if I can't sleep, then she shouldn't either."

"Be careful with that one. She's nasty," I say.

"Oh please, she may have a bark, but I've got bite."

That she did.

I keep driving ahead. It's just my luck that my gas light comes on five minutes into my drive. I'll have to stop for gas in town.

There are only two gas stations in town—the Mobile on Main, and Vic's. Greg works at Vic's, so I figure I'll kill two birds with one stone and see if I can talk to Vic about Greg. Grandma Marylin said she talked to him and he didn't know anything about Greg's whereabouts, but I figure it couldn't hurt. And anyway, Vic's is closest to the exit for the highway—Main street would be out of my way. I just hope it's open this late.

When I get to Vic's, there is a handwritten sign on the door to the small shop beside the fuel pumps that reads: Be back in ten minutes. If you know anything about small town business, 'ten minutes' means 'whenever I damn well feel like it'. I haven't seen Vic in a long time, but he was old when I was born—skeletal and pale with fake teeth that could chew through cow hide.

I lift the lever in the wheel well of the driver's side to pop the gas tank. A single street lamp illuminates the gas station, allowing me a little light to search my purse for my credit card. It's while my head is down that I hear a bell. I look up and there is a red pickup truck sitting at the pump across from mine. I didn't even hear it pull in. A breath later someone walks out of Vic's shop.

It's Phil Cooper. The tub-bellied plumber barges out through the unlocked door, stuffing a pack of cigarettes into his sagging t-shirt pocket.

"Well, looky loo," he says in a sing-songy tune. It isn't unfriendly, but I don't trust it either. This is the last person I need to run into right now.

"Hi, Phil," I say as I walk around to the pump. I slide my card, type in my zip code and select Regular. "A little five finger discount, huh?" I nod to the cigarettes in his pocket.

Phil walks over and readjusts a blue tarp over the cab of his truck, leaving nothing uncovered. "I've got a tab with Vic, don't you worry about me. Sounds like you've got enough to worry about with your boys missing."

There's no Grandma Marylin around for him to impress. What we have right here is Phil Cooper in the wild. "Wait, how do you know about that?" My finger weakens on the gas pump.

"Marylin called me. Asked if I'd seen them anywhere."

"Right," I say and tighten my grip on the pump. The numbers on the screen climb until the tank is full and the clamp stops itself. "And did you?"

"They're grown men. Grown men don't get lost. Wherever they are, it's because they want to be there. They're probably just grabbing a drink getting away from all you hens gabbing in their ears. They'll come back when they feel like it." He loudly gathers phlegm in his throat and spits a loogie next to his tire.

"I don't know why I asked," I say, rolling my eyes.

He leans his back against his truck, folds his arms, and watches me as I screw the gas cap back in. "You know, you look just like your Mama, now."

I pause in my tracks. Ice travels up my spine. There would be nothing insulting about this. My mother, despite her poor life choices and questionable character, was a beautiful woman. But the way Phil says it gives me pause. He's not the type to give out compliments. There's something else coming. I brace myself.

"She sure was beautiful. A good time too," he continues. "You know, when you kids went missing some people thought it was her that took you. That she came back. Wanted you back and took the others with her or something."

"Is that so?" I say, unamused.

"I never believed it though. I thought you four just ran off together. Figured it had something to do with that twisted relationship you all had."

"Twisted?" My keys are saturated with sweat and are digging into my palm.

"Don't think I don't know what a naughty little girl you always were." He winks and cocks a smile.

"What the hell are you trying to say, Phil?"

"Oh, don't be all coy. I know those boys passed you around like Thanksgiving sides." He laughs.

My cheeks flush with embarrassment and my ears grow hot with anger. "You're disgusting."

I take a step forward. My limbs are numb from the adrenaline. A vein in my neck shivers with each step. I'm toe to toe with Phil. My slight frame does nothing to intimidate him. He smiles as if he thinks the exchange is cute.

"Some backwoods piece of garbage like yourself would say that," I say. "Who thinks of children like that? Marylin might not see you for what you are, but the rest of us do. I see you for what you are—a gold-digging sack of shit lowlife who gets his rocks off picking on kids.

"And you want to know what? That's some bullshit about my mom coming back and getting us. You know what people really thought all those years ago? They thought it was you."

That gets Phil's attention. His nostrils flare and his upper lip sneers. I've hit a nerve. It's so satisfying that I can't stop. "Aw, it's not easy being the town creep, is it?" I pout sarcastically. "That's why Marylin will never love you. She won't leave you a dime. You know why she lets you around? Because she pities you."

His muscles tense toward me and his fists round. Sounding off was euphoric, but I'm suddenly keenly aware of how much larger he is than me. And how I'm also alone at a gas station at the edge of town- at night.

"Those are some fighting words," Phil says. "You ready to back them up you little princess?"

I force a smile, gather the last bit of gumption coursing through my veins. "Oh, Phil, if you think I'm a princess, shouldn't you be bowing?"

The sound of tires over gravel pops the tension between us. Phil keeps his eyes on me. His body settles back. Whatever he had in store for me a moment ago didn't include witnesses. The stranger in the silver

Ford Focus did their good deed for the day without ever knowing it.

I keep my eyes on Phil as I slip back into my car. With shaking hands, I start the engine and put it in drive. I want to slam on the gas and peel out of the parking lot. But I don't want to give Phil the satisfaction. So I go slower than I want, refusing to look in the rearview mirror. And all the while, I'm praying he doesn't follow after me.

My eyelids grow heavy as I drive. The woman's voice on my GPS is my only company. I turn on the radio and browse for a station music that will keep me from falling asleep at the wheel. I settle on an early Aerosmith song and crack a window, hoping the cool air will keep me awake.

My chest beats like a drum, and serves as a reminder of the shit-storm I'm currently in the middle of. My phone chimes in my lap. I flip it over, hoping it's a text message from Sawyer or Greg—but it's just a news article. At a glance, my eyes catch the name "Weston Cahill." Great.

I know I shouldn't look—not just because I'm driving, but because I'd sworn off caring. Breaking up with someone in the age of social media is hard enough. Trying to move on and forget them, without being assaulted by their latest post or picture is impossible. Breaking up with a celebrity is a whole other ball game. I could unfollow him on every social media app—and I have—but I still find myself getting updates about him. Take this article, for example: Now I know that Weston Cahill's New Action Thriller 'Gone, But Not Forgotten' has busted through record sales its opening weekend. Great.

I throw my phone into the passenger side wheel well. I'm ashamed for even looking at my phone in the first place. Even worse is that I'm slightly interested— even after everything he's done.

I've always considered myself to be a strong woman. I spent three long days in the dark, abused and taunted by a madman, but I survived. I was Mad-Dog Maura. But then I moved away from Settlers Hill and found myself on my own with no one to protect or harbor. And that's when I found out, the person I wasn't so good at protecting was myself.

Over the years, I fallen in and out of short-term relationships with men who were often condescending and controlling. And like a flower without rain in the slow burn of the sun, I nearly wilted when I met

Weston Cahill. I once read, in a black eyeliner graffit-ied bathroom stall in a club downtown, "What doesn't kill me will only weaken me for what will." And that's exactly how it happened to me.

I met Weston when he was set to be the centerfold for the magazine. It was my job to photograph him and after a long day of his overbearing manager chirping in my ear about Weston's "good side," Weston asked me out for a drink. He was impossible to resist. That movie star hair— dirty blonde and perfectly messy— and his sparkling eyes drew me in. He had the type of charisma that brought him the attention of every person in every room.

And he chose me. The relationship moved quickly. He opened doors, pulled out my chair at dinner, and sent me good morning and good night texts. He kissed my eyelashes before my eyes opened in the morning. He taught me how to shield my face from the paparaz-zi and convinced me not to read the comments on his social media accounts.

But once the honeymoon stage was over, when we got to the real meat of the relationship, Weston got controlling. He smacked me around a little after a few tequila shots too many. And he wrapped his fingers a little too tightly around my throat during sex—even when I asked him to stop.

I accepted his apologies and believed him when he blamed his behavior on exhaustion. Too many hours on set. I believed him when he said that he wouldn't have gotten so worked up had I not been such a bitch. I believed that I deserved it. And that cut the deepest.

Then things would be peaceful again and I would slip into the bliss of the early days of our relationship. I would forget. Forgive. Forget. Rinse. Repeat.

I don't think I really knew how bad it was. The bad times were seamlessly intertwined with the good times. The rationalization was almost hallucinogenic.

One day, Sawyer had called me up and said he was going to be in Manhattan for something work related. He tacked some vacation days on to the end of his trip so he could do the touristy things and, of course, visit me. We hadn't seen each other in almost a year, which was a long time for us.

I'd told Weston that I had a friend coming to visit me and apparently, I'd left out the small detail that it was a male friend. Weston knew about my past. He knew about Charlie and Greg and Sawyer and the barn. One drunken night, he tried to convince me to let him pitch it as a movie. I said no, closed the door on the subject and never talked about it again with him. It might have been the only thing I put my foot down on with him.

The night Sawyer came to the city, I had invited Weston to join us. He said he was working late, and said he would meet up with us later if he could. So, Sawyer and I got a few drinks at happy hour, which led to drinks with dinner, which led to after dinner drinks, which led to dancing like morons at a bar. I remember how the average age in the bar was twenty-two, and how it made us feel like grandparents standing next to toddlers. But we didn't care. We caught up, laughed and danced. I started drunkenly texting Weston. I was dying for them to meet, assured they would be fast friends.

Weston showed up to the bar just before closing. My eyes were red and dried out from the liquor and my hair that had succumbed to the humidity of the sweaty club, evolving into its natural lion's mane state. Weston's eyes turned to saucers when he saw Sawyer. I was in trouble.

Weston painted on his L.A. smile and politely had one last drink with us. Sawyer, countless drinks in, was his most social self. He asked Weston a ton of questions about what it was like to be an actor and cheekily told him to take care of 'his girl'. It was an innocent comment that I knew Weston wouldn't take well.

And so, we said our goodbyes, put Sawyer in a cab, and walked back to my apartment.

We were barely inside the door when Weston pinned me up against the wall and grabbed my chin so tightly I thought my teeth were going to collapse in on each other.

"You goddamn whore," he said through gritted teeth.

I tried to convince him that Sawyer was just my friend. That I didn't mean to be deceitful. I was desperate to be released and to quell his anger in any way I could. Tears streamed from my eyes and wet the crease between his thumb and pointer finger.

A shrill buzzing noise beside us brought a halt to the chaos. It was the front desk. The doorman. Someone wanting to be let up. It was three in the morning. Who would be coming that late? That early?

Weston covered my mouth with his hand so I wouldn't speak. I could barely breathe through the gaps of his fingers. He used his other hand to press the button to respond. The man on the other side said that there was a Mr. Sawyer Swenson here, asking to be let up. Weston said we didn't know anyone by that name and released his hold on the button.

"Nothing going on, huh? You're really trying to make a fool of me, aren't you?" he said and tossed me across the room.

My cheekbone collapsed against the cold kitchen tile. I may have been drunk earlier in the night, but I was pretty sober now. Pain has the powerful ability to bring the world into vivid focus. How did I let it get this far? I would never allow someone to treat my friends this way, so why was I folding to this man at every turn? Why was I taking it and turning the other cheek? Where was Mad Dog Maura then? I wanted to summon her from deep in my bones—that fearless version of my former self—to rise up and take Weston on, like she did other bullies. But Mad Dog Maura was dormant. In a deep sleep somewhere so far down that I couldn't reach her.

When I finally got the courage to part my hair from my face and glance up from the kitchen floor, I could see Weston pacing and running his fingers through his hair. It was his tell-tale sign that the downward spiral from rage to regret was beginning. And in spite of myself, I felt relieved. It was a sign that it was over for now. The apology would begin and it would feel so good, like a cool shower after a hot run, or like settling into bed after a long day.

Before I could get up, Weston knelt down and put his hand to my cheek. He ran his thumb over the tender bone and he furrowed his brow. "I'm sor—"

There was a knock at the door.

Weston whipped his head around, atonement stripped from his face. Before he could stand or I could answer, the door creaked open. It was Sawyer.

For a moment, nobody moved. Sawyer stood there, processing the scene before him like a computer loading information.

Weston spoke up first. The guilty usually do. "She fell. A little too much to drink," he said and gripped me by the elbow to lift me off the floor.

"Take your hands off of her," Sawyer took a step forward. He wasn't buying Weston's story one bit.

Weston took a step toward Sawyer. "Get the hell out of here. Don't tell me what to do with my girlfriend. Do you have any idea who I am?"

"You're out of your depth, buddy," Sawyer said. He walked around Weston and came to my side. He pushed the hair from my face. "You don't have to take this shit."

I couldn't have anticipated what happened next. Before I could answer, Weston crept forward, his face reddened with rage. I watched him as he wound up to punch Sawyer in the back of the head.

Weston's fist never made contact though. It never had the chance. Before his fist lurched forward, I had already shoved Sawyer to the side. I drove the palm of my right hand up underneath Weston's nostrils. I felt the bridge of his nose crack and collapse against my hands. Blood stained down my wrist.

Weston staggered backward, blood spurting from his nose as his back hit the door. "Damn it!" his gargled scream echoed through my tiny apartment. Sawyer grabbed Weston by the shirt, opened the front door, and dragged him like a rag doll out into the hallway. Then he slammed the door behind them.

I stood staring at the door, wondering if this was all a dream. My cheek throbbed. My wrist ached from hitting Weston. There was blood on the floor and on my hand. There was no noise coming from the other side of the door.

Sawyer walked back inside and closed the door behind him. "Are you ok?" he asked me. He looked me over. Examining me, he wasn't sure whose blood he was looking at.

"Are you ok?" I said. "Where's...where is he?"

"Gone," Sawyer said and walked over to the kitchen sink. He turned on the faucet and wet a dishrag. "Come sit," he welcomed me to sit on the couch in my own living room. He sat beside me and wiped the blood off my face, my hands, and pressed the cold of the towel against my bruised cheek.

"Why did you come here?" I asked.

"I knew something was off about that guy. The second he showed up to meet us. I didn't like the way he was looking at you. It was like he was a kid watching someone lese play with his toy. That and I saw the way he grabbed your arm when you were leaving. I didn't like it."

"I'm so embarrassed," I said.

Sawyer smiled. "I think we're past the embarrassment portion of this friendship."

And he was right. We'd been through hell together. We'd lived in a pile of our own filth together. We'd survived the aftermath of our abduction. So why was I so flustered in that moment, in front of Sawyer in my apartment?

Tears welled in my eyes and I bit my tongue to keep them in. Sawyer reached his hand behind my head and brought my forehead to his lips. "Want to hear something funny?"

I nodded, wiping the tears away.

"Fun fact: Big, tough action movie star Weston Cahill pisses his pants when he's got a real gun pressed to his forehead."

I cocked a half-smile. I didn't even know Sawyer had his gun on him. I guess they call it a concealed carry for a reason.

I don't know if it was the alcohol still streaming through my veins, or the adrenaline from the ordeal with Weston, but with no warning, not even to myself, I lurched forward and kissed Sawyer right on the lips.

There was a deep warmth in my belly. Blood rushed to my head and my toes all at once. And for a brief moment, Sawyer leaned into the kiss, his warm lips against mine, parting slightly. The heat of his breath welcomed my mouth deeper into his. But then suddenly he stopped, as if he'd given it a second thought and pulled away.

Breath caught in my throat. I wanted to ask what was wrong. Why he started kissing me, and then stopped? But who was I to ask that? I didn't even know why I initiated it in the first place—and I was too chicken shit to begin that conversation.

My face must have said everything.

"I can't—" he began.

"I'm sorry. I don't know where that came from. I'm a mess. I—"

"No, slow down. I want to. I really..." His eyes flickered down to my mouth and he bit his lip. "I really want to. But you've had a lot to drink and it's been a rough night for you. I want—just not like this."

I swallowed hard. I wanted to kiss him again. The urge wasn't entirely foreign—it'd crept up on me a few times in our long friendship—but I'd always been able to squash it. But in that moment, I had been stripped of all hesitation.

He was right. It wasn't the time. I nodded in agreement.

"I'm going to sleep on the couch," he said. "Why don't you go get into bed? I think we both need some sleep." He reached forward and kissed me on the forehead again, though this time his lips lingered just a moment longer than before.

When I woke the next morning, Sawyer was still sleeping on the couch. The morning light was tanning his left cheek as his long limbs hung over the sides of the couch. I knew something was different now. Even in the light and clarity of the morning, I wanted to kiss him again, there as he slept. It wasn't the alcohol or adrenaline after all.

But still, something in me wouldn't allow myself to do it. I left him a note saying that I had a shoot for work and wouldn't be back until later that night [a lie]. I told him to help himself to anything in the fridge. And then I added a 'ps' note that we would 'talk soon about everything and I'm sorry I had to run out', and I meant it.

We've texted since then, but never about anything serious. We only broached surface conversations, and hadn't even dared a phone call until Charlie's death.

I never heard from Weston again, but I did read in the paper that he'd broken his nose 'doing his own stunts.' I guess 'beat up by a girl' doesn't have the same ring to it.

I look up at the midnight sky. The memory has consumed me for most of the drive. At this point, it was a welcomed distraction. I should have told Sawyer how I really feel back then. I shouldn't have run out that morning. I can't help but wonder if that could have altered our fate and saved us from whatever the hell is happening right now. Charlie was alive then. Back then, I knew that Greg was in rehab. Sawyer was safe, right there with me. I pull into the Park and Ride that's a few minutes from Yates Federal. The aching in my chest and stomach is almost too much to bear.

My phone beeps. I try not to look down, thinking that maybe it's another alert about Weston, then realize it may be Grandma Marylin or Boyd or—in a fleeting hope—Greg or Sawyer.

But nothing's any clearer. The message is from Boyd. It reads: Nothing in the barn at the Salem farm FYI

He said he would keep in touch. I'm surprised when I see he's actually followed through with it. I figured he had just been saying that to get me out of his hair. I guess have to give credit where it's due.

CHAPTER 23:

2000

It's my fault, Sawyer thought. He'd been standing right next to Maura. Had he not run to hold the door open, adding to the chaos, then maybe he wouldn't have taken her. Or maybe he would have taken Sawyer instead. It was unbearable to think what could be happening to her on the other side. She was all alone. And now he, Greg, and Charlie were in their own hellish version of isolation—because they couldn't speak.

Every flutter of movement from his friends— shifting sitting positions in the hay, standing, pacing—sent his nerves crackling like droplets of water on a flame. *Except for Maura's,* he thought and immediately felt guilty. Greg and Charlie were his best friends. There was no doubt about that. And Maura was too. But Maura was the one that Sawyer longed to see most days.

Like when his moms took him on vacation to the Bahamas. It was before the cancer. He'd had the time of his life, soaking in the Bahamian sun and swimming with the iridescent fish in crystal clear waters. His moms were happy—holding hands, laughing, and taking him to outdoor dinners where flaming plates arrived, crackling to the table. He didn't even mind the strange looks they would get from some people, because there were two women holding hands with their son in tow. It was a happy time, but Sawyer found himself wishing Maura was there with him. There were odd moments when his mind floated to Greg and Charlie, but all roads led to Maura. She would have loved snorkeling. She would have bitten at his ankle underwater to scare him like she did in the pool. She would have made sure to order the fiery dish at the restaurant. And she would have found adventure in every corner of that resort. They would fight at least once a day, yell as they went their separate ways, only to mend fences before the hour was up and act like nothing had ever happened. But like any prepubescent boy, Sawyer always tried to push those kinds of thoughts of Maura from his mind. It made him uncomfortable to feel this way about her, though he didn't understand why just yet.

That longing was back now, there, as he was seated in that stable, but this time it was happening for a different reason. He didn't want Maura for her adventurous spirit or the comfort of her company or for the hours of laughter she brought. He wanted her back so she would be safe. He wanted to tell her that he's sorry he didn't do more to protect her. But she was too busy protecting him.

Stowed away in a closet across the barn, Maura shifted her weight from her right hip to her left, then back again. The space in the storage closet was tight. She lost track of the time. How long had she been in there? Hours? Days? Her sense of reality was slipping away. Maybe this was all a dream—or a nightmare. Her face still tingled from where the man's hands had smoothed it over.

A piece of her knew the door was about to open—call it instinct. When it opened, there was a dimmed light and the man stood before her. He was wearing all black and a black hood with only eyes cut out. He reached in and grabbed her by the front of her dress. He dragged her up toward him and flipped her around. He lassoed a cloth around her eyes and knotted it at the back.

Maura was too frightened to move. She swayed like a rag doll in his arms. His breath was heavy and smelled of cigarettes. There was a clumsiness to his movements. It was almost like he was as scared as she was.

He began to walk backward, dragging her feet across the barn floor, when something surged within Maura. A rush of adrenaline. She took a hard left from flight to fight. She bent her knee, raised her heel and donkey kicked it backward as hard as she could.

The man screamed a deep groan and his grip around her loosened. Maura took the opportunity to throw her body forward, but overshot it. Her nose hit the hard floor. She could hear the man grunting behind her. She used her tied hands to prop herself up onto her elbows. She geared her feet underneath her to lift her body so she could run. Even blindfolded, this was her best shot—and her only move.

She'd almost gotten it—balanced to her feet. She was ready to rocket forward. Her legs stung from the scratches. Her knee bones vibrated from the impact. The man's fingernails dug deep into her back. His hands slipped and fumbled, trying to grip her dress, her hair, anything he could hold onto to get her back.

She'd taken her chance and squandered it. She laid there, facedown, his knee driving further and further into her spine. Unable to breath, she tried to wriggle free. It was no use. The sharp point of a blade drove into the space between her shoulder blades. Long deep strokes cut into her skin followed by short curves. He was writing.

Maura screamed, but he brought his hand over her mouth. Pain ran down her arms and up into her neck.

When he was done cutting into her back, he stood her up. She gasped, her lungs reaching for air. He was holding her even tighter than before.

He stopped for a moment, shifting her position to free one of his hands. Then she heard the sound of a door opening. In one movement, he released her and kicked her tailbone, sending her flying forward. Her lungs sucked in a short breath before her face hit the hay. She felt the vibration of the door slam behind her. And before she could lift her head, she felt six hands on her—lifting her, sweeping her hair back from her face, removing her blindfold. Each movement was dreamlike. Tears streamed down over her cheeks. Sawyer, Greg, Charlie. She was back with them again.

Charlie thought Maura was dead when the man threw her back into the stall. Pain stabbed at the center of his chest.

Greg and Sawyer scooped themselves under each of her armpits and dragged her to a spot farthest from the door.

Charlie followed. He reached out to touch her, as if to assure himself she was real. But when his hand touched her flesh, he felt a warm liquid streaming down the back of her arms. It was congealing in the tips of her hair. No one needed to say what it was. They knew.

Greg asked, "Where is it coming from?"

Charlie ran his hands over his pants. Hay stuck to the blood, only making it worse. Hot tears streamed down his cheeks. "What did he do to you?"

They whipped their heads around in unison at sound of the door opening again. It opened swiftly and the light from beyond the door did little to illuminate the source of the sound. And then something—more than one something—collapsed into the hay.

Even after the door shut, they did not move. They stayed posted up in the corner. Maura's limbs hung over Greg and Sawyer.

"I tried to run away," Maura said, finally, through baited breath. "He grabbed me. Scratched my back, I think. Cut me. I don't know. It hurts so much." She shifted her weight off her friends to sit up.

To Charlie, Maura sounded more tired than hurt. Her failed attempt at escape had knocked the wind out of her sails.

"What did he do to you?" asked Sawyer.

"Put me in the storage closet. Gave me some food." She paused.

"What is it?" Charlie presses.

"I...I don't know. He just...when he first grabbed me out of here, the way he..." Her voice deepened as the words slipped past the saliva gathering thickly in her throat. "The way he touched me. It was like maybe he was going to...I don't know. I'm just happy I'm back here."

"Happy to be back here. How sick is that?" Greg said.

"I think it's food," she said.

"What?" said Greg.

"Whatever he just threw in here. I think it's food. He gave me food, too," she said, each word labored through the pain.

"We have to clean her up," said Charlie, remembering what their history teacher had told them last year when they were studying the middle ages. That before modern medicine, people could die from a simply cut.

"With what?" she said.

Charlie trotted through the darkness toward the stall door. He got down on his knees and patted the hay to look for what the man threw in. His hands found the plastic water bottles he'd prayed would be there. And then he felt another kind of plastic. It was thin crackling plastic. A sandwich bag.

There were four water bottles and four plastic bags. Inside was something soft, and slightly cold. It was spongy and circular. Charlie knew what it was. It was once of those prepackaged peanut butter and jelly sandwiches that defrost in your lunchbox.

Charlie hadn't eaten in two days, by his calculations. He bit into the sandwich and the sweetness of the peanut butter made his tongue tighten up and water. Beside him, there was a symphony of tongues smacking against the roof of mouths and gulping. Everyone was eating but Maura.

"Aren't you starving?" asked Greg, shocked.

"He fed me a little. I'm still hungry but I don't know when we'll eat again. I think I should save it," she said.

Charlie remembered her cuts. He cracked open his water bottle and crawled to Maura. "Come here, turn around. I'll rinse your back."

Charlie tipped the bottle gently, not wanting to waste any more water than he had to. Maura winced and stifled a cry as the water washed over her.

Charlie closed the water back up.

A groan of pleasure came from Sawyer. "It feels so good to eat."

Charlie agreed. The spike in their blood sugar had given them a moment's peace—a respite from the struggle they'd been enduring. But it didn't take long for that hopeful feeling to dissipate.

"So, what now? We're just prisoners?" Greg asked. "Locked in a cage like dogs? What, is he just going to feed us when he feels like it and beat us when we try to get out?"

"Well, our last plan went great," said Sawyer.

"So, what, we just stay here and die?" Greg asked.

"Someone will find us," Charlie said, remembering the siren. "Someone has to be looking for us by now. The town isn't that big."

"Yeah, but what if he kills us just before they find us? We don't know what this psycho is planning!" Greg stood and started pacing, kicking up hay as he walked.

"Oh my God, enough!" Maura yelled out. Her voice was painted in pain.

Greg stopped pacing. "Fine. I'll do it on my own."

"What is that supposed to mean?" Sawyer asked.

Charlie didn't like this. He didn't want them each to have their own plans. "Isn't that when people start dying in scary movies? When they split up? Greg, please don't do anything stupid. Look at what he did to Maura."

"Look?" Greg screamed. "That's exactly it! I can't even look. We probably have her blood all over us. We probably just ate it off those sandwiches. We're stuck in the dark and everyone just wants to give up."

"No one is saying that." Sawyer stood. "But getting yourself killed isn't going to help anyone."

"I'm stronger than Maura. Next time he opens that door I'm going through and I'm getting out. I'll get help and come back for you."

"It's suicide!" Charlie yelped helplessly. Greg was stronger than Maura, but he was slower, in mind and body.

"I'm doing it," Greg said. He inched toward the door, his body betraying his hesitation. They knew it would be a while before the door opened again—if it even opened at all. Greg was ready to go on the offensive, but Charlie was ready to do everything he could to stop him.

CHAPTER 24:

2018

I

t's only as I'm opening my eyes to the dewy glare on my windshield that I realize I'd fallen asleep. I check the time—8:00 a.m. In my sluggish half-awake stupor, I remember that I stuffed a half-eaten granola bar into the center console just before Charlie's funeral. In the days and hours leading up to his funeral, I'd lost all semblance of an appetite. I always wondered about those women who talked about sitting and eating a tub of ice cream when they were upset. Sadness, anxiety—all of my extreme emotions only ever stripped me of my appetite. Eating becomes a forced necessity and food always hits my empty stomach like marbles in a tin can.

The bar is dry. The peanut butter laced granola crumbles just as much into my lap as into my mouth, but it's just enough to bring my blood sugar to level.

It makes me uneasy to think that not far beyond the thicket of the Park and Ride is Rick Salem's home for the past decade and a half. I feel a shiver in my spine. The scars on my back tingle numbly. My eagerness to venture forward is tempered by my fear of facing Rick again. The last time I'd seen him had been in court, just after it all happened. I'd been surrounded by my friends and Grandma Marylin and had the full force of the town behind me—minus a few who spouted Rick's innocence. Even in the barn, in that stable, I'd had Charlie and Sawyer and Greg. The last time I was alone with Rick was when he threw me in that supply closet. My throat dries down to my chest at the memory.

I check my phone, hopeful for a string of missed calls saying that Greg and Sawyer have been found. I imagine that waiting for me there is some logical explanation for all of this madness. Instead, there is only a missed call and follow up text from Boyd. It says: Filed an official Missing Person's report for Greg and Sawyer. Call when you can.

It's strange to see his name light up my phone. In all the time I've known Boyd, this is the first time we've had each other's numbers. I'll delete it when all this is over, I tell myself. I don't want to call him right now.

I'm sure if he had any pressing information, he would have said it in the text, so I opt to text back. It says: Thanks. Busy, will call when I can.

Talking to Boyd would just psych me out even more. Grandma Marylin was the last person I spoke to and I want to keep it that way for now.

I roll down the window and let in a current of fresh air. It's cool and smells like wet grass. I start my drive.

When I arrive, security is wary of me. I'm an unknown woman parked outside the gate while the day shift guards sip their morning coffee. The man at the gate, who serves as the prison's first line of defense to the outside world, has grey hair with a beard to match. He has sparkling blue eyes that shine beneath his bushy eyebrows and his cheeks are rosy red. His name tag reads Tomlinson.

"Can I help you, Miss?" His coffee breath passes through my car window. I wonder if I can get a hit of that caffeine I need so desperately right now.

"I'm here to see a prisoner. Have visiting hours started?"

"You have an appointment?" he asks. His eyes peer over my shoulder and into my back seat. He's scanning for something, but I don't know what it is.

Shit. I didn't even think of needing an appointment. I have no idea how this works. "I don't. It's kind of last minute, I know. I'm sorry." I duck my head. Taking on a sheepish appeal can't hurt my chances of being let in, right?

"That's all right. You're lucky there are visiting hours today. But you're early. I need your license," he says as he looks at the computer in front of him. He takes the card from my hand without looking at me. "You're not in the system. Just going to have to go through a whole lot of extra security, that's all." He picks up the phone and says something into the receiver that I can't hear. Then the red and white striped barrier lifts. He tells me to park in the 'red' parking lot.

I'm surprised by how large the prison is, although I guess I really shouldn't be. Federal prisons are usually big. Tall gates with rounded electrified wire encase the property and there are towers posted at all four corners. The prison itself is a bright concrete building, giving it a corporate look rather than the Hollywood dark, dank look I'd expected. It's far less intimidating this way. I remind myself that it's a high-security, heavily armed office building with murderers and rapists walking its halls. Yates is maximum security prison, so it's no surprise that security detail is so heavy.

My purse is checked manually and via X-ray and then I walk through the metal detector. A female security guard is called for a pat down as a man seated at a desk behind bullet proof glass scans my driver's license. The female guard tells me that she's pleased that I know how to dress for prison. I look down at my simple Long-sleeved T-shirt and jeans. "The less skin showing, the better," she says and passes me off to the next guard.

Next, I sit in front of a desk across from a uniformed man. He wants to record my visit's intentions. I tell him I'm there to see Rick Salem and as soon as his name crosses my lips, I feel dizzy.

The man furrows his brow when I mention Rick. I desperately want to ask why he's giving me that look. I know better than to expect an answer.

He hands me off to a guard who looks like an ex NFL player turned super-guard. He ducks his enormous body through the doorway and escorts me into a room that looks more like a cafeteria than a visiting center. There's a vending machine humming in the corner. Tables are lined too close to one another, preventing private conversation. I'm the only person in there, aside from one guard standing by the vending machine. He sits me down and tells me to wait because the prisoners are finishing up breakfast. He's going to fetch Rick in a minute.

As I sit and wait, I watch the extra guard. I wonder what he's thinking. Does he think that I'm a family member of Rick's? Or maybe some girlfriend convinced of his innocence?

Every muscle of my body is clenched. The seat and table feel like cement against my skin. Each clap of footsteps in the hallway and ever creak of a door, startles me stiffer. But still, I wait for Rick. I wonder if they know that all this waiting is torture.

A long-gone therapist's words come to me. "When you feel afraid, lean on those you love. Imagine they are standing around you in a protective formation. Let them give you strength. You have the full force of their support."

I'm too nervous to close my eyes. I focus on a piece of dirt on the floor and imagine that Grandma Marylin is at my right and Harvey Barton is at my left. I imagine them closing themselves in around me, an impenetrable forcefield.

When Harvey cracked open that stall door and found us, half-starved and dehydrated, the clean air that billowed in and a look of glowing relief filled his face. It was the same look on his face when he stood between us and Rick Salem any time we entered the courtroom during the trial. That's what I picture when I imagine feeling safe. Settlers Hill feels less vulnerable without him at his post—after all, under Boyd's reign as sheriff, one of my friends is dead and the other two are missing.

But before my mind can travel down that road, the door to the visiting center swings wide open. My heart pauses. My eyes close. I must look ridiculous. A grown woman with closed eyes, sitting at what looks like a cafeteria table.

My stomach is butterfly house. Frenetic, flapping wings bump into each other, changing altitudes, ping ponging off walls and inanimate objects as kinetic energy builds and builds. I ball my fist and press it to my belly button, as if this might calm the madness. My heart beats in my ears. The guard's words are muffled, as if he's speaking through smoke.

My eyes snap open. "No touching," he says. Not to me, but to Rick Salem.

The man who approaches me is not what I remember of Rick Salem—in my last image of him, he was being escorted, hands cuffed behind his back, by the court Marshal. That was over a decade ago.

The Rick Salem in my memory was tall with tree trunks for legs and broad shoulders. He had shaggy dark brown hair that covered his eyes and a round face with permanently windburned cheeks.

The windburned cheeks are the only thing that are the same now. He's shorter than I remember. His body is round like a hard-boiled egg and his hair has been sheered to a crew cut, its color sucked out by age. I'm startled by his eyes. I can see them now that his hair is short. They're green, wide and friendly as he moves toward me, smiling.

As he and his escort guard separate, the guard gives Rick a wink that makes my mouth dry up. My bones vibrate and I concentrate on not shaking as he takes his seat. He looks pleased to see me—genuinely pleased. I want to speak first. I read something somewhere once—probably in the very magazine I work for—about assertion of power. Apparently, the person who speaks first leads the conversation, and therefore, maintains control. But I can't speak. My lips betray me and weld together.

With a big grin Rick says, "My Lord, another visitor. This is special."

Another visitor. He must mean Charlie. I stare back at him and say nothing. His voice doesn't match his body—it's the body of an overweight, middle aged man. His voice is the voice of a child—not in tone, but in temperament.

He rubs his thighs self-consciously under the table. "So how can I help you ma'am?"

It's then that I realize he has no idea who I am. This should make me feel better, but somehow, it makes me feel worse. Sick, even. Now I have to explain who I am. It's not only uncomfortable, but insulting. The man I see in my nightmares sees me as a stranger.

"I'm...I'm Maura," I say and I watch every upturned wrinkle in his face sag. The color drains from his skin.

He drops his eyes and refuses to meet my gaze. He's biting his lip and muttering half words and incomplete sentences before he settles on the right thing to say. "I swear on my Mamma and Daddy's life it wasn't me who did those bad things to you kids. I swear it." He clamps his eyes shut like he's in pain.

I want to be angry, to feel anything but the fear and sadness I feel right now. I skipped my chance to take control of the conversation, but I refuse to let the chance slip through my fingers again. I won't let him play the victim. I need to get angry. Get angry. 'Mad Dog Maura,' Sawyer coaches me in my head.

"Listen, I'm not here for a retrial," I say. "I'm here because I know Charlie came to talk to you. Before he died."

Rick's eyes raise to meet mine. His emerald eyes look even brighter against their red-stained whites. He no longer looks sorrowful, but shocked. "Died? What do you mean he died? I just saw him. He was here only last week. It was last week, wasn't it? Dead?"

I need him to stop saying that Charlie is dead. I clear my throat. "I want to know why he came to see you."

Rick is deep in thought. His eyes scan the table as if he's still questioning the date that Charlie came to see him. How dare he pretend to be sad! He tried to kill Charlie himself. I don't care if he considers himself innocent or redeemed, I know what he is and I know what he did.

I've had enough. I pound my palm to the center of the table and demand a response. "Why did he come to see you!" I mean for my words to convey authority, but instead, they sail in the wake of a cry.

The guard behind Rick takes a single step forward to assess the situation, but then he settles back. Rick sniffs back his tears. "He believed me. He came here because he believed I didn't do it."

This wasn't entirely news to me, but I never could imagine that Charlie would ever take his conspiracy theory this far. "So that's it?" I ask. "He drove over here one sunny afternoon on a whim to tell you that he thought you were innocent?"

"Kind of, well, I guess. He was really nice. He said he never thought it was me. That he couldn't say anything at the time because everyone was telling him I did it. He said he didn't know better then." His voice grows more boyish by the word.

"But why?" I say, gutturally.

"I can't really say. He said he couldn't really say either...said he needed more time. He said that he might have figured something out, or seen something he hadn't before. New evidence or something. But he wouldn't say until he was sure. He wanted to come here and talk to me to get my side of the story. And so, I told him. I guess my answer made sense to him."

Is it possible that Charlie uncovered something and kept it from all of us? As I try to make sense of my thoughts, I remember the barn. Charlie was set to sell the Salem place—including the barn where we were held captive. Did he find something there?

"Well, forgive me if I'm still unconvinced."

Rick reaches his hand to the center of the table where I've absentmindedly left mine. He sets his large paw of a hand over it. At the first sense of pressure, I snap my hand back.

"What do you think you're doing?" I look to the guard who'd said 'no touching' only minutes ago. But he's conveniently staring at the vending machine.

"I'm sorry. I mean no harm. I just...I never knew how to talk to people, even before this place. And this place hasn't made it any easier. I'm sorry. I didn't mean to scare you."

"I'm not scared," I snap. His chubby hands are folded at the center of the table. He fans them out then starts tapping, nervously. On his left hand, his thumb and pointer finger are shorter than the rest. On those two fingers there is nothing above the knuckle. On his right hand his pointer finger is bent at the top knuckle towards his middle finger. "Is all that from prison? The scars?" I can't take my eyes off of them.

He folds his hands over to look for himself and I can see that the palm of his hands are marked up too. They're scarred, callused and dry. "Those? Oh no, this is all from my farming days. I do some small janitorial stuff around here to keep busy—they give us jobs and stuff—but nothing that would do that." He flips his hand over and sets it down on the table to show me his right palm. Staring back at me is a large raised scar that spreads from the base of his pointer finger to the bottom left corner near his wrist. He fans his hand open and closed and I watch the scar redden and pulse. "That one's my favorite, only because it was so stupid. I was about fifteen and thought I'd show off to a girl. Told her I could flip an axe in the air and catch it by its handle." He chuckles to himself and tucks the hand back to his lap. "Not hard to guess which side of the axe I caught that day."

I've never truly experienced a flashback until this moment. Not a lucid memory, but a true flashback—a transportation through time, when all of my senses take the trip with me. I'm having a flashback now. I'm back at the barn, scared and alone with an arm around my waist and a hand over my eyes.

The hand is soft and smooth. It's long and stretches across the whole of my face.

The sound of metal crashing against metal brings me back to present. The guard has given in and gotten himself that Pepsi he'd been eyeing from the vending machine. "What about your fingers?"

"This one," he says as he raises his left hand, "happened when I was a kid. The tractor blade got all tangled and I was watching my dad fix it. He stepped away for a second and I tried to help. The blade kick started back up. Took some of me with it." And this, "He points to his bent right pointer finger, "was the dumbest. I was a teenager and was mad at my parents—I can't even remember what for—and I punched the wall. Hit it the wrong way. Doesn't hurt much anymore though."

A thought weasels its way in. "Can you write with your hands like that?"

"Not really. I can try to put the pen between my other fingers but no one can ever really read what I write. Just comes out at scribble. Why?"

"Just curious." I choose not to tell him what I'm thinking. What I can't believe I'm considering. The hand on my face, the man's right hand, was it actually Rick's? For whatever reason, I'd always remembered the smoothness of that hand. It had felt slimy against my skin.

I try to shake the thought off. I must be remembering wrong, I tell myself. There was a trial. It was in his barn. It was him. Don't let his sheepish charm fool you. I eye Rick sternly.

"But the no—" I stop myself, still reluctant to show any sign of doubt in his conviction.

The note. The one the man wrote to Charlie, Sawyer and Greg to keep quiet after he'd taken me, separated me out from the others. Charlie kept the note after we were rescued. I don't know if we even told anyone about it. At that point, what did one little note to stay quiet matter against everything else? Greg burned it when he found out that Charlie had it. He told him keeping it would just make him sick in the head.

Rick was twenty-three when he took us. His hands were already like that. Mangled. That note he wrote Sawyer, Charlie, and Greg when we were separated- it wasn't just written, but written in script. Neat, slanted, half-cursive.

I snap back to the present. "No, no, no" I say out loud, feeling my panic rising. Images flash before my eyes. Rick's rough hand. The note. Whatever Charlie had up his sleeve, if Rick wasn't the man who took us all those years ago, then it means the real man was still out there. Maybe Sawyer and Greg have gone missing because of him.

"Guard!" I yell out and he rushes over.

Rick Salem throws his hands up in innocence and slides his chair backward from the table. The guard asks me what's wrong. And then I throw up all over his shoes.

CHAPTER 25:

2000

The whisper of light through the slat in the stall disappeared. A symphony of insects buzzed, rattled, clicked, and hummed beyond the outer walls of the barn. Though they had designated a corner of the stall as a bathroom, the sour stench of their collected urine permeated the air. No one had a bowel movement yet, and Greg vowed not to break the seal on that one. The food churned his system, but he resisted the urge until it went away.

Greg noticed that Charlie hadn't spoken to him since his announcement that he was going to attempt an escape. Maura hadn't said much either. Greg didn't say much himself. His mind was occupied thinking about the scratches on Maura's back, because Charlie had told them about infection. His courageous spirit kept taking dips in the anxious wait for the man's next arrival.

By now, the second night in the stable, there was an unspoken understanding that they weren't going anywhere. Sleep would still not come easy. Maura and Sawyer spoke for some time in hushed tones, and though Greg couldn't hear all of it, he knew they were talking about him. Charlie hadn't said anything to anyone in protest. Even when Greg tried to reason with him—saying that the worst that could happen to him would be what happened to Maura, so he'd eventually be back there—Charlie only sighed.

Greg set himself directly to the right of the door, closest to where it would open. He figured that if at any time the man came back, he could catapult himself through and make his escape. He sat, leaning on hip with his arms folded and pressed his temple to the wall as he imagined the scenario. The man would return, most likely to give them more water or food, and that was when Greg would seize his opportunity and make a break for it. Lord knows Greg had plenty of experience fending off attackers—Boyd Barton especially. That was how he was going to think of this guy, he decided. Just a bigger version of Boyd.

If Greg could fend off the guy who put them in here, and single-handedly free his friends from this psycho, he would finally have earned the respect he deserved. Boyd Barton would never bother him or his friends again. He would be revered, and maybe even feared, by his classmates. He'd no longer be the butt of jokes about his red hair. No one would ask him stupid questions—like whether he'd found the pot of gold at the end of the rainbow, or if his insides are just "Lucky Charms".

Freeing his friends would shut his mother up for sure. She'd never be able to call him a "little wuss boy" again and she might even be proud of him. She'd parade him around town, because she'd be so happy to call him her son. At the thought of it, an electrical current snaked through his veins. He played endless scenarios in his head of his new future as Greg the Brave—no—Greg the Hero.

At no point was he conscious that he was asleep, not until Maura's hand on his shoulder startled him awake. "I think he's coming," she said quietly. She retreated backwards, pulling on Greg's shirt to follow her.

Greg looked to their only light source in an attempt to discern whether it was day or night. His eyes had grown so accustomed to the darkness that even the little light that entered with the morning sun seemed more like someone had lit a small lamp.

"Holy shit," said Sawyer.

Greg turned to find Sawyer and Maura's shadows pressed close to the light. Sawyer was squatting, staring at Maura's back.

"What?" Charlie and Greg asked in unison.

"What?" Maura asked, panicked. "What is it?" Her voice grew desperate.

"He wrote something. When he cut you. On your back," said Sawyer.

"What does it say?" Maura nearly screamed.

"You're not going to like it."

"It hurts so bad. Tell me anyway."

"Bitch," said Sawyer. "He wrote the word bitch."

Maura let out a sob, a deep cry from her stomach and Sawyer wrapped his arms around her.

Pain stabbed like a knife in Greg's chest.

And then he heard footsteps. He heard them growing nearer, his heart pounding in his chest. Each fantastical scenario that had flooded his mind the night before flew away and was replaced with fear and a deep desire to retreat.

But he'd be brave. He stood and squared himself against the opening, despite his trepidation. His knees were shaking. He put one hand against the wall to steady himself. Maura breathed heavily beside him in short, quick breaths that whistled.

"Don't be an idiot, Greg," Sawyer hissed from behind her.

Greg ignored him and kept focused. If he escaped, he'd solve their problem. In fact, it would solve all of his problems. He just had to do this one thing. That was all. Anyone can do one thing, he told himself.

The man was close. There was a clanking of metal as he fumbled with the lock. Greg tensed and then felt a piercing throbbing pain as his body was slammed against the wall and then dragged down to the ground. Charlie was on top of him. He'd taken a running leap to spear tackle Greg.

"I'm not letting you do this!" Charlie shrieked.

Greg tried to push Charlie off of him. Charlie used his wiry arms to thwart Greg's attempts. Greg used the heel of his foot to press off the ground and rolled on top of Charlie. At this point, Maura and Sawyer jumped in to break it up. Maura went for Greg and Sawyer dragged Charlie away.

The stall door creaked open.

Greg watched as it whined opened and knew this was his only chance. Maura had gripped his elbows behind him. He wrenched his torso to throw her off. Her body collapsed into the hay behind him and he bolted through the opening in the door.

The man was closer than Greg had anticipated. The light pouring in from the opened stable doors stung his eyes blind. He screamed as the man pushed him, belly down, to the concrete floor. Greg pressed his palms beneath him to prop himself up, but then there was a blinding pain to the back of his skull—a blunt crash that made him see lights before his vision turned to darkness.

He woke, gasping for air. Seated upright in a chair with his hands tied behind his back, stretched back so far his shoulders nearly came out of their sockets. There was a cloth tied around his eyes. The man threw a bucket-full of cold water at his face.

The man said nothing. He paced. It was quick and frantic, like a dog about to slip its leash. Shit, thought Greg, still groggy. The back of his head was aching. And in that moment, he didn't think of his friends. He didn't even think of the madman circling him like a shark. He thought of his mother. He was so desperate to make sure she wouldn't know about this. She would call him a loser. An idiot.

"Please, don't tell my mom," he cried out. The words bounced back to him off the concrete floors.

The pacing stopped but still, the man said nothing. Had he gotten through to him? Maybe inadvertently shown some humanity? The pacing resumed and Greg's hope sizzled.

"Please—just let us go. Why are you doing this?" He hated himself for pleading. This was not how this was supposed to go. In his fantasies, he'd even gone as far as to imagine that he would be brave like those prisoners of war he'd seen in movies, spitting at the feet of their captors and refusing to give up state secrets. Above all, he resolved to be brave. And yet, here he was, begging.

The man wrapped a cloth around Greg's mouth so tightly that it sank behind his teeth and dug into the corners of his mouth. He choked initially, but then he maneuvered his tongue forward and lapped it over the cloth. It tasted like it had been washed with too much detergent. The bitter soapiness made his mouth water.

When the man finally stopped pacing, he'd stopped at Greg's back. Greg could feel the man behind him. It sounded like he was rustling around in his pocket for change.

There was a snap, then pain—burning. Greg's hands were at his back, getting hotter and hotter until he jolted, his chest bowing away from the pain. He tried to move his hands but they were tied. He screamed and a muffled sound came through the cloth. The man was burning Greg's hands with some kind of lighter. Torturing him.

Greg tried to scream. "Please! Stop! Please!" But he couldn't hear his own the words through the cloth. His fingers writhed to be set free of their binding, but it was hard for Greg to move them while the flame was touching them. The stinging became unbearable.

Greg pounded his feet against the floor and without preemptive thought, he slammed them down in unison. The force sent the chair he was tied to flying back into the man.

And so there they lay, Greg and his chair atop the man. The man grunted in pain and in one motion lifted Greg and the chair off of him. Upright once more, Greg could think of nothing else but his stinging hands—the pain at the back of his head took a back seat. He dreamed of the man throwing that water on him again to soothe his seared hands.

Greg knew what the man was doing—punishing him for trying to escape like Maura did. He wished he could go back in time and listen to Charlie, Maura and Sawyer. Hot tears pooled in the cloth over his eyes.

The man picked up the chair with Greg still tied to it. He held it so Greg lay flopped forward. The pressure of the tie at his wrists cut the circulation to his burning hands. He tossed the chair into a stall, and Greg landed on his side with the chair choking his left arm. Hay poked into his mouth, and he knew immediately he was not back with his friends. He was in some other stall. The hay where he had been before was clean and dry, but this hay smelled of manure. He could hear flies buzzing inches from his face, and some even bounced off of it.

The stall door slammed and he knew he'd been left alone. His raw hands hurt. His head pulsated. His left arm was numb from shoulder to elbow. Any fight he'd had in him earlier had been burned out. It was beaten out—so he did the only thing he could. He laid there and cried.

CHAPTER 26:

2018

I leave the visitors' lounge of the prison in a dream-like state. Voices, of the guard and Rick Salem, dull to a hum and I'm desperate to break out into the fresh air.

After I vomited, another guard came in to escort Rick back to his cell. I don't feel the way I expected I'd feel. I'm not frightened. I'm not angry. I catch one last glimpse of Rick's face before he disappears to the other side and realize that he's the one who looks frightened. He's frightened and sad, and it feels as though I've left a lost child to fend for themselves.

I whip my head away from the disturbing sight. My mouth tastes like copper and peanut butter from the puke. My curdled stomach growls. I've exorcised the only thing I've eaten since breakfast yesterday.

The guard keeps his arm looped in mine to steady me as we walk toward the lobby. "You need help to your car Miss? You ok to drive? Is there anyone you want me to call?"

When I don't answer, he smiles warmly and says "You can sit here and wait as long as you need to." He points to a long wooden bench by the door.

I run my palm over my eyebrow and blink hard to regain focus. "No, thank you. I'm fine." I catch a glimpse of his shoes. They're black and painted in my peanut butter puke. "I'm so sorry about your...." I point down to his feet, and then reach into my purse to pull out my wallet. "Please let me give you money for new shoes."

The guard's eyes twinkle in the fluorescent lighting as he laughs. "Don't you worry about my shoes. Working here, they've seen worse days. Just take care of yourself."

"I'm so sorry. I don't know what came over me," I say. Tears stream down my face in part from exhaustion, both mental and physical. What just happened in there?

The guard guides me to sit on the bench and sets himself down next to me. He leans forward with his elbows on his knees. Each of his legs is the size of my torso. "Listen, I don't know what happened in there, and I know it's none of my business, but don't feel too bad. I've seen worse."

"What do you mean?"

"You know, fights break out, people jump across the table to start an all-out brawl." He leans back and gives a wry smile. "People try to touch each other, kiss, or worse. Some people cry, especially if there are kids involved. I hate when kids visit. I get it, the guests want little Billy or Sally to come see their daddy despite his heinous crimes. I guess a shitty father is better than no father, right?"

"Right,' I say, even though I don't agree. I'll take Grandma Marylin and no father any day over what I'd been given at the start.

"No matter if it ends in a brawl or a hug or tears or," he kicks up the toe of his boot, "vomit, people always come here because they need something. Comfort or closure or whatever. Some get it, some don't."

"Yeah," I say, not sure where he's going with all of this.

"What I'm trying to say is don't be so hard on yourself. Don't be embarrassed. It isn't easy walking into a place like this. It's tough with these guys, who are locked in here for years or the rest of their lives. And it's especially hard when you've got someone like Rick. Knowing he's done what he's done and trying to meld that with that gentle oaf before you. He was a monster on the outside, but a model prisoner in here. Hell, I wish all of them were like him—clean, polite and friendly. Like I said, I don't know why you came in here to see him, but—"

"You know I was one of the kids he abducted, right?" I say.

The guard's mouth drops open. "I...I didn't," he stammers. "I'm sorry. I thought maybe you were a family member. I...thought I was..."

"Trying to make me feel better by convincing me that he's not that bad?" I ask. "Charisma and charm don't make for good character. I thought you, of all people, would know that." I stand up and collect my things.

The guard tenses and wrings his hands together. "I'm sorry. I, I just didn't know."

I dig into my wallet and fish out forty dollars and slap it down onto the bench next to him. "For the shoes."

I walk out. As the door slams behind me, I feel a pang of guilt. That guard was trying to be nice, but his timing was wrong. Even still, my mind is reeling from what Rick told me in there, and from what I saw.

Rick's rough scarred hands were not the ones that touched my face all those years ago. Memory is funny like that. Some things I hardly remember at all, like all the bug bites we came out with. I don't remember feeling the bugs bite me, or the itching bites at all. But I do remember the doctors treating the small lesions on my skin when we'd been rescued.

As for the other things I remember now, I recall them in the way one remembers a dream. It was so dark in there that I instinctively came to rely on my other senses, like my sense touch. I remember the smooth hand across my face—so soft and dry, like a silk scarf across my cheek before it threatens to wring my neck.

My back aches. That bad word is carved into my back. Bitch. Even today, after endless laser treatments and with makeup covering up the scar, I'm marked for eternity. Boyfriends have seen it, of course. Weston, in his moments of rage, would claim that I was marked correctly. He once even said that Rick Salem should have put my name tag on my chest so that it would be easier to see.

And what if Charlie was right after all? What if Rick Salem, the model prisoner favored by guards, is innocent? That not only means that an innocent man has spent most of his life in jail, but it means that the man who abducted us—who tortured us mentally and physically—is still out there.

When I get back to my car, I take out my phone to turn it off silent. Waiting for me are three missed calls, two voicemails and a barrage of text message—all from my magazine editor, Rebecca, who also used to be my old college roommate. I don't bother listening to the voicemails because I know why she's calling. I was supposed to be back this morning and it's already 10 a.m. And I'm never late, so she knows something is up.

The phone rings once before she picks up. "Maura, where the hell are you?"

"I'm sorry, Bec. I should have called. Things have just been crazy here," I say.

"Here? Where's that? Are you not back in the city yet?"

"I wish. I just..." Where do I begin? How far do I go once I've started? Rebecca deserves an explanation, but I don't have the energy to give her one just now. Not after the prison. "Listen, I'm sorry. I know I should have called or emailed you or something. But I need this to be one of those times that you give me a free pass without an explanation. When I get back, I'll tell you everything and you'll understand why I couldn't get into it at first."

Rebecca sighs. Initially, I think it's directed at me, but then I hear her say, "We have deadlines for a god-damn reason, Tiffany." Her mouth is a few inches from the receiver, so I hear the reprimand in all its glory. "If you can't get your shit together, then I have a stack of resumes on my desk of people dying for your job."

A door slams and her voice softens. "Sorry, Maur. Of course, yes. You're one of my most dependable employees, not to mention one of my oldest friends. You do realize that I still need a photographer for today's shoot, though, right? That means that I'm going to have to use Loretta."

I let out a hard cackle that takes every ounce of my breath out of my lungs. It almost hurts to laugh that hard. It feels good. Loretta is a spunky, eager intern with the attention span of a fly on cocaine. She's the niece of a higher-up, so comes in three days a week to shadow me—i.e. follow me around as she tells me about her relationship drama and how much she drank the night before. She's always describing all these new online classes she's taking to become a certified something-or-other, even though none of it will never actually make her any real money.

"Your funeral," I say.

"Well, you leave me with no choice. Ugh, I bet this is all just a ruse—you're just leaving me hanging to show me how much I need you here. I see your game." She sighs dramatically. "I guess if you're not back by tomorrow, I'll have to find someone else to sneak off with at lunch for a mid-day Sake and sushi break."

"Believe me, I'd rather be doing that with you."

"All right, I've got to go and get a handle on this crappy rodeo circus. But in all seriousness, I hope you're okay. I know this is rough for you, with Charlie and all."

"Thanks, Bec. I love the hell out of you."

"I love it when you talk dirty. Au revoir." She kisses into the phone then hangs up.

I start the car and make my way back to Settlers Hill. It's a decent drive back and I'm exhausted—mentally and physically.

My phone dips in and out of service as I drive through different peaks and valleys. My first instinct is to call Grandma Marylin, but I know I'd have to relay everything that just happened, and all of my concerns and questions. It just feels too exhausting right now to take that on.

So instead, I call Boyd—someone to whom I owe no explanation. I know I won't be tempted to seek comfort from him. Our conversations can be kept black and white. I can ask him what I need to know—like, where the hell are my friends?

I'm three exits away from Settlers Hill when Boyd finally calls me back.

"Maura?"

"Hey," I say and try to keep my voice from shaking. I'm still not quite steady after my meeting with Rick Salem.

"You ok?" he asks. There's a rustling in the background. Is it paper, maybe? I can't tell.

"Yea. I'm fine. Any word on Sawyer or Greg?" I ask, getting straight to the point.

"The only good news I have is that since they're both officially missing persons, our resource pool has grown a little. We searched Greg's house and talked to Miss Winters, his landlady downstairs. I talked to Carlsen and the Judge. But so far, no one's seen or heard from him. Sawyer neither." My car beeps in warning that I'm crossing the edge of the lane. Boyd hears it. "Hey, where are you right now?"

"I just ran out to get some breakfast," I lie. "I'll be at Marylin's. Call me if there's any leads? I'm getting antsy. I can't just sit around and do nothing."

"You got it, boss. Now just try to stay in the lane there," he says with more charm than I'm willing to acknowledge.

My lie to Boyd about getting breakfast reminds me of how hungry I am. I head toward the deli across the street from Settlers Hill High School. It's a small brick building painted in a black and white cow print pattern. I think its actual name is 'Spellmann's Delicatessen' but everyone in town just calls it 'The Cow'.

The town feels different as I take the right at the light off the exit. Or maybe I'm different. For one thing, a new questions are swirling in my head: Could it be possible that Rick Salem wasn't the man who abducted and hurt us all those years ago? And if it wasn't him, then is the man who did it still here? Are Greg and Sawyer's disappearance connected? Or is it all just related to Greg's drug use?

I walk into The Cow. The air is filled with bacon-scented steam and sounds of the sizzling griddle, crackling over Motown music. A thin man with bottle thick glasses is hunched over the grill with bacon, egg and cheeses and a pile of rolls stacked as high as his eye beside him. He's rocking and bobbing his head to the music like there isn't anyone else around

There are two teenage boys on line. They're probably here on their free period, or more likely, are skipping from the sneaky looks they're wearing. An older man is sitting at another table, holding a newspaper and coffee. Coffee—that's what I need. Food is great and all, but I could do without it, as long as I have coffee. There is no one behind me in line, so I stagger over to the self-serve area and pour myself the darkest coffee they have to offer. I add a splash of half and half a bring the large foam cup up to my nose. The smell alone has brought me some life.

The bell over the front door rattles as it's pushed open. I quickly return to my spot in line to find Coach Carlsen standing right in front of me. What I first interpret as surprise on his face turns to malice. His cheeks redden. "You," he says through gritted teeth.

His tone catches the attention of the teenagers and the old man, who all turn to face us.

Carlsen squares himself to me and takes a step forward. He moves, not like a man, but like a brick wall on wheels. The air around him rushes towards me as he surges forward. I hold my breath and force myself to stand my ground.

"Heard you were talking some shit, little girl." Spittle flies out of his mouth.

I hold my coffee cup close, the heat penetrating the foam container and warming my chest. My cheeks burn. "What are you talking about?"

"Oh, don't act like you don't know. I've been getting calls all morning, and even got a visit from that piss ant, bootleg Sheriff. People keep asking me about your junkie friend. They're saying I was involved. With drugs and shit."

"And what does that have to do with me?" I make an attempt to snake around him and get back online. I refused to give him the attention he's seeking, but I also don't want anyone to see how my hands are quivering around my coffee cup.

He blocks me and cranes his neck down. He reeks of cheap cologne and his breath smells like coffee, covered up by a mint. "You and your other friend came to my place of business to ask me about that no-good junkie yesterday. And now, suddenly I'm getting harassed left and right? Now I'm accused of dealing drugs?"

My blood boils a few degrees hotter when he uses the word "junkie" to describe Greg. My nails make indentations in the foam cup. I force a snarky smile. "I wouldn't worry if I were you. No one would ever think that you were dealing drugs...to adults."

Carlsen stiffens and he stands taller. The small muscles in his arms twitch and he rears up his fist. But then he stops it at his waist, like he's using every ounce of self-control not to hit me.

Just then, the bell over the door rings again. And I hear my savior's voice before I can turn and see him. "There a problem here, Carlsen?" Harvey Barton booms in what I like to call his "Sheriff" voice.

I didn't realize the tension I was holding in my neck until the relief of Harvey's voice set it free. Harvey's a smaller man than Carlsen, but you'd never know it by his presence.

Carlsen takes a calculated step back from me. Now that he's moved, I can see that all three people on line. The cook and cashier have all stopped to watch the scene unfold.

Harvey positions himself beside me. "What's going on here?"

Carlsen looks anywhere but at Harvey. "Just having a conversation, that's all," he says.

"Oh, yeah?" Harvey asks. He folds his arms and shoots me a look out of the side of his eye. "What kind of conversation? I've seen boxing opponents with more love between them than the two of you."

"You're not the Sheriff anymore, Barton. Mind your own business," Carlsen says with the bravado and trepidation of a toddler who's taken a chance at talking back to their father.

Harvey smirks and steps forward. In a deep hiss he says, "You may be right, Carlsen. But just remember that even though this old man may be retired, he's still got more grit than you. I'm one hell of a shot. And, my son's the Sheriff now. I'd choose my next words carefully if I were you. You reside in this town because I allow you to do so. Don't you forget that."

The men remain in their stand off as I—and the rest of the patrons at The Cow—stare on with baited breath. Carlsen backs down first. Saying nothing, he storms out, but not before giving me a look that says "this isn't over".

The bell that rings with the slamming door acts like a pin in a balloon. It releases the pressure inside The Cow and everyone returns to their business, placing their orders, sipping coffee. The cook even goes back to rocking out to Chaka Khan.

Harvey grips my shoulder and gives it a little shake. "You all right there? Don't worry about Carlsen. He's all talk."

"Thanks," I sigh. I'm warmed by his presence. Harvey's got on jeans and a button-down flannel shirt with evidence of wood chips strewn across the front. "Yard work?"

He looks down at his clothes and wipes away some of the chips. "Yea, just getting some wood ready for the stove for when it's colder. Gotta do it now since I'm old and can't handle the cold like I used to." He smirks and his eyes twinkle. "The old house used to have electric heat, so I'm not used to this new system yet." He pulls his sleeve up to look at his watch. "I've got some time, so, want to tell me what all that was about?"

I open my mouth to answer, but am interrupted by the cook demanding my order. I ask for a bacon egg and cheese, and Harvey pipes up that he'll have the same. As if he already knew the orders, the cook flips the eggs. Then he piles on the cheese and bacon, and slides the food onto a fluffy white roll. He wraps the sandwiches expertly in tin foil and passes them to the cashier. I reach my card out to pay, but Harvey blocks me and throws cash for both of our sandwiches down on the counter.

Before he leaves the deli, Harvey grabs his warm sandwich wrapped in foil, kisses me on the cheek and says, "You look tired, kiddo. Take care of yourself, promise?"

"I will." I smile.

I scarf down my sandwich, hot cheese dripping onto my lap. I grab a napkin from the glove compartment, but the cheese has already soaked into my jeans. The rise in blood sugar gives me a moment's clarity. I feel it in my gut, despite all the internal sirens screaming for me to retreat from my ruminations.

Whoever kept us in that stable has to be the same person who is responsible for Greg and Sawyer's disappearances, and possibly even Charlie's death. I just know it in my gut...just like I know it wasn't Rick Salem.

I know I need to go see Boyd, so I can work with him on finding Sawyer and Greg, and see if he has any leads. But my mind keeps going back to the place where it all started: Greg's apartment. When Sawyer and I showed up there yesterday—how was that only yesterday? —we had been looking for Greg. We called out his name and then shortly after, found the hay in his bed. I was so startled—we both were—and I had no idea what to make of it other than to stifle the acid creeping up through my esophagus.

But now, I can't help but wonder if we missed something in our scramble. So, I decide to go back to Greg's apartment before I see Boyd. I wanted to go alone, because if Boyd was with me, I'd feel self-conscious and distracted. It isn't even noon yet, which means school is still in session and Miss Winters won't be there. There's a chance the police will have locked his door, I'm not too worried about it. I've picked a lock or two in my day.

When I pull up to the house, Greg's car is still there. I also notice that there's another car in the driveway, which I assume is Miss Winter's car. I park in front of the next house down so I can walk into Greg's place undetected. I would prefer not to see Miss Winters right now.

I snake around the yard to the side steps leading up to Greg's apartment. The door is locked and decorated with police tape. Does that mean this is a crime scene?

I turn on my heels and sulk back down to my car. But Miss Winters is at the bottom of the stairs looking up at me. My bones jump in my skin and I gasp.

"Oh! It's just you!" She clasps one hand to her chest. "Didn't mean to scare you. I thought maybe it was the police again."

"Sorry," I echo down and begin my descent as she comes up towards me. "I didn't want to disturb you, just came by to..."

Before I can finish my sentence, she is throwing her arms around me, just like she had done at Hannigan's after the funeral. She still smells like alcohol—like something sweet, like rum. She squeezes me hard enough to knock the wind out of me. I pull back.

"Oh, it's just terrible, isn't it?" she says. "The police were here earlier. No one has any idea where he is. I've been so upset I had to call out of work today!" As she talks, her arms wave wildly like one of those balloon street advertisers.

"I know. I was here yesterday. I just came back to...I don't know." I look down at my feet.

"You poor thing. Here, come down. Let's go to the kitchen. I'll make you a cup of tea or something to calm your nerves." She takes me by the wrist. I have to keep pace with her so I don't go flying down those steps.

Her part of the house is starkly different than Greg's. It's clean and smells as if she's been walking around all morning spraying some fruity perfume. The scent is pomegranate, or something else that's citrusy—I can't quite put my finger on it. Every light in the house is on and there is a loud buzzing coming from an old washing machine in a tiny room just off the kitchen. She shuts the accordion door between the rooms to drown out the noise.

"That old thing," she says, and tells me to sit at the kitchen table. She fills a tea pot with water and sets it on the stove. "You must be worried sick."

"I am," is all I can say without tearing up. Out of the corner of my eye, I catch two sets of keys hanging from a hook next to the refrigerator. The one hanging off a lime green lanyard has a label on it. I have to squint, but it looks like it reads "upstairs".

"So I'll tell you what I told the police when they came poking around here. I didn't hear anything odd. No visitors. No yelling. Nothing. This whole thing has just been so stressful."

"Has Greg been a good tenant?" I ask, trying to steer the conversation.

"Wonderful! Oh, and it's so lovely having a man around the house. Not that he's around the house, of course. But in a pinch, he's close by, if I need anything or if I'm frightened."

"Frightened?" I say. "Of what?"

"Oh, bumps in the night. The usual. It's never anything more than the wind. Just last week, I thought I heard something rustling outside my bedroom window. Must have been three in the morning. But I thought it was a bear! I called Greg and he came right down."

"Was it a bear?"

Miss Winters tosses her hands up in the air. "Who knows! It was something big. Probably not a bear though—more likely a deer or coyote. It made quite the mess and trampled my bushes!"

She walks over to the screaming kettle and pours two cups of tea. I take a sip too soon and burn my tongue. I scrape my burnt taste buds against the roof of my mouth. "That is strange."

"I just can't believe that the little boy I used to scold for talking too much in class is now the one I call when I'm scared at night." She leans back in her chair. "But so is the life of the spinster."

"You're not a spinster," I say. "I think spinsters stopped existing sometime in the early 1900s."

"You're sweet to say that. But no, I know that I've aged. Nothing makes it clearer to me than when I see you kids all grown up living your own lives, here I am needing one of you to pay my mortgage." She leans forward and puts her elbows on the table. Her expression softens in a way that makes me brace for impact. "I was a little older than you are now when you kids were abducted by that awful, awful Salem man."

I bite my lip and nod.

She shakes her head. "How ever did you all survive it? I have to tell you, I remember the first day you came back to school. I thought I was going to see these broken little birds, but then the four of you strolled into class! I swear it was everyone else who looked more nervous. I've never been so impressed. Me? I would have been in an insane asylum!" Her eyes widen as she catches her words. I can tell she desperately wants to pluck them from the air and shove them back in her mouth. "Oh my God. I'm sorry. I didn't mean to be so insensitive!" She slaps her hand to her forehead.

"It's ok," I smile. "People have said worse. And honestly, it was because we had each other. I think if we didn't have each other, we probably would have ended up in a mental health facility."

"Marylin has done right teaching you to be a such gracious young woman."

I smile, and then look back to the keys on her wall. "Hey, do you mind if I borrow those keys for the upstairs? To take a look around? Maybe I'll see something the police missed."

"Of course!" She jumps up out of her seat. Tea wobbles over the top of the cup and onto the table.

Greg's apartment smells different today, like stale bread and dust. I pace around the living room, scanning for something, anything that will give me a clue as to where Greg is. But there's nothing in his space, aside from an overstuffed ashtray, a pair of crumpled jeans next to the couch, and an empty remote under the coffee table. I hadn't noticed those things when Sawyer and I were here originally, but they ultimately mean nothing. Greg's a messy guy. It would be more suspicious if I had found sparkling floors and freshly vacuumed carpet.

Since there is nothing notable in the living room, I make my way over to his bedroom across the hall. All of my muscles tense and I almost turn back. Did the police leave the hay? Or is it evidence? I say the word again in my head: Evidence. It sounds so nefarious.

The bedroom door creaks as I open it. I think of Grandma Marylin and how she would always say, 'Could you imagine how much easier life would be if there was background music? Think of the girl in the horror movie, opening the door. The second she hears that doomy gloomy music she could shut it and run! The monster would have never had a chance.'

Where's my music? I need something to tell me whether to run. Instead, I take a deep breath and press onward. Light glares in through the window. The room a smoky sheen. Every piece of dust has been kicked up by the swinging door. The particles swim through the air and sparkle in the light.

I still smell it. The hay. It's been cooped up in here since before we found it and the smell has marinated the air. I bring the sleeve of my forearm up to my nose.

The hay is still in the bed, the covers peeled back from when Sawyer and I discovered it. The police must have left everything as is for the moment. I'm probably not supposed to be in here.

When I look back around the room, my eyes settle on the window again. That's when I see it. Was it there yesterday? The light was different then. It was later in the day. The sun catches the slick handprint on the window. A large one. I wonder if the police saw it, but I can't exactly ask Boyd. Then I'd have to tell him that I'd been here.

I get closer. The handprint most definitely belongs to a man. I touched it and it doesn't smear. It's on the other side of the window—the outside.

Miss Winters was just telling me that she'd heard noises outside her window. She thought it was a bear. But what if it wasn't? There's a human handprint right here. What if a person was outside her window?

I step back. My skin turns to ice.

Later, when I tell Boyd everything—about Rick, and that I spoke to Miss Winters—I leave out the part about the handprint. We're standing in the wind-smacked police station parking lot, and Boyd's looking at me with his half-mooned eyes. His phone rings upwards of three times, but he silences it each time without looking.

This time, he doesn't give me any sympathetic or thoughtful gestures. His expression is stern when I mention where I'd been all morning.

"So, that's where you were?" he asks and slides his hands to his hips.

"Yes," I say. Why do I feel like I'm in trouble right now?

"I thought we agreed you were going to stay put." Another cop peeks his head out the front door to the station and waves for Boyd's attention. "I'll be there in a minute, all right?" he barks over his shoulder. The young cop retreats back inside with his tail tucked between his legs.

"I'm an adult, Boyd. I can do what I want, when I want," I say. "Why does it matter to you if I went to the prison?"

"Oh, I don't know, Maura, maybe it's because two of your friends are missing and someone seems to be taunting you. I haven't even been home. I've been up all night working on this case. And for all we know, you could be in danger too. You said you recognized that cloth in the note, right? Someone clearly left it for you." As his frustrations grows, shadows of the old Boyd begin to shine through.

He says nothing for a moment and it's his silence that forces me to speak. "Fine, I'm sorry," I say for the sake of peace— even though I regret nothing. My apology seems to surprise and soften him. His bones settle back a little.

"So, what you're telling me is that you don't think Rick Salem is guilty? That he's a man wrongfully imprisoned?" He waves his hands in the air on the word wrongfully. He thinks I'm being naive. Maybe I am. "By that logic, the real criminal is still out there. Do you think he's involved in Greg and Sawyer's disappearance?"

"I don't know." I look down at my feet. Something happens when the words cross Boyd's lips; the whole thing seems far-fetched. Facts change and morph to fit a theory, rather than the other way around.

Boyd bites the inside of his cheek. "Do you think Natalee knew? You know, that Charlie visited the prison?"

"I have no idea. But this all seems too convenient not to be connected somehow, doesn't it? First, Charlie is selling the old Salem place—without telling us—then, he pays some unexplained visit to the man who tortured and held us captive, then he dies, and now, Sawyer and Greg go missing." I pause, considering whether or not to say this.

"What is it?" Boyd asked. "There's a look on your face. What are you thinking right now?"

My stomach aches. "I can't believe I'm saying this, but Rick Salem was different than I remember."

"What do you mean?"

"I know this is going to sound ridiculous, but he just seemed like...a big kid. Like a little boy in the body of a full-grown man. And the guards—don't even get me started on the guards— they all seemed to love him. I think one even referred to him as a 'model prisoner'."

"'Model prisoner' doesn't mean he's innocent." Boyd's lips curl smugly. "It just means he's smart enough to keep his head down and be nice to the right people in order to survive in there."

"Maybe. But I don't know, I think that—maybe just seeing him now, all these years later—I was having a hard time imagining the Rick Salem that was sitting across from me at the table was capable of carving the word 'bitch' into my back when I was a little girl. I don't think he would have set a little boy hands on fire or tried to kill us.

"And then there was his hands. Rick has rough farmer's hands. I could just be remembering wrong, but I've thought about those silky-smooth hands that ran over my face every day of my life. They weren't farmer's hands. And I can't just start doubting those memories now."

Boyd is staring a hole into me.

"What?" I shiver.

"It's just a shame what happened to you in there. You were just kids."

"Yeah." I stare at my feet. I'm beyond exhausted—both mentally and emotionally drained.

Boyd fell in line with the rest of our classmates at the time of our re-entry. It was one of the things about our life that we'd known before our abduction that would never be the same. When people saw Greg, Charlie, Sawyer and me, they saw our scars as deeply as we felt them. Scarlet letters adorning our chests in those cold grey hallways: V for victim.

Boyd stopped his relentless torment after our return—it was as if his hands would burn if he touched us. It's not like he tried to be our friend or was even nice to us. He kept his distance. At the time, I took it that we were being protected more than before—by teachers, classmates, any stranger on the street who recognized our pictures from the paper or the nightly news. People took notice. Children had fallen into the hands of a madman right under their noses.

Boyd shifts his weight from one foot to the other. "Listen, come into my office. I don't think we should be talking about all of this out here on the sidewalk."

When I walk inside, the once sleepy police station is now bustling, Greg and Sawyer's names are bouncing from mouth to mouth, twisting in the air like tornado winds picking up speed. At times, I even hear my own name, but I can't tell if it's because I have entered the room or am being associated with the other two.

I overhear a deputy saying that they've knocked on every door and scooped out every parked car. 'Going to need volunteers,' is the last thing I hear before Boyd opens the door to his office. He points me to one of the stuffed chairs in front of his desk and says, "Listen, I'll be right back. I just have to take care of something real quick. Just take a seat."

Boyd's desk is a nightmare. Stacks of paper and open manila folders litter what I imagine would be a nice desk—if it were ever to see the light of day. There's a picture frame with its back to me and I turn it around to see the person Boyd Barton looks at every day.

Nan. It's a picture of his mother. She's young here, holding what must be baby Boyd or Boyd's sister Jennie. I haven't even thought about Jennie since I've been here. She was a few grades below us and was Boyd's total opposite—a quiet bookworm. Not that long after high school, Charlie had told me that she left to pursue a law degree at Berkley. I never heard much about her after that. It seems odd to me now that Jennie never comes up, like she's some fringe character in my life. I remember thinking she was the luckiest girl in the world because she had Harvey as a father. But she also had Boyd for a brother, so maybe I wasn't always that jealous.

I try to place the frame down where I found it, but some of the papers and folders have shifted. As I nestle the frame back to its spot and sit down. That's when I see it. Charlie's name scribbled across the tab of a manila folder. There's a white label with black lettering across the front that says, 'Photos'.

My heart speeds up. I feel dizzy. I reach out for the folder, my limbs heavy. The door cracks open behind me. I jump out of my chair. I'm standing in the middle of the room like a toddler who's been caught with their hand in the cookie jar.

"You ok?" Boyd says. He closes the door behind him.

"Are those photos of Charlie? There? In that folder? Pictures of when you found him?"

Boyd looks at the desk and grunts. "Sorry, I meant to put those away. I'm sorry you had to see that."

"I didn't see anything."

Boyd exhales. "Oh, good. Here, let me get those out of here."

He reaches across the desk for the file.

"Wait." I grab his forearm. "Can I...I need to see them."

"I'll be straight with you, Maura—that's a bad idea. Believe me, you don't want to see these."

"Boyd, please. I can handle it. I don't know why, but I feel like I have to look." Every part of my body and mind is begging to see those photos. Maybe it's out of morbid fascination, or maybe...I don't know. But whatever it is, I need to see them. I need to see Charlie while he was still on this earth instead of six feet under it.

I settle down into the chair. Boyd cracks his knuckles on the desk and sits down next to me. "I wasn't the first one on the scene, but I wasn't far behind. I'm warning you it's...it's a lot."

"Where, not that it matters, I guess, but where was he? Like what trail was he on?"

Boyd's brow furrows. "He wasn't far off the Red trail."

I nod. "I haven't been up in those mountains since I was a kid. Since before..." There's no need to finish. What happened to us in that barn drew a universal dividing line in the history of our small town. Before and after.

"Really?" Boyd says. "I'm surprised."

"Why?"

"I don't know. It's just those mountains and trails—they're like a part of the town. It's like saying 'I haven't been to the grocery store since I was a kid'."

"We had a treehouse there, us four, before," I say. "Well, we almost a treehouse. We never finished it."

"Why'd you never go back?" says Boyd.

I pick at my nails. It was a nervous habit I thought I left in high school. "Having a place secluded from the rest of the world is appealing when you're a kid. It was fun to have a place you and your friends could call your own. But after...the idea of sectioning ourselves off into a tiny space...for us it just meant...it just rang too close to," I search for the word. There was "before" and there was "after", but there was no word for what had happened during. I settle on, "the stable."

"That makes sense," says Boyd. There's a softness in his voice. I don't bring up the fact that the treehouse was supposed to be an escape from Boyd-induced turmoil.

Boyd grabs the folder and inches the chair closer to mine. He drapes his arm over the back of my chair. I want him to open the folder and I don't want him to open the folder all at the same time.

He reaches to open the folder and I reach out to pat it back down.

"Change your mind?" he asks.

"No." My eyes are closed. "I want to do it."

Boyd lifts his hand and allows me the honors.

"But quick question first," I say.

"Shoot," he says.

"Why are there pictures of this anyhow? Like you said, it's not like it was a crime scene."

"Well, we didn't know what we were dealing with at first. We just followed procedure. Since we'd found someone torn up in the woods like that, there was no way to know what had happened at first. I wanted to be thorough, so I had our guy take some shots." He gave the folder a quick flick with his thumb. "If this was a crime scene, there would've been a hell of a lot more photos—I can tell you that."

When I finally gather the strength to open my eyes, I find that my hand is already in motion. I'm lifting the top sheet of the folder, as though my hand is its own master.

The first glossy print stares back at me at the top of the stack. But isn't of Charlie. It's a shot of the forest floor close to where they found him. It is difficult to make out, but I imagine the photographer took pictures of the ground to try to make out a possible footprint from an animal or man.

I know what the next picture in the pile is likely to be, so I slide the top picture quick, as if I'm ripping off a Band-Aid.

And there he is—barely a body. Blood is pooled beneath him, and his colorless skin reflects the flash from the camera. Blood has congealed and soaked into his clothing.

It looks more like a compilation of body parts that are torn and eaten. He's on his back with his chin tilted upward. His face is almost featureless. Skin has been shaved away by the animal's teeth. I half expected to see Charlie's final look of horror cemented onto his face. I never could have imagined there would be no face left. His clothes are twisted around his body. I snap my head back and look away, but then force my eyes back to the picture. I thought I would cry when I saw the it. I thought I might collapse to the floor, writhe and sob until my lungs could no longer support the rhythm of my despair.

But in place of heart-aching hysteria, my throat is dry. My face like a statue. My jaw is clenched. My fists are rounded into tight balls. I'm staring ahead. I can't stop staring.

Boyd flattens his hand against my back and starts rubbing in a circular motion. Normally, I'd swat away any affection from him, but I still can't move. He slides his hand to my right shoulder and cradles me toward him, like a parent would a child. My body collapses against his like a rigid corpse. My head is turned, and my eyes are still on the photos. Something is wrong with them. I can't see it yet, but I can feel it.

Boyd pets my hair and pushes it away from my face. Then, as if I've hysterically collapsed into his arms, he hums, "Shh, it's ok, it's ok."

"You know, Maura," his dry voice shakes. He coughs to clear the tickle. "This is hard, I know, but I'm here for you. I...I've always had a special place in my heart for you."

The words wake me from my catatonic state. I thrust myself away from him. For the first time, I've torn my eyes from the photos. "What are you doing?"

Boyd's eyes are wide, like he hadn't expected that response. No, like he'd worried that this new reaction was going to be the one he'd get. "I always loved you back then," he says, looking down sheepishly. "I think that was why—I mean, I don't think I knew it then—but I think that's why I picked on you guys so much. Why I gave those guys such a hard time. They were your friends. It was like they were the only thing standing in the way between you and me."

"Boyd, stop."

"You were never like the other girls. Even when we were kids. You liked to do all the fun boy stuff and you were always prettier than the cheerleaders and the girly girls. When I saw you after the funeral, it brought back all these memories. I didn't know if you would be the same girl I knew all those years ago, but now I see that you are and...I don't know, I feel like a little boy again."

At this point, I can't tell which of us looks more embarrassed by his words. But my embarrassment soon turns to anger. "So, you mean to tell me that I'm the reason you tortured Greg and Charlie and Sawyer? You did that because of me? No." I shake my head. "No. You cannot pin your violence on me, Boyd. That's not fair. You did all that shit all on your own. I'm not going to have you sit here and make it sound like your abuse was just some poorly translated love letter."

"That's not what I'm saying." His eyes narrow.

"You never thought about being nice to us? Maybe befriending us would have been the better option. It was grammar and middle school, not a goddamn gladiator ring."

"Charlie is my friend...was my friend," he says defensively.

Charlie. My eyes travel back to the picture. "Yeah? Then where's his watch?"

"What?"

"His watch. His father's watch. He never took it off. Ever. Where is it?" I point to his left wrist, one of the few parts of his body that was still intact.

Boyd shakes his head. "There wasn't any watch. All we found was his wallet and the clothes on his body."

I see it now. What my eyes had seen a moment ago, but couldn't fully comprehend through my tears. "Look at this," I say, rounding my pointer finger at the center of the picture. On the left side of the body the shirt is torn open. A patch of skin on Charlie's torso is exposed, just above the hip. That part of his body that is unbroken, clean like untouched snow.

"What am I looking at?" says Boyd. His voice is cold and sharp. He doesn't care for my digression.

I'm smiling like a maniac. I can feel Boyd's baffled stare on my cheek.

"This isn't Charlie," I say. Now the tears—the one's I had expected to come earlier—have arrived.

"Maura," Boyd says with sympathy, "I know it's hard to accept, especially since his face is...like that." He means torn beyond all recognition. "But that's Charlie. Those are his clothes. His shoes. We even found his wallet on him."

I shake my head, unyielding in my conviction. "No. And you know how I know?" I pick up the folder and bring it close to Boyd's face. I point to that patch of skin. "Charlie has a big ol' dark purple birth mark right here. Yup! It's shaped like the state of Florida. He's had it his whole life—you can't miss it." My voice builds like I'm about to announce the winner of a multi-bil-lion dollar lottery. I keep my finger planted on the picture. Boyd leans forward and squints at the spot above my nail. I lean in. "No birthmark here. Nothing. Not even a scratch. This. Isn't. Charlie."

CHAPTER 27:

2000

G reg had been gone at least an hour, though it was nearly impossible to tell the time anymore. How can you count without hands of a clock? Without meals or sun cast to shadows, signifying the passing of the hours? Maura wondered if it mattered whether Greg was gone for a long time. Did it matter that she was gone for a long time?

The word carved into the space between her shoulder blades pulsated with pain. Now that she knew what it said, she could feel the embedded letters pulsating. Her dress was damp and crusted with blood. Her calves chaffed against the dry hay. She felt it rubbing against her—even when it wasn't, like a phantom sending her hands swatting to her legs without reason.

No one said anything after Greg was pulled out of the stall. Even when they heard his screams, the three children stifled their own cries. Sawyer and Charlie remembered what that note had promised them, when Maura had been taken. One word from them, and Greg's screams could be silenced forever, too.

When Greg was finally returned, he was thrown into the stall with the brutality with which he was taken. The door swung open and his body flung through. He greeted him with whimpered cries as his limbs hit the hay. Charlie, Sawyer and Maura only dared move when they heard the lock on the other side of the door. It was as if the lock itself afforded as much protection as it did imprisonment.

Maura threw her body across Greg's. Charlie and Sawyer circled like sharks, unsure of what to do. Rain battered against the side of the barn. There was only a little grey light, and it landed on Greg's eyes—open, blinking, and barren.

"I told you not to do it!" Charlie said.

"Stop," Sawyer said.

"Greg," Maura shook him, "Greg look at me. Are you ok? What did he do to you?" Her eyes scanned his shadowed form in vain. She patted frantically around his body in search of another carving like hers.

Greg kept shivering. No answer. It was only when Maura's hands reached his that his silence broke, like a gasp above the break of water.

"What! What is it?" Charlie jumped.

Sawyer stepped forward. Greg writhed off of Maura's lap and screamed face down into the hay.

"What did you do?" Sawyer asked Maura.

"Nothing!" She shot up. "I just touched his hands."

Greg's voice came out in long streaming screams. His words were muffled beneath them. "It burns."

"What does?" Maura knelt back down. Hot tears rolled down her cheeks.

"He burned my hands! He lit them on fire," Greg shouted out.

Maura felt a bubbling in her belly. Greg's cries sent an electrical shock to her nerves, igniting her fury. "Enough." The word came out quietly at first. "Enough," she said, louder now. "Enough," she bellowed and bum rushed the stall door. She attacked it with every fury and fear she'd felt since they'd been trapped in that small square space. Her own pain took a back seat.

She did not feel the blood that dripped down her back as she shouted out to the man. She was sure could hear her because she'd never screamed with such force before. "Enough! Come in here and face us like a man! I'm not afraid of you! You're not going to get away with this. Kill us, do it! You're too chicken shit to kill us!"

She went on and on, as Greg's cries carried on behind her. Sawyer gripped her by the shoulders, begging her to stop. Charlie paced back and forth before he let out a startled scream that brought them all to silence.

Maura turned, still huffing in her rage. Suddenly, the light in the stable was sucked out of the stable. Something or someone was blocking it.

Then they heard a quiet scraping down, like something had been shoved through to their stall. But what could fit through a hole that size?

Their answer was lying on the floor just in front of the slit. On the end of a match, a small flame birthed itself, growing and growing, catching the hay strand by strand. It would ignite everything and turn them to dust.

CHAPTER 28:

2018

It was Sawyer who had broken the news of Charlie's death to me. I'd just returned from a Midtown Pilates class with a woman from work, Rita, who had sworn that the class changed her life, calmed her mind, and toned her body.

As I stumbled through my apartment door, I felt unchanged—outside of the ache in my lower stomach and the newly wound knot in my right shoulder. I popped two Advil and set a microwavable dinner up for three and a half minutes. Just enough time to change and select whatever TV show I was going to eat and fall asleep to that night.

When I saw Sawyer's name illuminate on my cell phone screen, I considered ignoring it. Rita had just talked my ear off on the way to and from Pilates, and it felt like I needed a month break from any socialization.

I let his initial call go to voicemail and intended to text him in an hour or so, telling him I was sorry I missed his call and I'd call him tomorrow.

But then, as an omen, he called a second time. Charlie, Greg, Sawyer, Grandma Marylin and I all had a code: One call may be ignored, returned at a later time. But two calls in rapid succession was not to be evaded.

Before I could say 'hello', Sawyer began, "Maura." He seemed to be speaking through thin pipes.

Instantly, lead formed in my chest.

"Sit," he ordered. "It's bad, Maura. It's really bad."

I collapsed into the kitchen chair and ignored the beeping microwave. "Sawyer," I said, begging him to tell me the reason he'd called.

There was no way I could have known that he was about to tell me—that our dearest friend, the boy I'd grown up with as a brother, the man who'd picked up all of my calls on the first try no matter the time of day—was dead. Of course, there was no way. But in that moment, before the words traveled out of Sawyer's lips and out of the tiny holes in the top of my phone, fear quaked through my veins.

I didn't believe him at first when he said that Charlie was dead. His words became even more fictitious to me when he told me how it'd happened. Found torn to pieces, likely by a wild animal, after he'd fallen while hiking. Visions of his body, splayed out over the moss-covered rocks like Prometheus, eagle-torn and bloodied, filled my mind. No. I pushed them away.

"There's been a mistake," I assured Sawyer with an authority that I assumed could change fate.

"I'm flying out of O'Hare tomorrow. But I can fly into JFK instead if you don't want to go back to Settlers Hill alone," Sawyer offered.

I refused. In my shock and grief, I'd taken his offer as a sign of my weakness. Did he think I would need to be escorted in my hysterical state? It wasn't until we sat in that church, when I saw Sawyer's thousand-yard stare past Charlie's casket, that I realized it was the other way around. He was the one who had needed to be escorted.

I was lucky, in a way. I didn't have to break the news to anyone. Grandma Marylin and Greg, living in Settlers Hill, knew first. They knew before the news broke out to the rest of the town, only after the authorities had informed Natalee. Greg made a call to Sawyer. And then Sawyer called me.

After Sawyer and I hung up, the walls of my apartment seemed to close in on me. I ran barefoot, still clad in my workout clothes, down the hall. I raced down the stairs, barreling past the building's doorman, and thrust myself onto the street. Only moments ago, the cool air had felt refreshing post workout, but now it twisted my lungs into braids. In the bustle of the after-work rush hour, a man stopped on the sidewalk and bent his head down toward mine as I panted at the pavement.

"Miss, are you ok?" he asked.

"Charlie's dead." I said. It was my turn to break the news after all.

CHAPTER 29:

2000

S awyer caught Charlie as he moved his body back from the flames. The fire ate at the hay. Embers jumped to the untouched strands. Flames danced, shaking off smoke.

Sawyer couldn't discern his own cough from that of his friends, if not for the stinging in his chest. It felt like a thousand matches were being held against the branches of his lungs. He held Charlie close. All four children backed thoughtlessly into the same corner—the one closest to the door. It was as if they had some small hope that the door might open itself out of sheer pity.

Greg drew his shirt over his mouth to shield it from the smoke. It was no use. His nose ran. Clean air was getting choked away by the second.

Now, in the light of the flames, they could see each other. The fire grew wilder—Maura couldn't believe how fast it was spreading. *We're going to die*, she thought.

Maura, Greg, Charlie and Sawyer stood pressed into the corner by the door. Their bodies rattled against one another. Then the door moved behind them.

The flames reached hungrily for the oxygen behind them.

All four of them ran out of the stable and into the alleyway. They coughed, falling forward. The flames were chasing them, not far behind. Sawyer's face collapsed against a pair of stiff, leathery shoes. He felt hands scoop him at the armpits. And before he could see a face, he was slung over someone's shoulder.

Maura cried out when she saw Harvey's face. She wrapped her body around his leg. He reached down and pried her limbs from him, shouting, "We have to get out of here!"

Harvey led the charge, holding Sawyer over one shoulder. His other hand gripped Maura's and forced Greg and Charlie ahead of him so they wouldn't get caught behind. He took all four of them out far into the field, and set Sawyer down. He travelled from one to the next, checking them over frantically and groaning painfully when he saw Greg's burnt hands and Maura's carved back.

Harvey stared down at the children then looked back at the barn. He wrapped his hands around his head. A vein beside his left temple throbbed. "Why? Why did this have to happen?" he cried out. That was the first time any of them had seen a grown man cry.

CHAPTER 30:

2018

"I hear what you're saying, Maura, but if this body isn't Charlie's then whose is it?" Boyd takes the photo from me for closer inspection.

"Your secretary—that woman at the front."

He eyes me warily, speaking slowly and clearly. "Maura, Midge is sitting right out..."

"No, I know. But when I first came in to see you—when I was looking for Sawyer—Midge said there'd been a grave robbery at the cemetery. She thought some kids messing around with the occult. What if it wasn't?" I ask, flapping the photo in his face. "What if this is the body from that grave? I think we should go to the cemetery and find out whose gravesite it was."

"Slow it down, Sherlock Holmes," he says with a smirk.

"This isn't a joke, Boyd."

Boyd waves me off like I'm just some hysterical woman. "I'm not saying that. Just calm down." The words are a kiss of death.

"Charlie is your friend, too, right?" I ask. It's the first time in over a week I haven't corrected my use of the present tense to past tense. "Don't you want to follow this lead? See this through? If this person in the photo isn't Charlie—and I'm willing to bet my life that it isn't—then not only does that mean that Charlie's alive, but it means that his death was staged. Charlie's missing, just like Greg and Sawyer."

I hate myself for what I do next. I play into Boyd's feelings for me, the very ones he'd just confessed to me moments ago. I place my hand gently over his fingers, which are cupped around his knee. "If we don't figure out what's going on, I could be next."

Boyd's face contorts to a sad smile. He's considering it. He draws in a long breath and lets it out. "Fine. I'll cut you a deal."

"Ok," I say, so eager that I've already agreed—no matter the terms.

"I will make this one last pit stop in the investigation with you. But after this, I need you to stay put. No more playing deputy. You sit tight at Marylin's house."

"Done."

We wade back through the sea of trilling phones and police chatter in the office—white noise over my racing thoughts. And then we head over to the cemetery.

Holy Rood Cemetery is one of two cemeteries in town. The other one is smaller, nameless, and filled with Civil War soldiers and nineteenth century sixteen-year-old mothers who died in childbirth. In Settlers Hill, unless you are cremated, Holy Rood is where you'll spend eternity.

Charlie is buried there—or at least, that's what I thought, up until now. Boyd doesn't seem quite convinced yet, but he's humoring me nonetheless. I stay stoically quiet on the ride over despite the fact that I'm screaming on the inside. My grief recedes from its shores and the sun pokes out from behind the horizon. Charlie is alive! I feel sure of that now. He might be in some other danger, so I'm not feeling overjoyed. No. I'm hopeful.

Not even Boyd's awkward confession of his love for me can slow me down now. What did he think would happen when he told me that? He clearly saw I was distraught when I was looking at those photos. He took advantage of that moment and unleashed his own emotional burden on me. It was like he thought I would spout joyful tears, accept his feelings and reciprocate them, or find flattery in his abuse of the people I loved in order to get closer to me. Did he think he could wipe the others out to leave me by myself, just for him?

Wipe the others out, I think again. I swallow past a knot in my throat. Here I sit, next to Boyd in his car, while Greg, Sawyer and Charlie missing. There's no way Boyd could have been responsible for what happened to us as kids, right? Sure, he tortured us, but whoever took us had to be a full-grown man, right? I'm no longer convinced of what I thought I knew for sure—that Rick Salem is one hundred percent guilty. I think to his rough, scarred hands, his fingers, to his lack motive. It doesn't add up.

Here I am as an adult, watching my friends get picked off one by one. I have to wonder, if not assume, whether the two events are related. But does it have to be the same person? What if the person behind my friends' disappearances is someone new entirely? A copycat. I glance sideways to Boyd. I don't want him to catch me looking. I fear that what I'm thinking is written all over my face.

Could Boyd have been hinting that he's currently doing the grown-up version of what he did as a kid, by picking off each of my friends to get closer to me? Here I sit, next to him—the deputy to his Sheriff in this investigation—spending more time with him than I have anyone else since I've been home. I need his assistance if I want to find out what happened to my friends. I'm in an emotional state because of the death of Charlie. I'm open and vulnerable, and who has been sitting beside me this whole time?

No, I tell myself, counting my inhales and exhales, trying to slow my heartbeat. I sound like a conspiracy theorist. Just because Boyd has feelings for me—which are pretty bogus considering he doesn't even really know me—doesn't mean that he's a kidnapper and a murderer. Just stay focused. And do not let on any suspicions.

I wipe the sweat from my palms onto my jeans as we pull up to Holy Rood.

A wrinkled woman with thin, curly hair cropped to her ears tells us to take a seat in the stand-alone pew by the door to wait for the director. When he emerges from the back, the man is Lurch-like—tall and thin with deep set eyes. Comically, he looks exactly like what you might expect someone who works at a cemetery might look like. It looks as though at night, he settles into one of the graves to sleep.

He reaches a hand out to Boyd, and then to me. "Roger Hughes, nice to meet you." His voice rattles deep and slow in his throat. His Adam's apple bobs hard with each swallow. "How can I be of service?"

"I just had some questions about the grave robbing that took place here last week," Boyd says.

Roger Hughes is surprised by the inquiry. "I am of course happy to help, but I believe I told the police everything I know."

Boyd nods. "Yes, of course. But we want to be as thorough as possible. You understand?"

"Of course. Come, follow me, and take a seat." He guides us to the back down a long brick hallway that smells like mothballs and formaldehyde. He settles in a robust red brown leather chair behind a mahogany desk. He clasps his hands deliberately in front of him. "That night, I'd left the cemetery around seven-thirty—"

"Sorry, Mr. Hughes. I don't mean to cut you off, but instead of focusing on the events of that evening, I'd like to discuss the body that was taken," Boyd says.

We've surprised Roger Hughes once more. He takes the reading glasses from his shirt pocket and puts them on. Then he turns to the computer on his desk and starts dabbling his fingers on the keyboard.

I'm too wound up to settle into my chair. I'm propped on the edge of the cushion with my elbows folded over his desk.

"You know, I was so resistant to this new-fangled filing system. Computers and such. They just aren't my milieu," he says, his face illuminated by the screen. Tiny letters roll in the reflection of his glasses. "Plot 197, yes. I'd forgotten his name for a moment. My memory isn't what it used to be. Don't get old," he says to me with a half-smirk. "It belonged to a young man by the name of Victor Burke. The burial was two weeks ago." He lowers his reading glasses and fixes his gaze on the wall behind us. "Yes, I remember that. It was a car accident. His parents, Alexandra and Victor Burke Sr., they'd had his body shipped from Galveston where Victor Jr was living. That was where the accident had occurred." He shakes his head. "I've worked in this industry all my life and I will tell you, one never gets used to watching a parent bury their child—no matter the age of the child. Imagine my plight when I had to tell those parents that their child's grave had been desecrated. That the body missing," Mr. Hughes says. I didn't think it possible, but his face has grown paler. "The police told me they would inform me of any leads about the body's recovery, but I've yet to hear back. As you can imagine, this is important to the parents. I'm glad to see you here today, Sheriff. It's good you're following up"

"Of course," Boyd says.

I know I should probably stay quiet and let Boyd take the lead, but I can't help myself. "How old was Victor, exactly? And how tall? Was he a large man? Skinny?"

Mr. Hughes is taken aback by my interjection, like I'm a mannequin that has suddenly come to life. I feel Boyd's cold stare on me.

Mr. Hughes' eyelashes flutter. "He was average in both height and weight, I would say. Around 5'10 or '11, and somewhere between 170 to 180 pounds, if I were to take my best guess. These aren't specifics we keep register of, you understand?"

"Yes, of course," I say.

Boyd stands. "I think that's enough. Thank you for taking the time—"

I cut Boyd off. "Was the body embalmed?"

Mr. Hughes frowns but looks more confused than angry. "He was not. His family chose not to. Why do you ask?"

Boyd reaches his hand under my armpit and pulls me to stand. "Thank you for taking the time to talk to us, Mr. Hughes. We'll be in touch."

This pleases Mr. Hughes and he shakes our hands.

Once back in the car, Boyd starts the engine and shifts in his seat to face me. He opens his mouth to speak and I cut him off. "Victor's around the same height and weight as Charlie, Boyd. He wasn't embalmed. Can you believe it? I knew it. I knew I was right."

"Slow it down. We don't know anything just yet," he says.

"Come on, you can't tell me that this isn't all starting to add up."

"Add up to what? What we have are a bunch of theories—conspiracy theories, you could say. I can see where you're coming from and I know you are grieving and worried sick, but we have to follow logic in an investigation, not feelings."

"The birthmark," I say through gritted teeth.

"Now, I can't explain that." He turns in his seat and sets the car in drive.

"Where are we going?" I ask.

"We had a deal. You're going home and staying put.

Shit. I can't argue with him. We made a deal. He kept his end, despite his doubts. I have to at least pretend to keep my end.

Boyd drives back to the station so I can get my car. I'm half way out of the passenger side door when Boyd grips my arm. "I'm having someone posted outside Marylin's house until this is all sorted out. You'll feel safer that way. And listen, what I said back there. "I mean it. Despite the circumstances, I've really enjoyed spending time with you."

Slowly, I slip my arm out of his grasp and paste on a smile. "Good to see you too, Boyd. Please keep me posted on the investigation." I can see the softness in his eyes and hear the sincerity in his voice, but my gut is telling me to get out of that car.

As I walk up the driveway Grandma Marylin's, part of me wants to rush inside to tell her what I suspect: that Charlie is alive. But first, I need more proof. I'm responsible for the state of my own hope, but I can't unleash that on Grandma Marylin until I'm one hundred percent sure. I head over to Charlie and Natalee's house.

On the way over, I consider what I need to tell Natalee and how I need to say it. I can't tell her that I think Charlie's alive and that I think the body she identified was not his. I wonder how she missed the birthmark, or lack thereof. But then I realize that she didn't want to spend too much time looking at a body like that, especially if someone told her it was her husband's.

When I pull up to the house, her car is right where Boyd parked it when we dropped her off at home last night. I ring the doorbell and get no response. It's only after the second ring that I hear the soft rush of footsteps toward the door.

It opens and Natalee is standing there, wearing bright purple sweatpants with CHEER down the left leg and a loose-fitting white T-shirt that's probably Charlie's.

"Maura?"

"Hi, I'm sorry to bother you. Can I come in?" I try to keep the shake from my voice.

She sweeps herself to the side to let me in. She looks confused already and all I can think is 'if she only knew.'

The house is a mess. There are shoes in the middle of the room and clothing on the floor. It smells like burnt food. As Natalee leads me past the kitchen into the living room, I sneak a peek at a pot on the stove that is crusted white from boiled over pasta. It looks like Natalee is on the grief diet, where you try to eat because you know you need to, but you can't get anything down. Your stomach refuses and deems everything poison.

Before I can speak, she sits and buries her head in her hands. "I'm sorry about last night. I'm so embarrassed."

"Please, I've done way more embarrassing things when drinking than call someone for a ride. It was good of you to call. You were right not to drive like that."

"I know, I know. I just...I can't think straight. Do you know we had plans this weekend? Charlie and I? There's a new restaurant that serves tapas and we were going to make a date night out of it. Charlie's been so busy that we hadn't gone out in forever. But now, I feel sick when I think of making those plans—thinking about how I didn't know we'd never make it. I feel like an idiot."

"If you're an idiot, then I'm an idiot. I keep thinking of when I talked to him last. On the phone. I wish I knew it would be the last time. I would have said so much more."

Natalee smiles softly. And just like that, we've begun talking like the old friends we never were. Not by my own efforts, but by Natalee's. When I feel vulnerable, I shut down, and apparently, Natalee does just the opposite. So, we dance through the conversation and I find myself letting her lead.

"It's sweet of you to check on me," she says, swiping some crumbs off the coffee table. "I'm sorry about the mess. I haven't been able to do much. Also," she smiles sadly, "Charlie was the clean one. I never realized how much he picked up until now."

She's assumed I'm here to check on her. It wasn't my conscious intention, but it makes me feel good that she thinks it was. It makes me feel less selfish.

We chat for a few more minutes, about memories of Charlie. We laugh at his little idiosyncrasies and miss them. Then, I finally ask her the question that's been pressing on my mind. Maybe it's insensitive, but I can't help myself.

"Natalee, I have to say, and I'm sorry if this is too much, but I don't know how you did it. How you identified the bod—I mean, Charlie—after they found him. That must have taken a lot of courage."

Natalee's smile has been wiped from her face. The color in her cheeks sinks away, back into a no man's land. She stares down at her feet. "I had to. I don't know if I ever would have believed it had I not seen it for myself. There wasn't much to see though, he was..." a cry forms in her throat.

"It's ok, you don't have to finish. I shouldn't have said anything. That was wrong."

"No, no. It's probably better that I talk about it because it was so strange. It's not like in the movies or crime shows, where you stand in a room full of strangers and nod yes or no after they pull the blanket back. Do you know who the medical examiner is now?" she almost laughs. "Rodney Gehan."

I snort. "Oh my God, didn't he blow up the Chemistry lab sophomore year?"

She raises an eyebrow and smirks. "Exactly. So you can imagine what it was like standing there—just me, Rodney, Phil, Boyd. It was horrifying."

I nod a moment before my brain catches up with what she just said. "Phil?"

"Yes."

"Phil Cooper?"

"Um, yes."

"What the hell was Phil Cooper doing in there?" I ask.

Natalee looks at me like I'm an idiot. "He's the one who found Charlie."

"What?" I nearly scream. "How come no one told me that? What was Phil doing in the woods? Don't tell me he was hiking for the beautiful view."

"Apparently he was hunting when he came across Charlie. He was the one who called the police. Come to think of it, I did overhear Phil talking to Boyd. He said he didn't want to be identified as the person who found Charlie, just in case anything was—what was the phrase he used? —oh, right, just in case there was any 'messed up shit' involved."

I leave Natalee's and make my way over to Grandma Marylin's. I'm no fool. I won't talk to Phil without her present. He'll be on his best behavior around her, which means it'll be easier to back him into a corner. I'll ask her to call him over and tell him that she needs him. Then she can help me interrogate him. I'll record the whole thing on my phone. He's involved—in one way or another. There is no way he wouldn't use the fact that he found Charlie's body to his advantage with Grandma Marylin—to garner sympathy or whatever.

Then it occurs to me. Sawyer's car, with the note and my dress, had been parked right by Phil's house. Had Sawyer figured out Phil was involved before he headed over there? Why didn't I think of it before? It all makes sense now. I feel like an idiot for being so blind. Why do what he did, though? Get us out of the way and get Grandma Marylin- and her money- all to himself? Who knows maybe he's just a sick son of a bitch.

I call Grandma Marylin to let her know I'm coming, but there's no response.

When I get to the house the front door is locked. I don't want to ring the doorbell in case she's finally getting some rest. I check the back door. It's unlocked and Grandma Marylin is not alone.

"What are you doing sneaking in like a burglar?" She's sitting on the couch, one arm craned over to look at me.

Harvey stands, smiling, to greet me. He kisses me on the cheek and I smell cigarettes on his breath. Since when does Harvey smoke? "Hey, kiddo," he says.

"I forgot my key and I didn't want to knock in case you were resting."

She waves me off. "I haven't rested since I was six months old, you know that. But while you're up, I will ask you to get Harvey here a cup of tea. He's kindly come by to check on us."

"Of course," I say. I can tell by her demeanor that she hasn't said anything to Harvey about Sawyer or Greg. I wonder if he knows—if Boyd's told him. Maybe that's why he's here.

I put a kettle on the stove and can overhear their conversation in the next room. "I can't even imagine what you're going through, Marylin," Harvey says.

"You're kind to come check on me, but it's the kids I really worry about. They've been through enough. Now this?" she says.

I pour the boiling water and bob the teabag in and out of the cup a few times until the water darkens. "Milk or sugar?" I shout out to the next room.

"Neither," says Harvey.

I walk back into the living room, careful not to spill on the rug. Grandma Marylin hates a mess.

"Oh, thank you." He smiles. "Nothing better than a hot cup of tea to soothe the nerves."

As his arm reaches out for the cup, his shirt sleeve gathers backward and the glass of his watch catches the lamp light. As the teacup leaves my hand, my eyes refocus.

The watch he's wearing—it's Charlie's. I'd know it anywhere.

I recoil like there's a snake under my feet. I'm unable to speak. Why is he wearing that? I look at Grandma Marylin. Her lips are tight. Her jaw is clenched. Her eyes bore into mine and then shift down to the space beside her on the couch before they float back up to mine. I follow her gaze to the gun laying on the couch, clasped in Harvey's right hand. It's pointing at her hip.

"Ru-," she begins but is cut short when the butt of that gun smacks the side of her head. I jump and her head snaps backward, a trail of blood running like a river down her left cheek.

I can't move anything but my eyes. And when I look to Harvey, he's smiling.

CHAPTER 31:

2000

The kids had been missing three days now and Marylin was on her last cigarette—including the spare ones she kept in the freezer and the emergency ones she stashed in her jewelry box. She'd smoked as a young girl, stopped during her years with George, and then started back up again after he died. She'd never forget the day Charlie came home from school and said 'my teacher said those are going to kill you.' Marylin had quipped back "Well, you can tell Miss Winters that those two-size too small dresses she squeezes into are going to cut off the circulation to her brain. That doesn't stop her, now does it?"

The Sheriff told Marylin to go home and stay put, just in case a call came to the house or the kids came running back. Harvey said it would be good if she was there to greet them. Besides, he and the entire town were out searching for them, so it wouldn't make a difference whether she joined them or stayed home.

So, Marylin dragged on her cigarette filters constantly, until the minty smoke laced her tongue. She didn't stop watching the telephone. But just like watched water never boils, a watched telephone never rings.

It was the not knowing that ate away at her like acid. At this point, even a ransom call would be welcome. Was that what this was all about anyhow? Sure, Marylin had her inheritance, enough money to buy the town, but Marylin wasn't showy about her money. She came from old money—railroad money.

People knew, of course, that she spent her youth rubbing elbows with the Vanderbilts and Rockefellers, her father picking up the tab when they'd go to dinner. But that had been a hollow existence for her. She never enjoyed the pressure to look a certain way, talk a certain way, or date the right boys from the right family.

Then George Tinton, a young man visiting New York for the first time, tapped her on the shoulder on the street one day. She'd dropped her lipstick and he chivalrously returned it— although she would later claim he'd pick-pocketed her to return the lipstick as an excuse to talk to her. It was George, the handsome stranger with soft eyes and rough hands, who rescued her from that vapid life. She would never admit it aloud, but it was love at first sight. What else do you call up and leaving your entire life to move off to a plumber's hometown only two weeks after meeting him? Her family was devastated—but not devastated enough to cut her off.

When George died, she thought she would never love again. Charlie was the first to prove her wrong. His wide doll-like eyes stared up at her each morning as she woke him for school every day after his parents' accident. Then Maura followed suit—Maura, who, after her mother left, would sneak into Marylin's room after a nightmare and cradle her body in the crook of Marylin's belly. 'You're my little hot water bottle,' Marylin would tell her.

Marylin adored Sawyer's mothers. Ramona was dry-humored and quick-witted and Shelly was sweet as butterscotch. So, when they asked Marylin if she could watch Sawyer in the summers while they worked, Marylin was happy to oblige. What was one more kid running around with Charlie and Maura? Marilyn hadn't expected to fall in love with Sawyer's smirk when he knew he'd done something wrong, or with the way he would thank her so sweetly for his peanut butter and jelly sandwich.

Greg sailed his ship onto the island of misfits last. Marylin despised Judge Bea. Bea was unkind, unfriendly and insincere. Marilyn didn't trust her. So on the summer morning when Charlie had asked Marilyn if Bea's son Greg could come play, she was hesitant to say yes. What would Bea's child be like? Should Marylin let her precious angels rub shoulders with the spawn of Satan?

But no, Marylin told herself to give the boy a chance. And she was glad she did, because after that decision, she seldom saw a day without Greg's face in her home. He was red-haired and rosy-cheeked, and as nervous as a rescue dog. And in time, his flinches stopped. Marylin was warmed by the honor of earning his trust.

My little toys on the Island of misfits, she would say—only in her head. She didn't want them getting a complex that they were misfits or somehow broken. We're all broken, she thought. Some more than others, but no one is without a rip or a popped seam.

Charlie and Maura never missed dinner. Marylin made a point of scheduling dinner at 7:00 p.m. most nights. She didn't care where the kids went after school or what they did—within reason—as long as their homework was completed and they were back by 7:00 p.m. sharp with washed hands and napkins on their laps.

She'd just put the water on to boil—Wednesdays were pasta night—when Shelly called asking if she'd seen Sawyer. Shelly was a worry-wort and Marylin slipped into her routine of telling Shelly that the kids were getting older and need some freedom to roam— it may prevent rebellion in the years to come. Shelly let Marylin calm her nerves and they finished their conversation by talking about who was going to bring the lemon meringue pie for the church bake sale in two weeks.

But when the grandfather clock in Marylin's dining room chimed briefly at 7:15 pm, a lump gathered in her throat. *They're just being kids*, she told herself and went to check the clock in the kitchen. Maybe the grandfather clock was off or needed to be wound. It was old, and had belonged to her grandfather back in the late 1800s. It was only natural that it'd be off by a few minutes. But time on the clock in the kitchen matched that of the old one in the dining room.

Marilyn opened the front door and let the cool night air wash her worry. *I'll give them ten more minutes,* she told herself. They are kids, and kids lose track of time when they're having fun. Though the thought crossed her mind, she'd decided not to call Shelly to ask if they are there because Shelly was most likely taking care of Ramona. They don't need any added stress. And she certainly won't call Bea. She didn't want to give Bea a reason to come down harder on Greg. There was no doubt in her mind that they were all together. Bea never noticed if Greg was home or gone—not unless someone brought it to her attention.

Then she heard what every Settlers Hill resident shudders to hear: the siren. It sung into its crescendo before bottoming out and echoing against the mountains. She knew what she'd been instructed to do in this scenario: Go back in the house, lock the doors, and wait for further instruction from the police or fire department.

But her children were out there, exposed to whatever the siren was meant to warn them against—whether it was a storm, a wild animal or a violent vagrant. Danger is most frightening when it does not have a name.

Her car keys rattled in her hand as she unlocked the driver's side door. She rolled down the driver's side and passenger's side windows so she could call for the kids as she drove—not that anyone would hear her over that Godforsaken siren. Marylin didn't feel frightened for her own sake. The kids were all that mattered.

She was only three blocks away from home when the siren stopped. She drove around for thirty minutes to all the children's usual haunts—the pharmacy where they bought candy, the skateboarding ramps at the park, even the pond where they would swim in the summer. It was too chilly for swimming, but it couldn't hurt to check.

The town was desolate. People were likely still inside after the siren. She circled back to her house, hoping that they'd returned while she was out. But the house was empty. The pasta sauce had grown cold on the dining room table. Her heart was racing. In a fog, she walked herself over to the phone and called the police station.

She asked for Sheriff Barton directly. Marylin was friends with his wife Nan—they'd taken some painting classes together—and she'd gotten to know him pretty well over the years. She didn't want to talk to some stranger with a badge would have felt.

"He's not here," the woman on the other line told her. "Can I get you someone else?"

"That's all right. I'll call him at home," Marylin said. "Hey, by the way, what was the siren for?"

Marylin could hear the busyness of the station beyond the receiver. The woman sighed jokingly. "Oh, that was nothing. But we're neck deep in calls about it, as you can probably hear. Some dodo over at the firehouse set it off by accident. We're sending people around and making calls to let everyone know it was a false alarm. Sorry we didn't get to you yet."

Marylin thanked the woman and hung up.

She called Harvey's home phone and Nan picked up. At the sound of Nan's voice, she poured out what was going on and her increasing anxiety over it. Harvey wasn't home, so Nan gave her his cell phone number. It was the age before every man, woman and child had a cell phone, but thankfully Harvey was one of the few who had one. Marylin could understand why he'd need one as the sheriff. He was a man on demand.

"All right, let's just take a deep breath," Harvey said kindly once Marylin had reached him and explained her concerns. "I'm sure they are just being kids and busting curfew a little. If it makes you feel better, I'll take a ride around and send another officer out. Maybe you can make some calls to the other parents?"

"Okay. Thank you, Harvey. Sorry to bother you."

"It's no bother. It's my job, on the clock or off. We'll find 'em, Marylin. Don't you worry."

Marylin breathed for the first time in an hour. She was still worried, but now she had some back up. She tried to imagine how embarrassed she might feel if they were to walk in the door any minute now. At this point, she'd be happy to be embarrassed if it meant they were back.

The door never opened, though. And neither Shelly nor Bea had seen them. Harvey and his deputy returned from their ride-arounds and came up empty. There's a twenty-four-hour holding period for reporting missing adults, but with kids, the hourglass gets turned immediately—the sand begins dripping down grain by grain.

She didn't sleep a wink those three days. Neither did Shelly or Ramona. Bea kept her distance from the other parents, but called Harvey incessantly and was the first to alert the media. Bea would never admit to calling the press, but it was her door the first reporters came to. Bea's face was the one on television, begging for her child's return in a downturned and sweet voice that Marylin had never heard from her before. It was as if Bea was auditioning for a role as a crestfallen June Cleaver when she was anything but.

The cameras of the media soon shifted once the children were found. Rick Salem was their focus. Harvey told Marylin he'd checked that broken-down barn himself. He told her that Rick must have moved them- possibly to the house- at some point before Harvey found them. And Harvey had only found them because he'd been making his way through the woods again. The FBI was in town and had all but taken over his investigation, so he'd decided to go off on his own and continue to manually search the town and its hiking trails.

At the bottom of the trail, Harvey had heard a faint shouting sound and followed it to the Salem barn. When he saw the smoke and heard the cries grow louder, he ran to the supply closet and grabbed an axe. He hacked away at the lock and took all four of the children from the barn. He called for back-up and the firemen came to hose down the barn. And then, a team of men in khakis and FBI-issued windbreakers came and escorted Rick Salem from his home.

Grandma Marylin brought Harvey cookies, cake, treats, and whatever she could whip up, for every single week for years after that. She didn't sleep until Rick Salem was locked away in maximum security.

Instead, she walked the kids to and from school and watched them as they slept. She only slept when they were in school and intermittently at that, keeping the phone close and the ringer on high. She bought them cell phones and made all four of them check in constantly. Her worst fear was that they would be taken again and that she would have to relive those three days. And though she did her best to be a pillar for Maura, Charlie, Greg and Sawyer, she lived her days as a woman haunted—by both past and present.

CHAPTER 32:

2018

Harvey is standing across the living room. His face is half-dimmed in the shadow of the lamp. His salt and pepper hair is ragged and his cowlicks are untamed. His eyes are sure and steady, and his mouth is pinched to a confident smirk. I've never seen him look like this before.

"What are you doing?" Every bone in my body is reaching out for Grandma Marylin, but the gun pointed at me keeps me from her. Cold sweat drips down to the small of my back.

Harvey sniffs, gathering snot and phlegm at the back of his throat. Then he clears it with a cough. "You really gave me a run for my money, you know that?" he says.

"Harvey, you're scaring me. What are you doing?" My jaw clatters.

Harvey throws Marylin's comatose body a smirk. "She's a spunky old lady, you know that? Well, of course you do. She raised you to be pretty spunky yourself." He seats himself in the chair across from me and rests the revolver casually across his knee.

My heart thumps in my throat. Spunky. He said the word in a way that makes me feel covered in dirt. I can't look at Grandma Marylin, so I take another look at the watch on Harvey's wrist. Charlie's watch.

My lungs nearly refuse to take the air I need for the words. "It's you, isn't it?"

"What's me, darling?" he asks. His Cheshire cat smile is strewn widely across his face.

"You took Greg and Sawyer. You put the hay in Greg's bed. Left the note on Sawyer's car with my dress. It was all you, wasn't it? Where are they?"

"Oh, come on, you've turned into quite the little Sheriff's deputy in the last couple days, haven't you? You know exactly where they are. It's where you're headed next."

The puzzle, the one floating over my head theses past two days, collapses to the floor, each piece falling into place. I can see the big picture. "It was you, even back then—wasn't it?" I'm trying not to cry, but the hot tears burn my cheeks. They roll off my chin and onto my chest. The word on my back burns itself into the fabric of my shirt.

"Smart girl." Harvey stands up and paces around the room proudly, like a cat who's lured a mouse into its home. "It wouldn't have been so bad for you four back then, if you had just stayed put. But you tried to escape -defying me every chance you got."

My eyes stay on his gun.

"No one really gave a shit about me in this town until I rescued you four. I needed people to see me for who I really was—a goddamn good cop. But then I realized I could get more. I could get people to see that I was a hero."

I want to ask where he's going with this, but I'm afraid that interrupting him will only bring the barrel of his gun to my forehead sooner.

He continues. "Everything changes when you have a child. I'd say you'd learn that one day," he chuckles to himself, "but that's not going to happen. After Nan and I had Boyd, I swore I'd never let anything happen to him—especially not what happened to me. I was tortured by my classmates and afraid to go to school. No. That wouldn't happen to my son.

"So, when I found out that you little shits were picking on my boy—after I saw the cuts and bruises he was coming home with—I knew I had to do something. Teachers, the principal, they all tried to spin it like it was Boyd's fault. Four against one and he's the bully? I don't think so. I'm not an idiot." He claps his hands together, the sound startling me further into the couch. "So, I put it all together. I figured out a way to teach you four a lesson about messing with my kid. You could get a taste of your own medicine. Then I would get to be the one who saved you. I would get the glory. It was the perfect plan. Everyone loves a cop who saves a kid."

"You think we bullied Boyd?"

He walks behind the couch to stand at my back. He glides his hand over my cheek, and his smooth palm glides like silk against my skin. Acid surges from my stomach to my throat. "Don't try to deny it or act all coquettish, ok? It won't save you now."

"You think we deserved what you did to us? We were kids."

"It wasn't supposed to be like that," he says through gritted teeth. "You were supposed to sit there in that goddamn stable. Get a little scared. Sweat it out. But you kept trying to escape. You came after me. I had to defend myself! I was a good person put in a shitty position."

"Carving 'bitch' into a little girl's back is self-defense? Not to mention, you let poor Rick rot in jail for your crimes! A good person does that?" The anger rises in my voice to meet his.

Harvey snaps hold of my hair and pulls it just tightly enough to wrench my neck back, tilting my chin to the ceiling. "I'm human. It pissed me off. If you had just stayed put, you would have been fine!"

"Are they dead?" My eyes throb from the pain.

Harvey releases my hair. A softness returns to his cheeks. He's regained control. "Oh, not yet. I thought how it would be poetic if you all went out together—you can thank your buddy Charlie for that one."

I can thank him. Does that mean he's alive?

"Oh, yeah?" I say, hoping he'll continue.

Harvey swings around and squats in front of me, the gun never taking its eye off of me. "He just couldn't let enough alone. He had to start digging into things and going to visit Rick. Not much happens in this town that I don't know about and I never ever took my eyes off any of you." He winks.

"I trusted you. We all trusted you."

"Oh wah, wah, wah, cry me a river. The little orphan girl thought she found a daddy figure in the man who rescued her, huh? How heartwarming."

This somehow hurts more than anything. Because it's true.

"Screw you," I say. Pain is a funny thing. Depending on where it's placed, it can paralyze or prompt.

Harvey takes the gun and points it between my eyes. Then he slides it over to Grandma Marylin. "No!" I shout.

"Going to lose another mommy, are we? Poor baby. Don't worry, you won't be alive long enough to grieve."

Without a second thought, I catapult myself off the couch. I ram my head into his stomach. He falters backward. The gun drops to the floor and slides under the coffee table. I roll off him and crawl over, reaching for it. But then I feel the full weight of Harvey's body on top of mine. We grapple for the gun, but he's stronger than me. His right hand finds it as his left hand keeps me pinned to the ground. And when it's in his grasp, he takes the butt of it and strikes me across the head.

Lights out.

The first thing I notice is the pain. The throbbing at my left temple is so disorienting that it takes me a moment to feel the sharp rattling of metal against my back. My body jolts upward suddenly. That was a speed bump. I must be in a car. I open my eyes to darkness—I'm in the trunk.

The air is dusty and tight—the kind of air that feels like there's a rope around your neck. My hands are tied behind my back, so the next bump in the road sends me rolling onto my chest. Like a turtle on its back, I can't roll over.

How did Harvey get me out of the house and into his trunk without anyone on the block noticing? The house—Grandma Marylin is there. What's happened to her? He didn't kill her initially, so maybe he hadn't planned to do it. After all, here I am, still alive and rolling around in the trunk of Harvey's car. The last I saw of Grandma Marylin, she was comatose and bound up on her couch in her own home, the one place that is supposed to be safe. My only safe place.

I hate him. I hate him for desecrating my home. And I hate him for what he's doing. For what he's done. And for what reason? Because Boyd was an even bigger little shit than I'd ever thought and ran home to his mommy and daddy every day, explaining away every bruise and cut on his skin as marks of *our* bullying? That's bullshit. Boyd was always getting in trouble with the teachers. He's the one who had all those visits to the Principal's office. You can't tell me that Harvey actually thought his son was some innocent victim.

But then again, I should have never doubted the twisted lies and crocodile tears of a child with the threat of punishment over his head.

No, there has to be another reason. A man who can do that to children—what Harvey did to us—maybe there's no logic behind that. I saw the look in Harvey's eyes. He's a maniac—someone who slipped under the radar, wanted power and found it, and enjoyed the sadistic road that took him there.

How did I not see it, all this time? My mind travels back to every interaction I've had with Harvey since I've been here. At the deli, his coat was covered in wood shavings. He said he was chopping wood for his house for the winter. Bull shit. Harvey was never a woodsman. I didn't see it then, because I was still reeling from my visit with Rick Salem and Coach Carlsen's attempt at assaulting me before breakfast.

The car comes to a stop. I know exactly where he's taken me. The trunk opens. Harvey pulls at my shoulder to roll me onto my back. I don't know why—call it gut instinct—but I decide to close my eyes, pretending I never woke up.

He grunts as he tosses me over his shoulder in a fireman's carry. His shoulder digs into my stomach. I try hard not to groan in pain and keep my body limp. Now that he can't see my face, I peek my eyes open. I watch as the heels of his feet snap twigs against the forest floor. The moonlight peeks through the canopy.

I hang over his shoulder with his hot breath against my hip. I've been upside down for so long that my head fills to the brim with blood. It grows heavy and my feet go numb from the lack of circulation.

When Harvey finally stops, he flips me off his shoulder and lays me down the damp ground. Small rocks dig into my spine. I try to keep the wince from my mouth and keep my eyes closed. This is going to be my one chance to escape. I can feel it.

I threaten myself with the thought of opening my eyes when I feel cold steel against my skin. My jaw clenches involuntarily and I pray he doesn't see. It feels like a knife. But then, when I feel the metal sliding over my skin and the coldness of the air kiss my stomach, my shirt splays open on either side of my torso and I realize that the steel I feel is a scissor.

He's cutting my clothes off.

No, please no. I wish I hadn't woken up. His soft hands peel my shirt away and I try not to shiver against the cold. He takes off my pants. Then I feel a cloth slipping over my head. Is he re-dressing me?

He only gets so far before he realizes that he can't slip my arms through the arm holes since my wrists are tied. He sighs in frustration and pauses, like he'd considered every angle in his plan except this one. *Cut the ties. Cut them you idiot*, I say in my head. His ignorance is starting to feel like a warm wind at my back.

The scissors saw at the rope around my hands. It's thick and takes a minute. Now that my hands free, he threads them through the armholes. The cloth fits to just above my knees. There are thin straps over my shoulders. No pants. It's a dress. I'm in a dress.

Then it hits me. *Please don't be a flower dress. Please.*

But that's what he did. He put me in the dress that I was wearing in the barn—or a similar one, since it feels as though it's my size. He wants everything to be the same. He even told me back at Grandma Marylin's house that he wants to finish what he started. Bile lurches up my throat. He's just sick enough to want to get all the details right. But this time, we aren't at the Salem Farm—that much I know for sure.

I hear him shift around on the ground away from me. This is it: If there's any chance of making it out of this alive, then this moment—right now—is going to have to be it. I can't risk opening my eyes slowly, because that will give him a chance to notice me and react. No, everything is going to have to work at once. I'm going to have to run, as hard and as fast as I can.

One, two...and on three, I open my eyes and spring up to stand. All of the blood that rushed to my head has made me dizzy and I drop to my knees, my hands planted in front of me. Shit. I didn't plan for that. So much for running.

He's heard me. I hear his feet rushing and snapping twigs along the way. I push myself up—only to fall to my side. I'm willing my legs to work. *Work. Please work.*

"Hey!" he shouts. I can hear the anger and panic in his voice.

I push myself up to stand again. There's something cold on the ground against my hand. The scissors. He was stupid enough to leave them right there next to me. I grab the scissors. Harvey throws his body on top of me. My forehead bounces off the ground.

We roll together, intertwined, ripping at one another. I fight, kicking as hard as I can. He rolls us over, gaining the advantage with his body on top of mine. He pins me down. We're chest to chest, his hand around my throat.

"It's going to be a hell of a lot worse if you fight back, little girl!" Spit flies from his mouth onto my face. I can't breathe. My legs won't move. My face is heating up and pulsating.

My hand—it's still holding the scissors. And my arms are free. I wrench my arm upward, praying for good aim. The scissors land right in the side of Harvey's neck. Hot blood pours like a firehose onto my face, slipping over my lips and up my nose. He stiffens. His hand loosens its grip on my throat.

As I gasp for air, it feels like a thousand tiny razor blades are cutting the inside of my windpipe. His other hand wavers over the scissors jutting out of the side of his neck.

Blood pools out of his mouth, his eyes are wide and focused on mine. It's like I've betrayed him, robbing him of his chance to kill me. That's the last look on his face before his eyes roll to the back of his head. He falls to the side and rolls onto his back. His body seizes twice as though someone has hit him with electric paddles, and then he shutters still.

I lay there for a moment until I can get air into my lungs. Then I roll to the side and spit Harvey's blood out of my mouth. My throat aches inside and out. My chest feels heavy on the left side. I think he broke one of my ribs laying on me. I manage to stand and take a few steps back from Harvey's lifeless body.

I stare at him. I know I didn't have a choice. He was going to kill me. But I feel sick over it all the same. I'm unsteady on my feet and manage to find a tree to lean against. I run my bloodied hands over the dress. There are flowers on it—yellow and big just like the ones on the dress I wore for three days straight in the stable. I was right. It looks almost exactly like that one. This was planned. Researched. Remembered down to the last detail.

I'm so lost in my thoughts and in trying to regain a sense of reality that it takes me a moment before I realize exactly where I am. I look up the hill that we just rolled down in our struggle. There is just enough moonlight for me to make it out.

Odin. I'm at the treehouse. The one Greg, Saw-yer, Charlie and I tried to build. It's bigger, built up... completed. I find my way over to it, leaving Harvey in my wake. I peek over my shoulder—and feel an over-whelming sense of paranoia, like in a horror movie where the bad guy plays dead and then wakes up. I pant through the pain in my chest, holding my rib to keep the pain at bay. As I get closer, I hear movement. I look behind me and Harvey's is still where I left it. There's sound again. But it's not just movement this time. A banging. It's coming from Odin.

I pick up the pace, pushing through the pain. My adrenaline works my feet for me. The sound grows louder until it sounds like knocking, hard and consis-tent. I'm right below the tree when I hear the moan-ing—and a muffled scream.

I keep one arm—the one on the side with the bro-ken rib—at my side and use the other hand to I climb the stairs up to the treehouse door. The pain is unbear-able and my muscles spasm under the strain. But the moaning and banging continues. It grows more fran-tic as I get closer.

"Hello?" I yell out against the door. There's a makeshift lock on the front that's made of two zip ties looped through the door's metal clasp. I rattle the door and the door rattles back against me. Someone's banging against it.

It's them, I tell myself. It has to be them. "I'm coming!" My voice echoes through the forest.

The scissors. "Hold on! I'm coming back." I struggle down the ladder and make my way back over to Harvey. He hasn't moved and the scissors are still stuck in the side of his neck. Their once silver sheen is now stained black red. I pause, reluctant to near him, as if removing them might awaken the dead. My ears fixate on the banging from the treehouse and I muster the courage to spring forward and pluck the scissors from Harvey's neck.

I run back to Odin—the scissors are slippery with blood in my hands—and ascend again. My breath shortens from overuse and the rib that's poking into my lung. I cut the zip ties and throw the scissors down to the ground. Moonlight pours into the darkened space. Inches away from my face is Charlie's.

His eyes open in recognition and relief. His mouth is taped shut and hands and feet are bound. I keel over against his body and collapse on top of him, sobbing. He buries his face forward into my shoulder and I cry harder than I've ever cried.

When I can manage to compose myself enough to lift my head up, I see Sawyer and Greg, laying down at the back of the treehouse with hands tied, mouths taped, and eyes closed. I reach up and tear the duct tape from Charlie's mouth.

"Are they—?" I ask.

He shakes his head furiously. "Drugged. Alive, but drugged." He smiles and I can't decide who is happier to see who.

Then panic washes over Charlie's face. "Where is he?"

"Dead," I exhale and my body collapses back over his. "It's going to be okay."

EPILOGUE

"Everything will be okay in the end. And if it's not okay, it's not the end."- John Lennon

To grieve is to feel the bottomless pit of sorrow at the loss of a loved one. But there is no word for the opposite of grief. The reverse of grief. Charlie was alive. And though I saw him with my own eyes and touched his face with my fingers, it was days before I could finally accept it. It was as though I was scared that once I finally accepted it, I would wake from the dream and be catapulted back into the harsh reality of his death.

Is there a greater gift? To regain what you thought was lost forever? No. I can tell you from personal experience that there isn't. The only thing that came close was watching Natalee see Charlie in his hospital bed alive. I was sitting at his bedside when a policeman escorted her through the door to Charlie's hospital room. Of course, they'd told her he was alive and explained what happened, but in a situation like that there is no believing without seeing. When she crossed the threshold, she dropped to her knees and could go no further. She was swamped by the joy and the grief spilling out of her. Charlie crawled down from his bed, dragging his broken leg and ignoring the pain from his broken ribs to lay down there, cradling his wife on the hospital's cold, laminate floor.

Sawyer, Charlie, Greg, Grandma Marylin and I were all released from the hospital on the same day. The reporters and paparazzi who had swarmed the hospital moved over to Grandma Marylin's house. Natalee came with us, clinging to Charlie's arm, and I wondered if she would ever let go. And Charlie reached down every few minutes to plant a soft, long kiss on her forehead.

By the time we were released from the hospital, our story was already in the papers, though none of us had spoken to anyone about it. But when the details became clear, the FBI released the information they wanted to the press.

Of course 'clear' is a relative term. Who will ever know the real reason Harvey Barton was such a monster? We may never know the why, but over the course of the few days they kept us in the hospital we learned how it had all happened.

I'd given my statement to the police. I told them what Harvey said that he'd sought revenge on us for what he perceived to be his son being systematically bullied. I told them he was looking for respect, and one of the FBI agents told me that was called Hero's Syndrome, where a person creates a chaotic situation that they can resolve in order to gain recognition by becoming a hero. By hurting us, Harvey accomplished what he'd set out to accomplish and became the ever-respected county Sheriff he'd dreamed of being.

Time had passed and Harvey had gotten away with it. Charlie had thrown a wrench into Harvey's plan when he'd set his sights on selling the Salem Farm. There had been another family living in the house. They moved in a few years after it all happened. The house had been renovated but the barn remained condemned. When Charlie was going over the old sale records he learned that Rick was already in the process of selling the property. Charlie couldn't imagine why Rick would kidnap children in his barn, days before closing when he knew there would be final walk through's and a new family inhabiting the place.

That moment was the spark to the powder keg that set everything in motion. This new information fueled his doubts about Rick Salem's conviction. Charlie's near fatal mistake was going to talk to Harvey about his doubts over Rick Salem's conviction. Charlie visited Rick in prison and was further convinced that he wasn't the guy. He didn't want to tell us initially, in case it set off any unnecessary emotional alarms just in case he was wrong—especially considering Greg was in rehab at the time. So, he set off as a one-man mission. Harvey told Boyd that he'd left town to tend to his sister, but in reality, he never left Settlers Hill. He was going after Charlie.

Charlie had been working on the treehouse over the course of the past year. He returned to Odin and set out to build it up to the original vision our treehouse. I guess he wanted to surprise us with it come Christmas time. He didn't know that Harvey had been stalking him everywhere he went ever since he revealed his doubts. Harvey approached Charlie on his way up the trail one afternoon and hit him over the head with a crow bar. Harvey had stolen a body from the cemetery by digging it up in the middle of the night. He had transported it to the forest just before abducting Charlie. Once Charlie was unconscious, Harvey must have stripped Charlie's body and put his clothes on the dead body. Then he proceeded to tear it apart as a wild animal would have—though I would argue a wild animal did.

He put the dead man's clothes on Charlie and stowed him in the treehouse, returning every so often to give him enough sustenance to survive and nothing more. He drugged him into unconsciousness. Harvey died up there on that mountain, so we're left to speculate whether he'd planned to take Charlie's watch for himself. The FBI agent explained to me that sometimes killers will take an object as a souvenir.

It was safe to assume that this was when Harvey decided he needed the other three- the original cast of his sick little play. Harvey broke into Greg's home in the middle of the night after the funeral and brought him to the treehouse at gunpoint before drugging him as well. I was mistaken to think that Sawyer had ever made it close to the police station. Harvey intercepted him in Grandma Marylin's driveway. Harvey stuck

Sawyer in the neck with a needle and then it was lights out for him. He woke up in the treehouse.

Harvey had stuffed Sawyer in the back seat and drove off with Grandma Marylin and I none the wiser. He must have known I would come looking for Sawyer and left me the note with that ragged piece of dress tucked inside. It was almost like he was having fun with it all.

It seems I'd thwarted his plan by spending so much time with Boyd, making it nearly impossible to whisk me away. And I often wonder, even now, why he didn't take me that day outside the deli. Maybe he wasn't ready for the cat and mouse game to end. Maybe it would have been too easy. Or maybe he wanted to watch me squirm a little bit more.

Boyd reacted to the news about his father not as I'd expected, as any of us had expected. I thought he would want me dead, or behind bars at the least. I'd killed his father, his idol, the man whose footsteps he followed into the job he had today. But it seemed that after some convincing, some calming down, Boyd's memory opened up. He began to see his childhood in a different light. His father's had unaccounted for absences at the time of our abduction, a personality change after we'd been found and loads of anger. Plus, Boyd noted that they could never quite keep a pet—and how the animals' deaths were always of brutal or mysterious circumstances. Something was very wrong with Harvey Barton from the very beginning.

Boyd kept his distance from me after that night. No visits from him in the hospital, no calls or texts. I can't say I blame him. In a way, I feel sorrier for him now than I do for myself or my friends. We gained a sense of real closure whereas Boyd's world came crashing down, and doubt seeped in through his every pore.

Rick Salem was released from prison and was given his family's farm back. It was too worn down to run, so Charlie helped him sell it. Rick used the money to move out of town and change his name. He went somewhere where he could start over—where no one knew his story.

Greg returned from his stint trapped in the treehouse reborn. "You know you're not Jesus, right?" Sawyer poked at him. Greg found God in that treehouse, bound and drugged. Finding out it was Harvey who'd been behind it all, he found a sense of closure he'd never been able to feel before. He said something happened to him in there—his mind slipped in and out of a drugged haze of consciousness, that it felt like God was giving him a second chance. He bargained with God that he promised to get cleaned up, went to church, and dedicated his life to God's word if God would rescue him this one last time. He believed that God delivered on his end of the bargain, so Greg made it his life's mission to deliver on his end.

So, he continued on with regular therapy and meetings, went to church, bought himself the Bible, and volunteered to help others. Ultimately, he decided to move out of Settlers Hill once he earned enough money at the gas station. He enrolled in a trade school and became a successful plumber—Grandma Marylin was so proud. He moved two towns over, so he could still be somewhat close to Grandma Marylin and Charlie. He even met someone. A widow with three children who all adored Greg and accepted him, past and present.

As for Bea, Greg told me that his first conversation with her after he got out of the hospital went a little something like this:

Bea skipped over the sentiment of concerned mother. "You're an adult. How could you let this happen to yourself? You're going to end up in rehab again in no time. Well, don't come to me for help."

Greg smiled.

"What are you smiling about?" she asked.

"Mom," he grabbed her hand. She recoiled and tried to pull away but he held tight. "I forgive you."

"Forgive me? For what?" She sneered, her upper lip curled.

"I forgive you for not wanting forgiveness." And just like that, he said he'd never felt freer.

And as for Charlie and Natalee? Well, they picked right up where things left off. They even announced that Easter that they were pregnant and expecting a baby girl.

But who bought Old Salem Farm? Well, Grandma Marylin decided that she'd had enough and that the farm needed a facelift. She bought the place and had the house and the barn mowed down to the grass-line. She was happy to think of it as an investment in Rick Salem's new life and donated the property to a non-profit organization that used farm animals to help children and adults with disabilities.

With Sawyer, I knew the moment I saw him in that treehouse, asleep, what I needed to say to him when he woke up. So, the next day in the hospital, I sat at his bed side.

"I have to talk to you about something," I said, placing my hand on his forearm.

"What's wrong?" he asked. He pushed down on the hospital bed to sit up straighter.

"When you went missing, I didn't know if you were dead or alive. I thought Charlie was dead. I didn't know where Greg was. But it was different with you. All I could think about was how I wanted to go back to that night in my apartment, to the next morning actually, so I could stay instead of running out. I..." I paused. "I wanted to tell you that I love you. And not in the way I love anybody else. I wanted to kiss you. But you were gone. I was too late." The sides of my lips quivered into my cheeks as I tried to stifle my cry.

Sawyer just smiled, leaned in close, and said 'I've loved you since I was seven-years-old. There's no such thing as too late, Mad Dog. I'd crawl out from my grave to come find you if you called for me.'

I reached over and kissed him, our lips fitting like puzzle pieces. Warmth shot down to my toes. He winced from the weight of my body on his bruised torso and when I inched back, he scooped his hand around the back of my head and held me tighter to his lips. Not long after that, he put in a transfer to New York and we haven't spent a day apart since.

Before. After. It was how I described our first abduction. Everything was either before or after. Happiness was before—pain was after. But now that's all changed. I guess now, you could call it happily ever after.

Acknowledgements

Support for a writer comes in many forms and from many places. So, thank you:

To my parents, Bill and Michele Simonetti, who fostered my love of books from the beginning and would give me an hour to read past my bedtime even though they said, "ten minutes, then lights out." They gave me the paper to write on, the computers to research on, and the confidence to dive into any subject that interested me with the full force of their support behind me.

To my sisters, Jennifer Simonetti-Bryan and Elizabeth Simonetti, and their love of stories, be it movies or comics or books, opened my world to all the stories out there waiting to be told.

To my husband, John Gemma, who pushed me to keep writing whenever I wanted to give up. He taught me that simply wanting something isn't enough and that if I wanted to be a writer, I had to make time for it, drive forward, and work harder than I wanted to.

To my dearest friend Erin Grdovich, who read my first draft the fastest and remains the wind at my back through every uphill battle and meets me on the other side for sushi and reality TV reruns.

To Michaela Penna, who woke the dormant writer in me, one sleepy Tuesday morning, by giving me a Writer's Digest Competition slip she received in the mail. Her talent and bravery in her own art inspired me to put myself out there and call myself a writer.

To my editor, Laura Apgar. She met my characters, got to know them, and got right down into the grit of the writing process with me, all while instilling confidence in my writing ability.

To Mike Colesanti, of Revolut1 Graphix, who created the artwork for my cover. He not only managed the impossible task of isolating an image from my scattered brain, he then improved upon it ten-fold to give me exactly what I was looking for.

I couldn't have done any of this without you all.

Made in the USA
Columbia, SC
18 November 2020